# OUTLASTING THE TRAIL

# OUTLASTING THE TRAIL

*The Story of a Woman's Journey West*

MARY BARMEYER O'BRIEN

**TWODOT®**

GUILFORD, CONNECTICUT
HELENA, MONTANA
AN IMPRINT OF THE GLOBE PEQUOT PRESS

# A · T W O D O T® · B O O K

Text design by Lisa Reneson
Base map by Tony Moore © The Globe Pequot Press

Library of Congress Cataloging-in-Publication Data
O'Brien, Mary Barmeyer.
  Outlasting the trail : the story of Mary Powers's Oregon Trail
journey/Mary Barmeyer O'Brien–1st ed.
    p. cm.
  ISBN 0-7627-3065-X
  1. Powers, Mary Rockwood, d. 1858—Fiction. 2. Overland
journeys to the Pacific—Fiction. 3. Oregon National Historic
Trail—Fiction. 4. Women pioneers—Fiction. 5. Wagon trains—
Fiction. 6. California–Fiction. I. Title.

PS3615.B76087 2005
813'6—dc22

                                                  2005040394

Manufactured in the United States of America
First Edition/First Printing

*For my mother, Dorothy D. Barmeyer,*
*who taught me*
*the fine art of letter writing,*
*the meaning of "being at home with oneself,"*
*and to "never underestimate the power of a woman."*

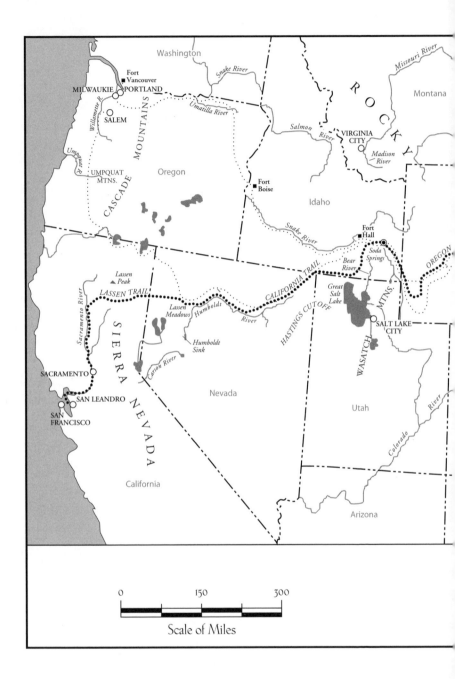

Washington

*Missouri River*

Fort
Vancouver
MILWAUKIE ■ PORTLAND
*Snake River*

ROCKY

Montana

*Willamette R.*

SALEM

*Umatilla River*

CASCADE MOUNTAINS

Oregon

*Salmon*
*River*
VIRGINIA
CITY
*Madison River*

*Umpqua River*

UMPQUAT
MTNS.

Fort
Boise

Idaho

*Snake River*

Fort
Hall

OREGON

Lassen
Peak

LASSEN TRAIL

CALIFORNIA TRAIL

*Bear River*

Soda
Springs

*Sacramento River*

Lassen
Meadows

*Humboldt*

*River*

Great
Salt
Lake

HASTINGS CUTOFF

WASATCH MTNS.

SIERRA NEVADA

*Carson River*

Humboldt
Sink

SALT LAKE
CITY

SACRAMENTO

SAN LEANDRO

SAN
FRANCISCO

Nevada

Utah

*Colorado River*

California

Arizona

0            150            300

Scale of Miles

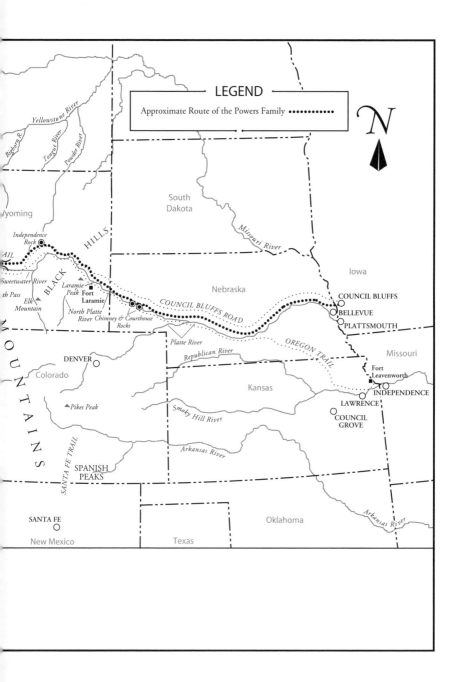

# OUTLASTING THE TRAIL

## AUTHOR'S NOTE

Few pioneer accounts are as compelling as the true story of Mary Rockwood Powers, who undertook a covered wagon journey to California with her husband and three young children in 1856. In a remarkable narrative written for her mother and sisters back home, Mary described her family's trip, which began from their home in southern Wisconsin. What started as a promising adventure deteriorated into a grim struggle for survival soon after the family embarked upon the overland trails at the Missouri River.

Mary's husband, Americus W. Powers, was an experienced, middle-aged physician when he decided to go West. Historical records hint that he purchased expensive Canadian horses to pull the covered wagon, but before the Powerses even reached their jump-off point near Omaha, Nebraska, the animals had begun to fail. By the time they had worked their way deep into Nebraska Territory, the horses—and consequently, the Powers family—were in serious trouble. Perhaps it was the terrible stress caused by this event or simply the intense rigors of a cross-continental trek that caused Dr. Powers to begin displaying possible signs of what we recognize today as an episode of severe depression.

Mary was a refined, intelligent, and delicate woman who was distressed and frightened not only by the perils of the journey itself but by the changes in her husband. Day after day, she watched him become more withdrawn, hostile, irrational, and ineffectual. Like most women of her time, she had almost certainly been raised to submit uncomplainingly to her husband's wishes and to follow his lead. When Dr. Powers's poor decisions and unreasonable behavior continually put her family in danger, Mary was forced to reexamine her convictions. How she resolved the conflict between her cultured, traditional upbringing and her family's treacherous situation on the overland trail is the heart of this story.

Mary's original handwritten narrative was a detailed account, part journal and part letter, intended to describe her trip west and reassure her worried family back in Wisconsin. Her work has been published both privately and publicly throughout the years. With a bit of searching, readers of western history can still locate it and study Mary's own version of her dramatic story.

It was Mary's account of her desperate journey—and her extraordinary, courageous response to it—that inspired this work of fiction. Although these pages generally follow the westward trip of Mary and Americus Powers, many of the circumstances, names, locations, events, and details are imaginary. It is the author's hope that, were Mary Rockwood Powers to read this fictionalized account of her westward journey today, she would find it true to the actual story she herself penned a century and a half ago.

She couldn't say how far they had traveled in miles or days—she had lost track of both—but she could measure the terrible distance by the distressing changes in the Doctor's mood.

They had come too far, he insisted, to turn around and inch back home, so day after weary day they labored farther into these gray, windy grasslands, away from every speck of civilization.

Tonight, crushed in the covered wagon bed with her sleeping family, Mary Powers opened her eyes to absolute darkness. After a moment, she realized the weight pressing down on her chest was her husband's arm thrown across her like a fallen log. Curled against her other side, little Celia sighed sweetly and turned, pressing a sharp elbow into Mary's ribs. She could hear Cephas and Sarah shifting restlessly as another night stretched on to the morning. Quick tears came to Mary's eyes. She knew she would lie awake, chilled by fear, until the sun lightened the skies along the Platte River.

Suddenly irritated, she lifted the Doctor's heavy arm off her chest. Whatever had the man been thinking to drag his family to this godforsaken Nebraska Territory? How dare he put them in this alarming predicament and then overnight become a stranger to her? Ever since they had left home, she'd felt married to a scarecrow or a stick man who had lost every shred of his usual warmth and congeniality—a stranger with a recent string of poor decisions that put them all in danger. Mary bit her dirty thumbnail. Surely there must be an explanation for his behavior.

Something moved outside the wagon's flimsy canvas sides. She strained to hear. Logically it had to be the horses, she told herself, but her heart beat fast. She buried her icy hands beneath the covers and tried to peer across the children's heads through the opening in the canvas. Nothing but utter darkness. She listened again and silently began to pray, beseeching God to keep her family safe.

It seemed an eternity before the eastern sky glowed faintly. Mary slid from beneath the dew-dampened quilts. She stepped down the wooden wheel spokes to the ground, her bare toes silent on the splintery oak. She was the first one stirring in camp, and she stretched her slender arms above her head and breathed deeply. Then, pulling her shawl closer, she stood for a moment, watching the pink sunrise hide the stars.

By the time the sun glowed round and yellow above the prairie, she had rekindled the fire and made a charred breakfast for Americus and the children, who clambered sleepily out of the wagon, their hair poking up in all directions, their clothes pressed into unbecoming wrinkles. Mary sent twelve-year-old Sarah with Cephas and little Celia to wash their faces in the river while she climbed back into the wagon, determined to make use of this opportunity to dry the patchwork quilts. Sunlight seeped through the overhead canvas. One day of this weather would be enough to rid the wagon of its musty smell, dry out the few remaining beans and the bedding—and give her the strength to carry on.

Outside the wagon, the Doctor sat beside the dying breakfast fire staring at the embers. The other men in this small wagon train were tending their livestock, striking tents, and making quick repairs to their wagons. Occasionally Americus lifted his eyes to watch them. Even the fragrant morning coffee hadn't made him stir. Mary had poured a tin cup full for him, but it sat brimming on the ground, cold as the nearby river.

She heard footsteps approaching the cook fire. At first she thought it was Tessie DeFrance, the capable new friend she had made soon after leaving the settlements on the Missouri. Mary felt as though she had known Tessie for years. Out here, she discovered, friendships formed quickly and solidly. People got right down to the business of caring for one another in these rough conditions, where the smallest good deed might mean the difference between life or death.

The footsteps were too heavy for Tessie's. Mary rose to peek out of the puckered opening in the wagon cover. It was Captain McFarland, the leader of this small train, his thin auburn hair lightened by the sun, his solid frame moving purposefully. He approached the Doctor, who remained seated on the grub box where his skinny shadow fell across the bare ground, thin as a skeleton's.

"Doctor Powers." Isaac McFarland's deep voice held a hint of reluctance, despite its decisive tone.

There was no response at first. Americus Powers shifted on the grub box and cleared his throat.

"Morning, McFarland."

"I've come to tell you—I'm sorry, but we have to go on without you. The men voted this morning."

There was a stony silence from Americus. Inside the warm wagon, Mary felt her body go cold. She pressed a hand over her mouth and sank again onto the bed.

To travel alone along this dangerous trail was a terrifying thought, especially with the Doctor in his present frame of mind and the horses so exhausted that they nearly collapsed every time the wagon stopped. Despite Mary's attempts to stretch the dwindling supply of beans, the children were getting hungry. The Doctor had no rifle: He had let a stranger borrow it, and the man had taken it for good, leaving them no way to shoot game or protect themselves. Mary doubled over and clutched her knees. They wouldn't last a day out here alone.

"The problem is your horses," the captain continued. Mary could hear him scuffing a hole in the dirt with his boot, and his voice seemed muffled, as though he weren't looking at Americus. "Those fine animals of yours are beauties, but they weren't meant to pull a 2,000-pound wagon. They're holding us up. We're concerned about the delays."

Mary peeked out again, just in time to see the Doctor jerk to his feet and shout, "Go ahead, leave us! See if we don't travel better alone anyhow!"

Mary cringed and groped in her apron pocket for her handkerchief. The captain went on evenly, "We want to be sure you'll be all right by yourselves. Send Mrs. Powers around later, and we'll share our beans with her before we leave. Then you folks should turn around and go back home. Face the facts, Powers."

"I wouldn't take your beans if I were starving. And I'm not going home." Americus's voice trembled with wrath. "I never want to see you or your wagon train again." He stalked off toward the horses picketed in the distance, his back rigid. The other man watched him for a moment, then turned and walked away.

Inside the wagon, Mary pressed her fingers to her temples. It wasn't the horses the men wanted to leave behind.

Mary knew that as well as she knew the pages of her well-worn Bible. The horses were agonizingly slow, but each day the wagon train went on ahead, and the Powerses caught up to join their circled encampment as the moon rose to silhouette the black prairie. No, the group wanted to be rid of Americus, whose strange behaviors and angry tirades were becoming daily events. These good people were intent on one thing: reaching the far-distant western valleys before blizzards blocked the fearsome mountains ahead. The Doctor's sullen moods, odd decisions, and lack of provisions put them all in harm's way.

A fly buzzed frantically against the stained canvas overhead, caught inside the crowded wagon by the cinched-up ties at front and back. Mary understood that panicked quest for freedom. Never in her life had she felt so trapped as she had on this fearful trip west. She longed to burst free of the journey's treachery and flee back home—back to Wisconsin, where her mother and sisters went about their quiet, cultured, orderly lives as she herself had once done. Back to Wisconsin, where the Doctor had been a kind husband and a thoughtful father. Out here he was a changed man, to say the least.

She'd better act quickly, while he was off with the horses. Her fingers fumbled with the wagon cover as she enlarged the opening enough to crawl through. She felt like a beggar slipping through the circled wagons to implore Captain Mc-Farland to give them another chance, but she purposely held her head high and thought of her children. They were in danger of starving out here without the kindness of the other travelers. From the first, these fellow emigrants had noted the Doctor's failure to cope and had embraced Mary and the children in the circle of their protection. Yesterday, Mr. DeFrance had brought a fat skinned rabbit to stew, and Tessie had given her flour for dumplings.

"I'm sorry, Mrs. Powers." Isaac McFarland was kind but firm as she stood before him, trembling. He spoke with feeling. "If it were up to me, I'd make another decision . . . but the men voted. I'll be honest with you. They're afraid your husband will have more of his moods. And your horses will only get sicker, slowing us all down. A few days of rest is what you need. And food. I've got a sack of beans for you. Then you need to go home. You're only about a month from civilization." He paused and then said again, "You need to go home."

"The Doctor won't hear of it, Captain. I know he won't hear of turning back. I'd better take your beans, for the children's sake. With our thanks, of course."

Mary ducked her head, her cheeks hot, as the captain shouldered the bulging sack of beans. Accepting charity and pity was one more part of this journey that chafed as badly as a sharp sliver in a tender finger. The cold sweat of embarrassment trickled down her back as she led the way to her wagon and showed the captain where to hide the beans under the bedding. He nodded his good-bye. "Go home, I implore you, Mrs. Powers."

After he was gone, Tessie DeFrance rounded the corner of the wagon, her blue eyes wide. Typical of Tess, she hadn't taken time to secure the fly-away strands of hair that had fallen from her hairpins, and her apron was streaked with campfire soot.

"I just heard. Oh, Mary, I can't bear the thought!" She hugged Mary hard. "Whatever will you do? Jacob tried his best to persuade the other men to give Dr. Powers another chance, but you know my Jake. He's not much at speaking out when there's a disagreement." She paused to search Mary's face, her eyes showing the shiny beginnings of tears. Then she grabbed Mary's hand and tucked a gold coin into it. "I want you to have this. Please take it, Mary. You're going to need it."

"Oh, Tess!"

"Try to stay close behind us," Tessie begged. "If you can possibly stay near . . ."

Mary leaned heavily on her friend's solid shoulder. She could smell the campfire smoke in Tessie's hair and feel the strong arms around her. "The horses—they won't be able to keep up. Poor Lucretia nearly toppled over from fatigue yesterday, and Blackey isn't much better." Her eyes filled. "Tessie—thank you. Thank you for everything." Her words felt ordinary and inadequate, like a gift too small for the occasion. She could never tell Tess how much she appreciated all her kindnesses: the food, the friendship, the support. Tessie had watched little Celia by the hour while Mary tried to cope with the travel chores that Americus couldn't manage.

"You have to be the husband on this trip, Mary," Tess blurted out, tears now brimming in her eyes. "You have to take charge and be the husband." With a quivering smile, she said good-bye and was gone.

The husband? Mary thought about it as she piled more bedding over the new sack of beans. The chill she felt wouldn't leave despite her wool shawl and the sunshine, and her head ached. Her tattered handkerchief, once crisp and white but now stained a sooty gray, was damp with tears. It was entirely possible Tessie was right.

How does one take charge, she wondered, when taught from birth to be obedient and submissive, to defer to her man's wishes and obey his command? Her marriage vows seemed long ago and far away, but Mary had always believed they governed her role in life. Her husband was to make the decisions and she was to follow—with patience and deference and self-sacrifice, if necessary. For a woman to take charge was not only unseemly, it was contrary to everything she'd been taught.

It was only minutes before the others finished loading last-minute things, rounding up stray children, and offering Mary their awkward good wishes. They fell into line along the rutted trail, leaving the Powerses' wagon alone, a dirty gray speck on the wide expanse. Tessie's blanched face kept looking back in sympathy until it was lost in the distance.

The Doctor led their limping horses to the traces, harnessing Lucretia and Blackey but leaving the big bay, St. Lawrence, free. Quietly, Mary took a deep breath and, lifting her faded skirts slightly, climbed the front wagon wheel into the driver's seat. Driving was more than she was accustomed to, but Americus insisted.

She clucked to the horses and turned out onto the Platte River Road while the Doctor and the children walked alongside. The day stretched out before her, as endless as this monotonous trail, while she urged the faltering horses along the tracks. Every hundred yards or so she stopped to rest them, then urged some more.

At midday Blackey and Lucretia failed, as they did every day now, and Americus hitched the big bay alone to the wagon. The good horse shouldered the load a few feet at a time, drooping with exhaustion whenever the wagon stopped. Overhead the hot sun crept by, hour after hour.

Mary wondered if they had covered even three or four miles by the time it was dusk. Light winds blew through the grasslands, and coyotes yipped in the distance while she warmed a scant supper in the fading evening light. Americus brooded silently as she worked. Even the children were subdued, and when the stars came out, they settled willingly into the wagon. Mary took them a single plateful of biscuits made with the rest of Tessie's flour. She gave them each a drink of warm coffee, since the river water by itself tasted of rotting vegetation and gritty silt. As much as she hated to give coffee to little Celia it was better than nothing. At least one could imagine that the grit was coffee grounds, not disgusting river dirt.

She heard the Doctor scraping the bottom of the flour sack, looking for a few mouthfuls to feed the horses for strength. She'd never dreamed when they left home with those 100-pound bags of flour that the horses would eat most of it. Now it was used up, like Mary's strength and her patience. Pressing her lips together, she put the children to bed fully dressed, heard their prayers, and kissed them one by one. Then she lay down herself on the narrow spot that was hers in the cramped wagon, pretending to be asleep when the Doctor climbed in beside her.

Mary had memorized enough of the guidebook tucked under the straw-filled mattress to know how dangerous it was to travel alone. Before they left home, the book had reassured her with its comforting words about a westward journey filled with camaraderie and adventure. Tonight it mocked her with its promises that overland parties would never consider leaving one of their families behind.

*Tomorrow,* she thought, *I'll look at the Doctor's map and see how far it is to the nearest fort. And I'll try to figure out what day it is.*

Americus Powers peered down from his wagon seat at the turbid water flowing past the iron-rimmed wheels. These blasted horses! Were the dimwitted beasts such weaklings that they couldn't pull the wagon out of this stream? His family and all their possessions were mired here in a deep, deserted creek, and this time there were no other travelers with their extra oxen to help. He could feel the now-familiar anger rushing in like wind before a rainstorm. It gripped his tall, lean frame with a tension that made him tremble. His knees felt weak, and he had an unnatural strength in his bony hands. Even his throat seemed to close tight, making him choke on his words. He took a deep breath and tried to calm himself, but it was no use. Everything was against him, especially these horses he'd once admired. Now they seemed like demons.

"Get out!" he barked, ignoring his wife's shocked look of dismay and the frightened whimpering behind him. Little Celia was becoming a sissy, crying every time there was a problem. He'd have a talk with the child. At three years old, it was high time she had some training about proper behavior. He shouted again, "Get out of the wagon!"

"Yes, Americus," he heard Mary murmur above the rippling water and the blood roaring in his head. He stood and glared at the horses as she held her long skirt above her bare feet, and, white-faced, stepped down the wheel spokes into the cold current. She called in a soft voice, "Celia, come with me. I'll carry you to shore." No wonder the child cried all the time. Mary babied her too much.

She took the toddler in her arms and started for the nearest creek bank behind them, avoiding the deeper water and faster current ahead. Still holding her skirts and balancing carefully on the slippery rocks, she nodded at seven-year-old Cephas and at Sarah, who obediently followed. The children held hands as the water rose higher on their legs, both looking straight ahead to the muddy shore. Cephas slipped and fell, but Sarah kept her grip on his hand, her thin arm straining against the current's pull. The boy struggled up again, shivering in the cool breeze.

Now, the horses, Americus thought. He'd show those horses a thing or two.

The creek was colder on his bare feet than he thought it would be, and the spring rains had swollen the current until it was over his knees. It felt as though it came straight from the Rocky Mountain snow fields he had read about in the guidebook. So far they'd seen no mountains, only the vast prairies and the low hills of Nebraska Territory that seemed to go on forever. He wondered if the Rockies really existed. Those guidebook writers, he had discovered, had put down some big lies. Maybe they'd never traveled this treacherous route themselves but sat in cozy houses back home and imagined it all. Well, they had imagined wrong. This was not the simple adventurous journey they had described. This was near-suicide, taking a family through Sioux country so wild and rough a man felt as though he were fighting for his life every moment.

Maybe those authors had only invented the Rocky Mountains.

He'd dragged his family so far by now that he felt they must be near the end of the continent—or at least near their destination in California's gold fields, where, he'd been told, nuggets were waiting to be plucked from every stream. But as far as he could tell from the map, they were still plodding along the Platte, not yet even to Fort Laramie.

The stream made his feet ache and his long, thin legs go numb and white. The sound of it rushing by, causing the wagon to sink deeper and deeper into the stones and mud, enraged him. Only twenty feet or so, and the wheels would be on shore again, but the creek bank ahead was steep. It was wet, too, although others had obviously traveled up it before. As much as he'd admired his glossy animals back home—and was sure they could handle a simple overland trip—they had failed him.

Sunlight glinted off his wet hand as he slapped Lucretia's flanks. The horse jerked, startled at the unaccustomed treatment. He did the same to Blackey and then to the bay. He could see now why other travelers chose those ugly, clumsy oxen. At least a team of four oxen could pull a wagon through a little creek. He wasn't about to be beaten by a few lazy horses. His voice shot through the air. "Pull, you wretched animals!"

Their muscles strained, although Lucretia wobbled from exhaustion, but the wagon moved only an inch or two. Americus ran his hand through his thinning dark hair, and stumbled, splashing and slipping through the current, to urge the horses from the front. This time Lucretia nearly collapsed into the cold water.

Red faced, Americus yelled again, struggling to stay upright in the hissing silt. He caught a glimpse of his family behind him, lined up on the creek bank watching him, wide eyed and silent. Sarah's face had turned white, and she had her hands over her ears. Cephas was biting his lip, trying not to cry. Mary spoke to them and tried to divert their attention from his tirade. Never mind. He had business to attend to. Now they'd have to unload the wagon, and they'd better do it quickly.

"Mary!" he yelled. "Help me unpack."

She looked at him across the stream and seemed to be considering something. "Perhaps we could try pushing from the back," she called, her soft voice barely discernable above the rush of water. "Do you suppose that might be enough?"

Americus looked at her. How dare she question his judgment? Wasn't he the head of this household? Wasn't he in absolute charge of this expedition? His voice was stiff when he replied, "I said, come help me unpack."

Mary spoke to Sarah, and Americus knew she was instructing the girl to watch little Celia and keep her away from the dangerous water. That enraged him, too. "Sarah, you come here and help. You too, Cephas," he shouted. His voice climbed higher than he intended. He could feel the blood in his face and the irritability that was like a caged bird within him straining to get out in some bigger way.

He saw Mary start to protest. Someone needed to watch Celia. Well it was high time that child took care of herself. Couldn't a child of three keep herself away from danger? "Come here this moment!" he demanded, and this time Mary spoke firmly to Celia and pointed to a place on the ground well back from the stream, where she was to sit. Then the three of them waded slowly toward the wagon. Americus could see Cephas's teeth chattering and his small wet body shaking. Mary no longer tried to keep her dress dry. The long, blue calico skirt was being tugged downstream, and the dark stain of water reached her hips.

They unloaded the tent and the bedding and carried

them to the shore ahead. Americus went back for the provisions box. Mary's gray eyes looked glazed, and Americus knew one of her headaches was coming on. For now, she worked hard enough, despite her slender, petite build. Already she was a lot more muscular than she'd been back home, and her face was more angular.

He sent Cephas ashore with the wooden keg and the iron frying pan. The boy strained under the weight and the pull of the fast water, but he deposited his load on high ground, and then with a furtive glance at his father, crossed the creek to the far side to remind Celia to sit where she had been told. Mary took a small wooden chest ashore herself, clutching the box close to her chest, fighting the current sucking at her soaked dress.

"Now, push," Americus demanded when they returned. He wasn't sure the horses had rested long enough, but knew he had to get them out of the frigid water. He tried not to see Mary's shocked expression as he jerked relentlessly on the harness. "PUSH!" The word exploded from him so loudly his throat hurt. He watched as Mary and Sarah set their shoulders to the wagon box. Cephas was too small to be of much use, but he did as he was told, teeth still chattering and eyes downcast. Slowly the wagon moved out of the creek and started up the steep bank.

As soon as they were above the swift water, Americus could hear little Celia on the far bank, too close to the stream, screaming and crying. The idiotic child thought they were leaving her behind! Mary took one look and abandoned the wagon, racing down the bank before it was too late. This time she ran through the stream, slipping and catching herself, arms outstretched, water splashing her face, until she reached her child. Americus sprang to her place and continued to push. Inch by inch the wagon ascended the last few uphill feet. Finally it stood on flat, high ground, its wheels dripping and mucky. The horses' sides were heaving; Lucretia trembled. Well, at least they had made it. Americus watched Mary gather Celia into her arms. She buried her face in the little girl's neck. Celia clung to her, sobbing.

Now, to reload and be on their way. He spoke sharply to Sarah and Cephas to quit resting and load up the belongings.

Mary brought Celia to the wagon and covered her cold feet. She handed her a biscuit left from breakfast and soothed her with a quiet voice. Mary's eyes were red, but she was calm. She squeezed some of the water from her skirt, which had mud and sand around the bottom edge like a grotesque brown trim. Americus noticed she wouldn't look his way, and that she kept pressing on her temples.

Suddenly his anger was gone and he wanted to take her in his arms, but he knew he had ruined the day and destroyed whatever shred of trust she still had in him. Why was everything against him? Every moment of this trip—this adventure he had embraced so enthusiastically back home—was poisoned. He detested it all: the tiresome drudgery, the baffling toil that every inch of this blasted trail demanded, even the nagging presence of his family that made it necessary for him to keep pressing onward when all he wanted to do was lie down and be rid of it all.

Wearily, he sank onto the wet earth and covered his face with his hands. Even with his medical training, he couldn't imagine what was wrong with him. He wasn't himself, that was for certain. These days he was dead tired all the time, when just a few short weeks ago he'd been filled with energy and enthusiasm for the journey. Melancholia draped itself over him like a heavy black blanket.

Back home, he'd gladly practiced medicine, drawing

people from all over the countryside to his small, clean office in town. After he was finished for the day, they dropped by just to talk and enjoy his company. Out here, though, he couldn't seem to get anything right, and he felt like a tyrant. He knew he distressed Mary with his grim complaining, his angry outbursts, and endless sulking. He himself railed against the anger that flared without warning and the grinding fatigue that dogged him every moment. Almost everything overwhelmed him and depressed his mood. He was ineffectual, too, an odd feeling for a man used to being in control.

He flexed his skeleton hands and felt the power drain out of them as surely as if his life's blood had poured out onto the ground. His strength was gone, every last bit of it. He felt he couldn't—absolutely couldn't—stand up again and get the wagon moving along the trail. He couldn't face Mary, the children, even the horses. He wanted to sit here beside this vexing creek until he turned to stone.

Mary slipped her pencil and a precious leaf of paper into her apron pocket and hurried toward the river where a patch of undergrowth would finally afford her some privacy. Sarah was watching Celia for a few minutes before they had to start supper, giving Mary a rare moment alone. At last she could pour forth her thoughts into a letter that she would somehow, somewhere along this trail, find a way to mail to her mother.

Mother! Just the thought made Mary's throat tighten. How she longed to sit in the familiar old parlor with its gleaming mahogany furniture, rocking and sipping tea from a china teacup, while she told her mother about the troubling changes in her husband. No, not "troubling"—that wasn't a strong enough word for these appalling developments. Alarming, she might say, or even terrifying. Mother would smooth Mary's clean, brown hair from her forehead and offer her usual sympathy and wise advice. Mary tried to imagine what that advice might be, but her mind hummed with confusion. There seemed no way out of this dreadful mess she was in.

She found a rock beside a low bush, and clutching her pencil like a lifeline, began to write in tiny, neat script. She was proud to be able to put the date down first; she'd spent most of one sleepless night figuring out what day it was and had kept a careful count ever since.

*June 18, 1856*

*Dear Mother,*

    *I'm sitting on the banks of a creek, somewhere in this vast wilderness near the fork of the Platte. It has been raining again today, and the ground is cold and wet, as is everything else, including the children. I can't remember when we've been truly dry on this miserable trail for more than a day or two.*
    *We are traveling slowly—more slowly than we should—because the horses are so sick. You remember how strong and shiny Blackey was before we left home. Now he has worked so hard he is nothing but bones, and he can't pull long before giving out. The big bay, St. Lawrence, isn't much better, and, oh! how sad I am to tell you that Lucretia has died. I suggested to the Doctor that we ought to trade the remaining two for oxen when we reach Fort Laramie, and he promised he will. For now, though, we're continuing to hitch up these poor half-dead beasts day after day. So we're struggling on, making only a very few miles a day. At this rate, we'll never get to California.*
    *The Doctor is acting so strangely, Mother! I can't fathom his behavior. You wouldn't recognize him, he is so changed from the kind man you knew. He is taken with fits of anger, sometimes over the smallest things, and at times his rage seems uncontrollable! Mother, he shouts at the horses— and the children—every day, if you can imagine that.*
    *I've begun to shoulder more of the responsibility for the*

*travel, since the Doctor seems unable to do so. He stopped*
*setting up the sleeping tent, even though that means we're all*
*crowded into the wagon at night. And I hesitate to tell you*
*this because I know it will worry you, but the wagon train*
*has left us behind. The Doctor's uncharacteristic outbursts and*
*unpleasant interactions combined with the sick horses caused*
*the split.*

*Sometimes I wonder if God is punishing him for trying*
*this dangerous trip with a wife and children. He suddenly has*
*so much anger in his heart—and Mother!—yesterday he even*
*cursed in front of Cephas! Back home he would have sooner*
*died. Whatever has happened to my kind, God-fearing*
*husband? What has happened to the man who used to sit with*
*me and watch the sunset? Sarah and Cephas remember the*
*days when he used to take them for walks and find them*
*pretty rocks and hawk feathers, but I am afraid little Celia*
*won't remember her father as he was before we left—how he*
*would roll down grassy hills with her or bounce her on his*
*knee. Instead she will remember this strange man who barks*
*at her over the tiniest infractions, and who is cool and distant*
*all other times.*

*We are nearly out of money (except for a gold coin I*
*have secretly hidden away) and almost out of provisions. The*
*horses are suffering from the absence of the Doctor's usual*
*faultless care, and the poor children are frightened, as am I.*

*But lest I alarm you too much, I want you to know that*
*our health is good, and I am leaning heavily on my faith in*
*Almighty God, who sustains me in my darkest hours. Sarah*
*has been a great help, too. I wonder what I would ever do*
*without my precious children?*

*I miss you terribly, Mother. Not a moment goes by when*
*I don't long to be back home with you. I pray that I might be*

*allowed to see you again someday. For now this letter must suffice.*

*My deepest love to everyone,*

*Mary*

She folded the paper, filled on both sides from margin to margin, and tucked it into her pocket.

It seemed as though she and her family had been following this muddy trail for decades; in truth, it hadn't been more than a few weeks. As the wagon jostled over every stone this everlasting journey put in their way, the days blended into each other as surely as the colors in a fading sunset. By now her hands were red and coarse from scrubbing dishes in the cloudy river water. Her complexion, she was sure, was tanned and windburned, although she hadn't had the courage to fetch her looking glass and find out for certain.

This trip west had changed more than just her skin. Even her prayers were different—desperate pleas for courage and strength instead of the joyful thanksgiving she had offered back home. Mary wondered what her mother would think of her stained calico dress, already patched where she had caught it on the rough wagon seat. Had all those years of careful schooling and lessons in gracious living come to this? She ran her fingers over her windblown hair, which she had jabbed into place with hairpins yesterday. It felt dusty, like the rest of her, and matted. She must take time to brush it out. She wished she could find a secluded place to wash more than just her face, too, but the lack of vegetation made the most private of endeavors a public spectacle.

She knew she should return to the children, but she couldn't, not yet. Her head ached, and when she tried to stand she felt dizzy, so she sank down again onto the uncomfortable rock. A sudden ray of sunshine washed over her. She closed her eyes. She hadn't felt this tired since she was expecting Celia.

She let her thoughts drift back home again to the neat bungalow in Wisconsin where she and the Doctor had set up housekeeping. Roses—both pink and scarlet—thrived beside the door and tried to take over her well-tended garden. Her clean windows were framed by the muslin curtains she kept crisp and white. Sunlight glinted off the winding creek that ran near the little country cabin. She could still see the path that Americus had worn through the green fields as he walked back and forth to town each day, faithful as the church bell that rang every noon. His clothes had been pressed then, and he was tall and energetic. Even his name sounded eminent: Dr. Americus W. Powers. At sunset he would come striding across the grasslands, whistling a tune or craning his thin neck to watch the blackbirds. The children would run to greet him.

The day he had announced his intentions to take the family to the California gold fields, Mary had actually cried out, her hand over her mouth. She knew better than to protest her husband's will. Hadn't she vowed to honor and obey him? He had, she remembered, gone for days with only catnaps, working until dawn making a wooden grub box or leather harness. Sometimes his thoughts about going to California had tumbled out so quickly that Mary had a hard time even keeping up with his words. He convinced her that the trip would be an all-summer picnic, just an extended camping trip in the pure beauty of a new territory. Nothing could stop them and their nearly perfect horses, and they would be in the California gold fields before they knew it.

Still, Mary had wept privately for days. Separating herself from her mother and sisters seemed like ripping out a piece of her heart. Today, sitting on this boulder, she felt the empty place all over again. Even the sunshine couldn't touch her there.

Reluctantly she stood, but nausea swept over her, strong and unexpected as a snowstorm. She knelt on the ground, certain she was going to be sick. Her head ached—it had ached for days—as the realization overcame her. Oh, no, dear God. Could it be? Another baby? Not now. Not here.

Sarah had collected more of those disgusting buffalo chips when Mary returned to camp and had tried to get a blaze going with them. She had succeeded in starting a small flame, which she fanned with her dirty sunbonnet. Celia sat nearby eating a cold biscuit. Mary gave her older daughter a grateful smile as she fetched the cookstove, once so shiny, but now blackened and scuffed. Would it be beans with bacon or beans without for supper? Mary wondered if she could swallow either one.

"Sarah, dear, thank you. You are such a help to me." Mary put her arm around her daughter's shoulders. "This trip won't last forever, you know."

"Mother, I don't think we're going to get to California! I think the horses are going to die, and we're going to run out of food. I looked in the flour sack. It's gone!" Sarah's thin face was pinched; little Celia looked up with big eyes.

Mary looked hastily behind her to see where Americus had gone. He would be terribly angry at Sarah if he heard her utter such words, but he and Cephas were nowhere to be seen.

"Don't you worry about that, dear. That's your father's responsibility. Surely the horses will make it to Fort Laramie— it's only a week or two more—where we'll buy more provisions. Wouldn't it be fine if we could get some oxen, too? They're clumsy, ugly creatures, I know, not nearly as nice as the horses, but they're much stronger and more dependable." Mary tried for a smile, but Sarah wasn't persuaded.

"And what if the Sioux come! We don't even have a gun!" she blurted.

"Sarah, hush! You're frightening Celia. God won't let the Sioux harm us."

Sarah bent over the fire again, and Mary looked down at her daughter. The girl could see straight through Mary's false cheer. The poor child had been tremendously patient. She hated being wet and dirty, as she always was now, but she rarely complained. Her hair hung in stringy brown braids framing a face that, even in the sunshine, looked pale. Her green eyes, once so lively, were dull and resigned. Soot blackened her slim, chapped hands, and she had given up cleaning the dirt from under her fingernails. The gray wool dress she wore—a child's dress, inappropriate for a twelve-year-old—stopped midcalf; the sleeves ended several inches above her wrists. Mary had told herself a hundred times to cut some muslin into a new summer dress for her, but she never seemed to have the energy to get started. Maybe at Laramie she could have a day's rest.

Laramie was the answer to her prayers, an oasis of supplies, a safe resting place, her family's salvation. It was civilization, and there, she thought, they would finally be able to trade the horses. Even in their pathetic condition, the gentle animals would bring a good price. They were fine horses, carefully bred and trained, and they were sweet natured, too, despite the recent hardship. Anyone could see their potential. The Doctor could trade for a strong team of oxen, and still perhaps have enough left over to buy an old rifle and some ammunition. Tessie's gold coin would replenish the provisions.

Mary bent over as another wave of nausea passed and then hurried to the wagon to get the evening's allotment of beans. Sarah was absolutely right. The horses could hardly be expected to make it all the way to the Fort. If they made it as far as Chimney Rock, a few days ahead, it would be fortunate. They would die, sooner or later. What then? Could she expect God to protect them, when they had done almost nothing to protect themselves?

Angrily she scooped the beans from the bottom of the sack. The sun was gone now, hidden behind a ridge of gray clouds, and a chilly wind blew from the creek bottom.

# CHAPTER 4

# SARAH

Sarah dabbled her bare feet in the swift-running North Platte River. At least her feet could be clean, even if the rest of her felt grimy. She wanted to hide forever behind this bush, watching the sparkles on the water. Most of all, she wanted to hide from the feeling that gripped her middle like a hawk's talons. It was the same nervous, sick feeling she used to get back in Wisconsin when she had to recite poetry in front of the whole school. Now it was stronger, and it never went away.

She wished she hadn't sneaked the guidebook from beneath the mattress and read the part about the Sioux. She hadn't thought about Indians much out here until she read the book's warnings. Now she made a point as she walked beside the wagon—first along the dull Platte and now beside the North Platte—to watch for them. Every shadow that moved in the breeze made her heart race.

She and Cephas and Celia couldn't ride in the wagon any longer. Father said the horses couldn't pull the extra weight. Sarah's feet were calloused from walking, and her right heel was stone-bruised, but there was nothing to be done. Her soles were so dirty, even after soaking in the stream all this time, that Sarah imagined they would never come clean. Sometimes she wanted

to sit down in the middle of the trail and refuse to go a step farther. But she was afraid of the way her father yelled when he got
angry, which seemed to be every day now. So she limped on,
piggybacking Celia when her little sister's legs got tired.

Father acted as if he didn't even care that Indians might
be lurking about, or that her heel hurt, or that Mother didn't
feel well. He acted as if he didn't care about anything. Sarah
could feel her cheeks get hot just thinking about the way he'd
go for whole days without speaking to them or offering to help
Mother with the chores. Some nights he even forgot to water
the horses, so Cephas took the poor beasts to the river in the
rustling darkness.

At bedtime, when Mother read the Ten Commandments
aloud, Sarah always cringed when she heard the one about
honoring your father and mother. She had no trouble honoring Mother, but Father was much harder. How could you
honor someone who was so unfeeling and who wouldn't even
say good morning? He hadn't smiled once since the Loup
River, barely a few days from Council Bluffs. And he got so
angry at her, red in the face, every time she scorched the beans.
It was hard to cook beans over a fire without burning them
once in a while, especially since she had to breathe that horrid
smoke from buffalo chips. Sarah was the one who had to scrub
the cooking pot anyhow.

Once Cephas left his only cap where Father stepped on
it, and Father threw it in the fire. Poor Cephas fished it out
with a stick, but the crown had burned through making it useless. Cephas wore it anyway.

Sometimes Sarah tried to speak to her father, but he either ignored her or stared at her with that blank look and
didn't answer. It made her angry, but it puzzled her, too, and
made her cry into the Rising Sun quilt at night when everyone

was asleep. She remembered not long ago, back in Wisconsin, Father had always been so kind. He had gently tugged her braids and took her and Cephas for walks to collect pretty rocks. He helped Mother cook dinner when her headaches bothered her, and he swept the floor for her.

Now he was like someone else—someone who had given up. He acted as though he was just marking time until they starved or the horses died. Between spurts of anger, he walked around with his attention somewhere else. It embarrassed Sarah whenever they met anyone on the trail. Father acted so rude, even though Mother tried to make up for it by being especially gracious. And his hair hadn't been combed for weeks. It shot outwards in all directions, wild and snarled and dirty. It made him look like one of those mountain men she had read about. Whiskers made dark stubble on his face, and his forehead was streaked with dirt. He barely ate despite Mother's encouragement, so his bones stuck out all over.

Sarah's feet were getting cold, and she knew she should return to camp. She didn't want to go back to the wagon, even though Mother would be getting worried that she'd been gone too long. If she went back, she'd just have to cook beans again, or pick grass out of Father's boots, or search for more firewood or buffalo chips. She'd had enough chores to last a lifetime. When she grew up, she was never going to do chores again. And she certainly wasn't going to attempt any wagon trips to California.

Sarah snapped off a twig and found a few blades of strong grass. She'd make Celia a stick doll while she was sitting here. Father would say that there was no time for silly child's play, but the bright look on Ceely's face would be worth the price. Deftly, she crafted the little doll, tying its rough arms and legs in place with twisted grass strands. She would surprise her little sister with it tonight when Father was off by the river staring at the map.

Sarah slowly walked back to the wagon, the stick doll in her apron pocket. Maybe if she helped Mother with supper again, the two of them could swim in the river after dark and wash away the trail dirt. Mother had said they mustn't bathe in the daylight. But poor Mother was so tired lately—maybe she wouldn't want to bathe. She had promised to make Sarah a new summer dress, but Sarah was still wearing her old winter wool, and it was nearly July. Sarah sorely disliked the way it itched. It showed too much of her legs, too, and offered little protection from the clouds of mosquitoes that swarmed along this stretch of trail. She always dipped her knees when they saw other travelers, hoping to make the skirt reach closer to her ankles.

There was Father, stretched out in the shade under the wagon while Mother worked over the cook fire again. Father looked like Ceely's stick doll lying there with his arms flung wide, a skeleton covered with leathery, sun-darkened skin. The wagon wheel cast the shadows of its spokes across his rising and falling chest and across his closed eyes, dividing him into segments.

# CHAPTER 5

## MARY

In the fading daylight, Mary could see Fort Laramie on a low bluff across the river. Its small buildings caught the sunset's orange glow, making the settlement shine like a flash of hope. Finally, after weeks of struggling, they could find a fresh start here: trade the horses, buy flour, post her letters. She had anticipated the fort for so many weeks that it felt as though this rough seedling of civilization were heaven itself.

Blackey stumbled against the bay. Mary pulled on the reins to give him time to rest. After all this time they could finally put an end to his torturous work and offer him freedom from the wagon's dead weight. The Doctor said that even one of the horses would trade for a team of oxen. Blackey was on the verge of collapse, but despite his pathetic condition, his value was indisputable. He was a good horse, too, and faithful, obeying his master's commands without protest or question. For all his simplicity, this quiet animal held the quality that Mary worked to attain every day of her life: pure unquestioning faith in her Master.

"The grass is too poor here to stop." The Doctor's voice interrupted her thoughts. "We'll have to camp upstream and come back in the morning."

Mary rubbed the back of her neck. She could see that the grass was gone from this popular rendezvous spot, but she could hardly bear to pass by the fort, even temporarily. Nevertheless, she acquiesced and gave the horses the signal to move on.

It wasn't until they had driven three miles upstream in the darkness that they found adequate feed. There was a new wagon train camped there, a large ox train of 30 or 40 wagons they hadn't seen before. Americus halted the horses with a sharp command when it came into sight and then grabbed the harness and started up again, making a wide arc around it. Mary yearned to greet the women who waved from their campfires, but Americus seemed intent on getting past as quickly as possible.

It was then that Mary noticed Captain McFarland's train, too, farther up the river. Even in the darkness she could recognize Tessie's wagon, familiar as a favorite old shawl. Tessie was crouching over her crackling fire poking the embers and adjusting the lid on her cook pot, and Mary could see Captain McFarland sitting on a wagon tongue repairing something in his hands.

"Americus, that's our old train over there. Would you mind if I visit Tessie for a few moments?"

Her husband barely nodded his agreement as he pulled the horses around so that the back end of the wagon faced the group and halted. Mary lifted Celia into her arms and hurried over to Tessie's fire.

"Tess?"

"Mary! Oh, is it really you?" Tess rose quickly and took her hand, drawing her away from the smoke that stung their eyes.

"Oh, Tess! I'm so happy to see you. You can't imagine how much I've missed you."

"How are the children? How are the horses doing?"

"We're getting along. The children are well, but the horses are bad. Blackey is worn to the bone; he wobbles when he pulls and leans against St. Lawrence for support. The Doctor says he'll trade him for oxen in the morning. I can barely endure the waiting. I feel despicable driving those pathetic beasts every day, and I'm afraid we'll be stranded."

"I wish I could persuade our train to wait for you," Tessie answered. "It's hopeless even to try, though. We've been delayed for a few days, and by now the men have already done their trading at the fort. They said to be prepared to pull out before sunrise and make quick progress to the Sweetwater River."

"Perhaps Americus can be quick about his trip to the fort. Then we may be able to overtake you again, Tess." With fresh oxen in the harness, anything seemed possible.

It was late when Mary finally hugged her friend and carried Celia back to the wagon, but her mood was light as she thought about morning. Americus would visit the fort early and take care of all their needs. Crossing the North Platte with the children was an unnecessary risk, so the Doctor would go over alone, leading Blackey through the current.

In the morning she prepared a dinner for the Doctor to take along and found the letters she had written to her mother and sisters. How many weeks had they not heard from her? They must be worried to death at her long silence. She had promised her mother she would write often and keep a journal, and she had succeeded at writing the letters. Why hadn't she realized that this land was so remote that posting her letters was nearly impossible?

The journal was another matter. At first she had blithely recorded each day's date, the details of the trail and events that seemed remarkable, but as the trip grew more grueling her time and strength faded. She had envisioned long pleasant days riding in the wagon reading aloud to the children and writing down her thoughts in her beautiful script. Now she was doing the work of a hired hand instead. Her fingers, rough and stiff and chapped, had a hard time even gripping her pen.

She curried Blackey until he shone as she had seen the Doctor do, and patted him gently on the neck, promising him freedom. On impulse, she tied a bit of shiny red ribbon into his dark mane. It made him look cared for, and it took one's attention away from the sharp bones sticking out from beneath his hide. She watched as Sarah kissed his velvety nose and whispered her good-byes into his flickering ears.

Then Mary went to the wagon and pulled the gold coin Tessie had given her from between the pages of her Bible. She hoped the surprise of it would please the Doctor so much that he wouldn't be angry with her for accepting charity. It was a good thing Laramie was situated where it was. They had to have flour and other provisions if they didn't want to starve out here. And a rifle. To think of having a gun again! Americus wasn't a practiced rifleman, that was certain, but he could use it for protection and could shoot a deer for meat.

The Doctor climbed onto Blackey, although Mary wished he would walk. He looked down at them all, his close-set eyes squinting in the sun, and nodded a curt good-bye. Mary handed him the gold coin.

"This is for flour to last us until the next fort," she said quickly, half expecting him to explode with wrath at her secret. "If there's enough, I hope you'll bring salt pork and dried apples, as well."

Americus looked incredulous and started to speak, but he clenched his jaw and said nothing. Then he rode off down the trail. Mary wished she had thought to comb his hair, which stuck up in its usual unruly tufts. After he had gone,

Mary saw Blackey's red ribbon lying trampled in the dust.

Tessie's train was miles up the North Platte by now and the ox train had pulled out early, too. Nothing was left of them except the trodden grasses and the old, smoking fires in a rough circle on the landscape. The place looked stale and used, littered as it was with the left-behind debris of a thousand travelers before them. The riverbank was trampled into hundreds of muddy hoof prints. Mary wondered briefly how the Sioux felt when their grasslands were spoiled like this.

Indians. That was a frightening thought. Here she was all alone with the children. She tried not to think about the recent skirmishes with United States soldiers she overheard Captain McFarland talking about. Hadn't God protected her family so far? She made herself concentrate on tidying the wagon and putting more beans on to cook. Tess had told her about a new way to fix them by mashing them and patting them into a block, making a loaf to slice. At least it would be a slight variation from the same old dinner fare.

It was lonely here, especially after the camaraderie of last night. The only sound was from St. Lawrence. The horse seemed not to notice that Blackey was gone as he cropped the grass or snorted through his nostrils. It was so quiet that Mary could hear his tail swishing. The children were down at the river, poking sticks at something in the water.

By midafternoon, Mary began taking short forays to the river to search for signs of the Doctor returning, but each time only the silver water greeted her. Finally, in the heat of the day, she saw him coming far off. He had crossed the river again, and he seemed to be riding something up the wagon tracks. Mary felt her stomach lurch. He wouldn't be riding oxen. Certainly he wouldn't have traded for more horses after all the trouble they'd had with Blackey and the bay.

Sarah came to stand beside her, holding Celia's hand to keep her away from the current.

"Do you see him, Mother?"

"Yes, I do. But I can't tell about the animals he's bringing."

Sarah looked where she pointed and squinted her eyes against the glare of the river. After a while she said, "It looks like Blackey to me."

Could it be true? Mary stared harder. Her hands started to tremble as she realized her daughter was right. It was Blackey, his head drooping from the short walk. Mary stood rooted to the spot, her hand over her mouth, until he got closer. Then she could see there were no sacks of flour. Her letters were poking out from beneath the saddle blanket.

Thoughts jumbled in her mind. There must be an explanation. Perhaps the traders were gone, the fort deserted. No. In all likelihood, Americus had failed to cope with the trading.

"Now, Mary, don't say a word." he said. "There's a trading post a few miles up the river, and we can do our business there just as well as at Laramie. In the morning, we'll head up there."

"But, Americus! Surely Laramie must have the things we need, and . . . ."

He interrupted her. "We'll do it in the morning, I said."

Mary stopped. It seemed as if her heart had quit beating and words stalled in her brain. She felt as if her body would never move again. What had happened at the fort? Another quarrel? Maybe her husband hadn't gone there at all but had curled up on the ground for a nap instead. Now what? She knew Americus. He would never tell her what had transpired, and he wouldn't waver in his determination to pass by the fort. All she could do was hope there truly was a trading post—and that it had supplies and oxen.

Before dawn the next morning, Mary gave up trying to sleep. She crept from the wagon to watch for the sunrise. Even when the eastern sky lightened and turned a soft yellow promising a beautiful day, she couldn't relax. She hurried the children through their chores and fixed breakfast quickly. The sooner they were on the trail, the better. Mary couldn't swallow coffee or any of the new bean loaf but promised herself she would try to eat once they reached the trading post.

The post was roughhewn and dingy, but to Mary it was a welcome sight. There were oxen scattered around it. When they drew near, the Doctor instructed Mary to stay with the children while he went to negotiate by himself. Mary buried her misgivings, determined to be obedient and keep the harmony.

"Come, children. Into the wagon with you, and I'll read some of *The Pilgrim's Progress*. We haven't read together for a long while, and it will make the time go faster until Father returns with our new oxen," she said a little louder than she needed. She watched the Doctor pick up Blackey's reins and walk off, his shoulders hunched like an old man's.

Celia squirmed on the quilt as Mary read, but Cephas and Sarah listened to the story with their full attention for more than an hour until they heard slow hoof beats on the ground. Mary looked out.

This time her husband looked angry as he pulled Blackey back to the wagon. His face was red, especially at his sharp, high cheekbones. Mary's heart began pounding. She needed to find out what was wrong before Americus made them leave this place of relative safety. Quickly she stepped down from the wagon and walked toward him.

His eyes were focused straight ahead, and his hand was clenched around the leather straps that held the horse in tow. He stood tall with his shoulders thrown back.

"I couldn't make the trade, Mary." It was all he said, but he spoke with finality. His tone invited no questions. "We'll overtake that ox train and get some provisions from them. Maybe they have an extra animal or two."

Desperation hit Mary with a feeling like suffocation. Whatever could her husband be thinking? Or was he being mindful at all of the nearly dead horses and the miserable hungry children? There was no flour. No rifle, no oxen. There might be no more civilization for hundreds of miles and certainly no chance of overtaking the ox train. The dreaded hill country lay ahead, "treacherous, isolated, and harsh" according to the guide book.

Fear was prodding her like the horns of a nasty bull. No one in his right mind would make the decisions the Doctor had made these past two days. She knew that before the day was over she would plead, beg, and reason, asking him to change his mind.

And she knew without a doubt that he would not.

# CHAPTER 6

## MARY

Descending this cliffy ravine near the Sweetwater River had been frightening enough, but climbing back up looked impossible. Mary wiped her perspiring hands on her apron and lifted another mound of bedding from the wagon. At least it wasn't raining today, which made unloading less of a chore. She wondered how many times had they unpacked in the 600 or so miles they'd traveled from the Missouri. Even empty, the wagon was so heavy the horses could barely drag it to the top of these deep gulches.

Americus was inside moving things to the back where Mary could lift them down. Her back hurt today, but there was no help for it. She unloaded the butter churn, Americus's medical bag, the cook pots, and what remained of the beans.

"Mary, what in hell's name is in this wooden chest we keep unloading?" he asked, hauling Mary's oak chest with metal hinges from under the bed.

"It's Granny's silver teapot and a few of her other heirlooms."

"Teapot? That silver teapot?" Her husband looked at her as if she were out of her mind. "These horses are hauling a silver teapot across the continent?"

"Americus, it doesn't weigh but a few pounds, chest and all. It's a treasure to me." Something fluttered in Mary's head, a small warning.

"Treasure or not, we're leaving it here." His voice turned sharp. "Find a place by the trail. We're not bringing it another foot."

"Oh, Americus! No! Please! I can't!"

"These horses are getting weaker by the day. What do you intend to do, Mary—hold tea parties on the frontier? Leave it here, I said."

No proper woman would argue with her husband. Mary could feel tears gathering, and her chest tightened. It wouldn't do to scream and protest the way she wanted. Maybe she could calmly appeal to her husband's sensibilities. Long ago back home, that would have worked.

"Americus, please. It's a family heirloom, irreplaceable. And it's such a little thing. I'm willing to leave the churn behind—and even the Dutch oven—but not the teapot. I want to pass it on to Sarah someday."

"Absolutely not! It will be utterly useless in California. I don't know why you brought it in the first place." Two red spots appeared on his concave cheeks.

She must, of course, defer to her husband's wishes and preserve the peace. But she wanted to clutch the chest to her and put it back in its place. She wanted with her whole being simply to defy him!

"Americus." She adjusted her voice, mindful of the children. "This teapot has been in my family for fifty years. It . . . it reminds me of home. Of family. I cherish it . . . I need it."

"Mary." His voice was barely controlled now. "Leave the churn and the Dutch oven and the teapot. Do as I say! And get rid of those spare wool blankets while you're about it. And that packet of your writing paper. It's heavy."

Her heart was thumping violently now. Her face was red, she knew, and she could hardly breathe for the wild resentment filling up her chest. She started to speak, but caught herself just in time. A cultured woman always kept her self-control.

She turned and blinked her stinging eyes and tried to swallow the lump in her throat. It wedged there, big and firm as a river rock. Slowly she turned back and took the wooden chest Americus thrust at her.

She'd seen belongings abandoned along the road, of course. Bedsteads and dressers and spinning wheels. Walnut chairs. Fine dresses and someone's mirror, broken into a million shards. Until now, she hadn't known the heartache.

She carried the chest to the side of the road and placed it under a bush of flowering sage. It seemed like a coffin. She stood beside it for a moment, her head bowed, then straightened her shoulders and walked back to the wagon. Americus was gone. She grabbed her bundle of writing paper, wrapped it in a clean cloth, tied it with a red ribbon from home, and tucked it into her apron pocket. At least she would keep her paper! She would carry it with her, bear its paltry few ounces of weight herself! Her thin leather Bible, too, for that matter.

She grabbed her set of white wool blankets and stuffed them in an old flour sack, which she tucked under the bed. They weren't heavy. Certainly it wasn't unkind to expect the horses to carry their small weight. She wanted them for trading, or for keeping the children warm when they crossed the mountains in the fall. They might mean survival.

Perhaps she could smuggle the teapot in, too. Leave the heavy wooden chest here and hide the teapot in the trunk. But she feared her husband's wrath if ever he discovered it. He was such a changed man. There was no telling how he would react if he found that she had disobeyed his wishes.

Maybe even her heirloom teapot wasn't worth the risk.

# CHAPTER 7

# AMERICUS

It had been days since they'd started along the Sweetwater. Americus saw the land ahead ease upward, reaching away to the horizon in a grand, long sweep dotted with that odd, blue-green sagebrush he'd never encountered until this trip. It tufted up like scrawny miniature trees across this barren land. A rough gray sign staked into the hard-packed dirt said "South Pass," but Americus wondered. South Pass, according to the deceptive guidebook, climbed over the Continental Divide, the high ridge that cut the country in two, sending rivers on one side crashing into the Pacific and on the other side rushing toward the Atlantic. This gentle, almost unnoticeable incline couldn't be South Pass.

He sat in the dust near the wagon and stared at the map. His body felt stuck to the ground as surely as if he'd been sewn there by his trousers. In a few minutes he'd get up and harness the horses to see if they could make a mile or two. In a few minutes. For now, he couldn't move, couldn't muster the energy to put his feet beneath him and shove himself off the hard earth.

What difference did it make if this was South Pass? The horses were too jaded to pull the wagon uphill, no matter how imperceptible the slope. He tried to think what to do, but fatigue gripped his mind, deadening his thoughts. The answer seemed as mysterious and remote as the cold stars that stared down at them each night and laughed at his pathetic efforts to reach California.

He wished his leg would stop aching. He couldn't remember injuring it, but it hurt. Last night he'd dreamed that Blackey had trampled it. The horse had reared up and purposely dashed it with his forefeet, a glint in his horse eyes Americus had never seen in real life. Maybe it was revenge for all the recent toil. Whatever it was, it was unsettling, even though he'd quit being so irritated by the horses and their constant faltering. Now he just felt a detached remote indifference to them, with no more affection than he felt toward that idiotic stick doll Sarah had made for Celia.

It was his family who annoyed him now. It seemed odd how much energy he had all those times when he was angry— strength that seemed as boundless as this vast continent. Mary with her white face and hollow eyes, and Celia, who cried too much. Sarah, constantly scratching her forearms beneath those too-short sleeves and burning the blasted beans all the time. Even Cephas, who left his belongings everywhere a person would trip over them. He wondered how long he could put up with them all, especially if they were to be stranded here beside the Sweetwater.

Sweetwater! Whoever had named this river surely hadn't been in his boots. If he'd been naming streams in this hostile country, he could have chosen something more fitting: the Hellwater or Devil's Creek. Torment Divide instead of South Pass. The name "Sweetwater" had even misled the children, who had run ahead and sneaked a taste of the cold current, hoping that the water would, indeed, be sweet. But it wasn't the slightest bit out of the ordinary. It tasted no better than the sluggish, turbid Platte. As for a sugary treat, they had been sorely disappointed.

He looked out over the land behind them. From where he sat, a short way from the place the horses had failed last night, he could see forever. In the distance, white clouds inched their way across the huge sky. A restless herd of buffalo—thousands of them—swarmed the distant swells, and the river wound through the dry land like a piece of gigantic rope that stretched for miles. Miles that had taken a huge toll, and not just on the horses. He felt a hundred years old, decrepit and made of marble. All that enthusiasm he'd had back in Wisconsin was gone, every last ounce of it. Those days seemed as far back as childhood.

He remembered his mood in the weeks before they'd started out. He'd had boundless vigor. Mary's tears had seemed minor, a temporary trifle to be endured. He felt dauntless, as though all those warnings in the guide book were simply words on a page. There was no doubt in his mind that his strength and ingenuity would carry the day on the trail, and the horses he'd chosen so carefully would rise to the occasion, even though his acquaintances kept insisting otherwise. Get oxen, they'd said. Tough, plodding oxen, strong and reliable. He had known better. These horses were the best stock he could buy. They could manage a little overland trip. It couldn't be too difficult. After all, thousands of others had traveled the trail before him and had made it to California.

They'd be invincible, he and Mary, so the miles would slip by like a sleigh ride. An all-summer picnic, he'd told her. He had envisioned them rolling across the green prairies, a sparkling river beside them, helping the other poor emigrants who had broken wagons or sick families. They would make good time, arriving in California late in August. The children would swim or play hide-and-seek along the way, and roast their nightly steaks over fragrant campfires.

This, though, was about as far from his imagined odyssey as could be. He couldn't fathom where his vigor had gone and why the simplest things seemed overwhelmingly difficult. In the past, occasionally his customary good humor seemed to flee at times, leaving him with nothing but a desire to sleep. Those times were mild in contrast to the malaise and dark thoughts and dead tiredness that affected him now.

Mary was—what was she doing? Loosening the picket stake on Blackey and leading the limping creature toward the wagon. Certainly she wasn't going to hitch up herself! But he remembered she had watched him carefully yesterday as he put St. Lawrence into the traces. She didn't look his direction. Instead she lured Blackey to the wagon, talking to him in a soft voice and stroking his dusty neck. Why couldn't she just let a man rest?

"Americus," she said when she got close enough, "We need to get on the trail. The sun's been up for hours."

"I know." His words were short. "It's no use, Mary. They can't pull uphill, and it's got to be uphill ahead. South Pass."

"Well, don't you think we should make an attempt? We can't just sit here."

"We need to lay over a day, let Blackey recover."

"Americus, we've been laying over and over and over. At this pace, snow will catch us on the wrong side of the Sierra Nevada. We're so far behind our schedule!" Her voice climbed a notch. "It's dangerous, this slow pace. And we're almost out of provisions. The beans are nearly gone." The Doctor saw her glance to the wagon where the children were tidying up.

Anger swept over him, lending him strength. He rose to his feet, snatching Blackey's tether from Mary's small hands.

She took a step back, but then held her ground. Americus heard her take a deep breath.

"We've got to trade these horses, Americus. We'll die out here if we don't. We've got to stop at the next settlements wherever they are, whether you want to or not, and trade for oxen."

He stopped, shocked. He detected a tone he hadn't heard from her before, different from her usual gentle words and her habit of deferring to him. Her chin seemed stronger this morning, too, as though it had a mind of its own in her face, jutting out in a certain way to let him know she meant what she had said. She took another deep breath. Inside the wagon, the children were silent. "But we've got to get there, first. We've got to hitch up and get there."

He didn't answer. His anger faded, surprisingly, and again he was too tired to move. She was right, of course. Forcing his feet to take a step, he led Blackey to the harness. Mary went to the bay, dozing in the sun, and loosened his picket stake as well. The day had started, whether he was ready or not. The children were jumping out of the wagon, ready to trudge along the dusty ruts. Sarah smiled a shy smile as she glanced at her mother. She'd heard, of course. She'd heard Mary take charge, if even for a brief second, but he was too tired to care.

"Children," he heard Mary call. "Did you say your Bible verses to each other?"

"Yes, Mother," Sarah replied. "I helped Ceely remember hers."

"Thank you, dear. Now let me look at your heel, Sarah. Is it still sore?"

"Yes, but look at Cephas's foot instead, Mother. He cut it yesterday on a rock. It's an ugly gash, but he didn't say anything. I think it needs dressing."

The Doctor heard the conversation in a daze. Blackey was hitched, and St. Lawrence stood ready. His hands worked so slowly he felt as though his slim, calloused fingers were detached from his body, doing some slow-motion dance of their own. The sun was high in the blue sky, and the breeze was gone. His balding forehead and long, straight nose were scorched and tender. The wagon's left brake dangled at an odd angle after he'd accidentally knocked it askew with the grub box yesterday, but they probably wouldn't need the brakes today anyway. He could fix it later.

Cephas was sitting on a flat rock while Mary rubbed grease on the sole of his foot and bound it with a rag. She looked up at the Doctor and nodded, a bob of her head that told him she would be ready in a moment. Cephas's face looked peaked like Mary's, and the boy was skinnier than ever. Now his foot was in trouble. Well, that was unfortunate, but the horses couldn't pull another ounce. Cephas would have to be a man and walk like the rest of them. Americus spoke to the team, leaning his bony shoulder against the wagon to push. The wheel moved an inch and then two, and then a few yards.

The ruts etched in the dry earth pointed the way. They slid off into a hazy distance that seemed to Americus like infinity.

M ary stood on the summit of South Pass looking out over the landscape ahead. The high plateau seemed to stretch on forever, a vast ocean of undulating plains, blue–gray and gold and muted green. She had earned this panoramic vista, earned it inch by inch with the struggle that got them here. For a while it seemed as though they would be stranded on the Pass's eastern slopes, the horses too jaded to pull any longer. Somehow, inconceivably, Blackey and the bay had risen to the occasion, pulling and faltering, stumbling and stopping, dragging the wagon until it felt as if ascending the gentle incline over the Rockies went on for centuries. Finally they reached this magnificent viewpoint where the trail seemed to halt its uphill slope. Ahead of them, the land was gently, mostly, downhill.

The sage was low to the ground here, scrubby, Mary supposed, from the constant winds and winter's cold. It stretched as far as she could see, turning the landscape into a nubbly sea of blue. Here and there it bloomed with thick, fragrant clusters of flowers, their greenish yellow a contrast to the smoke-colored leaves. They were subtle flowers, but beautiful in a way Mary wasn't used to. Not showy red or pink like her roses back home.

They blended with the land, holding their glory in check but lending the air their wild and delicate fragrance.

The trail was scoured so deeply into the landscape that it was flanked with banks of reddish brown dirt, cracked and dry now in the August sun. Mary knew that dust would roil up behind a sizeable wagon train in a choking cloud before the wind caught it and blew it into the distance, and she made a conscious note to be grateful that their slow, solitary pace stirred hardly any dust at all. Behind them, the bare rocky summits of the Wind River Mountains rose on the northeastern horizon.

The sky pulled her gaze upward, as it did every day on this vast expanse. Enormous and ever changing, it reached down in all directions to touch the earth. Today it was filled with huge gray and white clouds, billows and billows of them that floated above the lonely landscape, constantly changing shapes and shades of color. Sunlight streamed from behind them in visible rays, illuminating the plains between cloud shadows.

To the west, though, a bank of black thunderheads hung low. Silent mist fell from them, dissipating before it reached the ground. Mary knew the signs of an encroaching thunderstorm and she knew, too, how quickly storms advanced across these plains. They frightened her with their violence. She grabbed the harness and hurried the horses along the blessed downhill slope—thankfully not steep enough to require the brakes—into a hollow. It wouldn't do to be caught by lightning standing alone against the sky at the top of South Pass.

Almost immediately the wind began to gust, pushing against Mary's skirts and rippling the canvas wagon cover. The smell of new moisture and sage blew from the west and dry grit stung her face. Celia ran to bury her face in Mary's apron. Mary lifted her into her arms.

"Let's get in the wagon, Celia," she said. "Find Cephas and Sarah, too. It's going to rain." Americus would see to the horses. Already they were white eyed from the approaching thunder.

As she and the children climbed into the wagon, Mary cinched up the forward end of the wagon cover and watched the storm advance rapidly. In less than a minute the wind was gusting so hard that it seemed strong enough to blow the wagon top off. She could imagine it snatching all their worldly belongings and scattering them across the plains like lost children. On the horizon, a flash of lightening cracked straight from the clouds to the ground. Thunder, low and rumbling, followed.

Suddenly the lightening was all around them and deafening thunder boomed. The children, even Sarah, put their fingers in their ears and hid their heads under the quilt. Mary peeked outside at the Doctor, who was wrestling with the horses. He had succeeded in unhitching them and tying them to the back of the wagon, but with each crash of thunder they tried to rear. In their panic they yanked the wagon with sudden sharp movements. The light faded as the first huge raindrops hit the canvas, leaving large splats of water that quickly turned to mud as they mixed with the powdery dust collected there. From inside the wagon, they sounded as big and powerful as the enormous grasshoppers that often flew onto the wagon cover and bounced off again. At first the canvas stayed dry and the dirty drops slid harmlessly down its contours, but soon they soaked the oily fabric, collecting in the low places. It wasn't long before water began dripping through, making wet patches on the bedding.

The thunder and lightening were moving past, progressing across the plains like a determined regiment, but Mary could tell that the rain had settled in. Sarah sat miserably on the trunk, her shawl over her head. The front end of the wagon was leaking badly, but Mary wanted Celia—and perhaps Cephas if he would—to nap. The poor children were damp and cold, and it would be far better if they could sleep through the rest of the storm. Snatching a blanket, she moved to the front of the wagon and knelt just inside the opening to hold it over the bedding and keep the two of them as dry as she could.

The large drops pelted harder, driven by the cool wind. It blew through the small opening in the canvas and dripped from above, soaking Mary's wool shawl and her dress and dripping down her back as she held the blanket over the children. At long last, Celia and then Cephas drifted off to sleep. Mary didn't want to move for fear of waking them, but she could feel her muscles stiffen as the wind chilled her wet clothing. The rain seeped down her shoulders until it was running in icy rivulets into her bodice and sleeves. Then the hail began, its stinging particles of ice pelting the wagon's flimsy canvas and Mary's back. She glanced over her shoulder and saw it building up on the ground like snow, turning the plains white.

Mary wasn't sure how long she knelt there keeping the children dry. She was astonished at how stoic she could be in bearing discomfort now. The trail taught hard lessons but it taught them well. Back home, she never could have endured such prolonged misery; out here she could triumph over it.

The Doctor finally quieted the horses. He climbed into the wagon to wait out the storm. Mud was spattered up and down his legs, and water streamed from his windswept hair and dripped off the tip of his nose.

Eventually the rain let up and stopped. Mary tried to unknot herself from her awkward position but her arms were as rigid as oak sticks, and her teeth chattered even when she clenched her mouth shut. It was as if she had become a statue kneeling over the children, protecting them as a stone angel would stand guard over a churchyard. The Doctor came to her and tried to help her stand, but Mary collapsed onto the bedding. He sat beside her and wordlessly rubbed her arms until she could move them again and covered her with a blanket in a futile attempt to warm her.

Mary lay on the damp quilt while darkness fell. Sarah was asleep now, too, and Mary moved closer to her warmth. She was still shivering, but her clothes weren't quite so wet and her mind was quieting.

*The power, and the glory, Lord,* she thought. *We have seen Your world and all its ferocious power. Please help us survive its terrible glory until the end of the trail.*

# CHAPTER 9

## SARAH

It seemed to Sarah as if the small wagon train appeared from nowhere. St. Lawrence was creeping along through the deserted ruts, as usual, taking the wagon's weight. Blackey was leaning on his teammate, barely able to keep up. The land ahead looked level in the twilight, but suddenly it dropped away into a hidden hollow. That's where the circle of wagons nestled. A group of oxen grazed nearby.

Mother, high on the driver's seat, saw them first. She gave a little cry and covered her mouth with her hand. By the time Father looked up, she had stopped the horses. Quickly she ran her hands over her hair and asked Sarah to wipe the soot from Celia's face. Then, without a glance at Father, she urged the horses down the slope to join the group.

Several men stood up when they noticed the wagon rattling toward them, and the women turned from their chores to look. Sarah cringed to have so many strangers gazing at them. Mother, though, was perfectly suited to the occasion. Already a smile lifted her face as she waved to the stalled travelers.

When they reached the camp, Mother stopped the horses again and stepped down the wheel spokes, her skirts carefully hiding her ankles. Sarah watched her approach the strangers.

Father hung back in the shadows, but Sarah found the courage to scoop Celia into her arms and follow.

While the men and women greeted Mother, Sarah saw several children about Cephas's age scampering about, ragged and brown as biscuits. There were also two tall boys, both with worn trousers badly patched at the knees. Finally, a girl her own age approached with a shy smile. She had a delicate upturned nose and blonde fly-away hair that looked as though it had been braided against its will. Her feet were bare and her dress was too short. Sarah smiled back.

Compared with all the other evenings they had spent on the trail, this one was just as she had imagined. In the flicker of the campfires, there was talk and laughter. The good smells of stew and coffee and fresh biscuits mingled with wood smoke and crushed sage. One tall, angular woman with capable looking hands brought Mother a tin pan filled to the brim with rabbit stew, and a large round loaf of bread. A tall young man with blond hair to his shoulders sat on a wagon tongue playing his banjo while others sang. Their voices rose into the black sky where the full moon shone down as though protecting them from the darkness of the plains. Sarah hadn't always felt that way about the moon. Other nights it had seemed cold and far away.

Later, as she curled up beside Ceely—in the roomy sleeping tent, not the wagon for once, thanks to help from one of the nice men!—she could hear the night guard pacing around the camp with his watchdog. She fell asleep thinking about this stranger protecting them, alert to any possibility.

The new travelers and their captain, Mr. Hendricks, didn't know that Blackey and St. Lawrence would barely be able to pull the wagon another day. It was up to Father, of course, to tell them and ask to borrow their spare oxen. But he didn't, and in the morning, he was in one of the moods Mother politely called "sober." He scowled as if daring anyone to say a word as he hitched Blackey and St. Lawrence to the wagon.

It wasn't long before St. Lawrence began faltering as he obediently pulled. Sarah wondered when obedience stopped being a good trait. Perhaps it was like peppermint sticks—nice in small amounts but bad in large doses. Obedience had its limits, that was for certain. Her whole family—even the horses!—was obeying Father, who wasn't acting like himself at all. It was as if a stone-faced stranger had taken his place.

The other wagons disappeared into the distance ahead. Blackey and St. Lawrence staggered to a halt every few hundred feet before they could press forward again. Sarah thought they could stumble on forever and never overtake the others.

The long day passed. At suppertime, Mother kept driving. Finally, after it had been dark a few hours, they caught up with the train. By then the travelers were asleep, the fires were low, and Mother had to situate the wagon outside their protective circle. Deep sand was interspersed with that odd bluish-green sagebrush, so Blackey and St. Lawrence ate the few blades of grass Cephas could scrounge in the dark and a handful of hay Sarah slipped from the straw-filled mattress.

Her stomach growled. It was too late for supper, of course, but Mother handed them each a small chunk of last night's bread and a cup of cold coffee.

# CHAPTER 10

## CEPHAS

Cephas couldn't believe his eyes. Father was hitching up Blackey and St. Lawrence again! Poor Blackey was too sick. St. Lawrence was worn out, too. The new folks had extra oxen, but Father didn't ask to use them. Mr. Hendricks was so busy that he didn't offer.

Cephas peeked through the crack beneath the wagon cover. Mother was putting things away. She gnawed the inside of her cheek. Maybe she would speak up about the horses like she did that day at South Pass. Cephas remembered the look on her face and the new sound in her voice.

This morning, though, Mother's mouth stayed clamped shut.

Back home, Father always took good care of his horses. They had a warm barn and the best feed, and he curried them every day. Now he even forgot to fetch water for them. He got cross when they were slow, too. Sometimes he yelled words that Mother didn't want Cephas to hear.

Cephas rolled over on his back and kicked the quilt off his legs. It was starting to get light, but he didn't want to get up. Yesterday he walked until his legs felt heavy as rocks. He wiggled his toes in the morning air. He wondered if Mother might have a warm breakfast for him. Then he heard her speak outside the wagon.

"Americus." Her voice sounded like it had at South Pass. "If you don't arrange for some oxen this morning, I am going to. I'm not leaving this camp with those poor horses pulling us. I'm not."

There was a silence, and then nothing but the sound of Father's boots stamping away. Cephas peeked through the crack again. Mother was sitting beside the fire, her face in her hands. Maybe if Cephas put his arm around her neck, she would feel better. Perhaps she would even smile at him and say some cheerful words. He scrambled up and jumped from the wagon bed. Mother glanced up at the sound, but she didn't look as though she wanted a hug after all. Cephas dug his toes into the dirt. He didn't see any breakfast.

In a few minutes Mr. Hendricks led two teams of oxen to their wagon and hitched them up.

"Good morning, Mrs. Powers," he greeted Mother. "How about giving your horses a rest today?"

"We're very grateful for your help, Mr. Hendricks." Mother replied. Cephas didn't think her voice sounded angry any longer, just worn out instead.

"Here, Cephas," he said, lifting the boy and setting him on Blackey's bare back. "Take this poor horse out with the extra stock. He can follow along today. I knew he was spent, but I didn't realize he was so far gone. You folks will have to borrow these oxen for a while."

Cephas did as he was told. Sarah came behind him, leading St. Lawrence. When they reached the dusty spot where the other animals were, Cephas slid off Blackey's back. He stroked the warm place under both horses' manes. Then he lugged the sloshing bucket to them so they could drink. He wished the water would seep down their throats with a magical power that would turn them frisky again.

Mother said Cephas was too young to stay back behind the train to help herd the extra stock. Cephas wished he could. The older boys tended the animals until they thought no one was looking. Then they held foot races, dived into the rivers, and played tricks on one another. It was much better than keeping pace beside the dull wagon day after day, as Mother said he must. She said the big boys got into trouble back there.

It was time to pull out. The train jerked to a clanking start. Mr. Hendricks's oxen pulled as if the wagon weighed hardly anything. They limped, and their hips stuck out, but Cephas thought they pulled better than all the horses in the world.

# CHAPTER 11

## SARAH

Sarah reached deep into the mattress. Mother hadn't yet noticed it was getting flatter and flatter as Sarah sneaked handfuls of its hay to the horses. The straw smelled as sweet as the clean, fresh mornings back on the prairie, but its edges had dried sharp enough to slice her fingers. She pulled out a matted handful. This time she pressed it into the murky water in the bucket. Perhaps if she soaked it overnight, she might soften it enough to braid a straw hat for Cephas. She'd never tried working with straw before, but it seemed simple enough. Such things came easily to her, like drawing and sewing, and molding river bank clay. She didn't even have to pay attention to what her fingers were doing. They moved on their own, twisting or braiding or sketching. In fact, if she started thinking too hard, they got muddled. It was better to let her mind wander and her fingers have free rein.

For now, she'd best get ready for bed. For once she didn't mind retiring early. Mr. Hendricks liked to start the day long before sunup. Today the sky hadn't even been turning gray in the east when his raspy call awakened them. He didn't know how hard it was to crawl from under the quilts when it was still dark! It was true, though, that they were making plenty of progress. Those ugly oxen kept up a steady pace.

At rest stops, Mother went about chatting with her new friends or making little jokes with Cephas. Sarah noticed her brother laughed more easily now, and his eyes didn't dart after every sound he heard. Father, though, avoided even his family and ate his meals alone. Sarah could tell he shrank from accepting charity, especially the use of Mr. Hendricks's oxen. The other women had found out that Mother was out of food so they were sharing their supplies, too. Mrs. Newel brought over some sweet dried apples and a chunk of whitish butter she had made by simply hanging her churn beneath her lurching wagon all day. Mrs. Clark delivered two kinds of beans, and the banjo-playing young man brought a big lump of fresh-killed antelope. Mrs. Hendricks slipped Mother a packet of black pepper and another of allspice. Mother, her cheeks red, borrowed flour from her as well, and from Mrs. Turner.

Sarah tried not to eat much in order to stretch what skimpy provisions they had. Her stomach ached from hunger. She made sure Celia had enough, though. The guide book said there were trading posts along the way where Mother could trade for food. Sarah had seen a few falling-down shacks, but Mr. Hendricks said that most of the traders had long since given up and gone back East.

As she set the straw-filled bucket under the wagon, she saw that the men were gathered around Mr. Hendricks's campfire. Father, surprisingly, was among them, perched on the edge of a water keg. The conversation sounded uneasy, and something was making Mr. Hendricks frown. Sarah walked nearer to hear their words. Suddenly Mr. Hendricks's incredulous voice shouted out.

"Powers! Your horses can't pull you another mile, and you have no provisions. It makes no sense!"

"Why would you want to travel alone?" Mr. Turner

asked, baffled. "It's dangerous, Powers. Even if you don't care about yourself, think of your family."

From where she stood, Sarah could hear Father start to rave, his mouth hissing words into the firelight. She put her fingers in her ears, but she could still see his long, narrow nose and pointed chin stuck out in defiance. As she watched, he stood up abruptly and began pacing as he counted something off on his fingers. Mother stood nearby, shocked into utter silence while tears streamed down her face. Mrs. Turner and the other women discreetly moved away. Mrs. Newel grabbed Celia's and Cephas's hands and hurried them off to the river.

Sarah turned and ran into the darkness. From a distance, she could still hear the furious voices shouting back and forth. At least she couldn't make out the words above her own hard breathing. Now everyone would despise them and be glad to leave them behind.

It was much later when Sarah saw the men scattering to their own dark campsites shaking their heads. By then, she was huddled on the ground, chilled and exhausted from crying, so she made her way back to camp. Mother looked gray, as if she had been dragged along the trail in the dust. Sarah gave her a wan smile and climbed into the quiet, black wagon.

In the early morning, Mother went about with her eyes lowered, packing the dishes while Father harnessed Blackey and St. Lawrence. Mrs. Turner came by and took Mother's hand to bid her good-bye. Sarah felt as if she were watching a funeral. One by one, the women paid their respects, wiping their eyes with their apron corners and carefully avoiding Father. Several furtively slipped provisions under the wagon cover.

Then the train turned back onto the trail, and once again Sarah watched the last wagon rumble out of sight.

# CHAPTER 12

## MARY

*Dear Mother,*

*I hesitate to tell you what has befallen us, but I must unburden my soul. Writing to you soothes me so, and I try to imagine what wise counsel you would offer me if you could be a bird in the heavens watching our progress from above.*

*The terrible truth is that we have once again been left behind to fend for ourselves. Americus quarreled with the leaders of our new train (I forbear giving the details), and now we are again alone in the wilderness. All my efforts to establish our position with our fellow travelers and to make ourselves congenial were for naught.*

*I cannot say exactly where we are, nor what day it is, for I have lost track again, but we may as well be stranded on a remote desert island somewhere in an immense ocean. I shan't grieve you with tales of all our hardships but shall simply say that the horses are nearly dead, our food is gone (all but a few provisions my friends from the ox train left with me), and although I can see for miles in all directions, there is not one sign of civilization—just mile after mile of bleak and uninviting desertlike land stretching to eternity.*

*I am dispelled of hope tonight, for I am certain we shall*

*perish. Even the weather has been contrary, presenting us with another hard storm that completely soaked and chilled us. We are camped in a low hollow where we concluded to stop this afternoon when the horses could go no farther. The children have gone to bed hungry, but I know if I lie down I will not sleep for fear and worry.*

*My health is not good, Mother, although I have not actually taken sick. We have had a great deal to endure, and I fear it has stolen my vitality. For a short time, I thought I might be expecting another child, but that has proven to be untrue, much to my profound relief. Yet even walking tires me and the lightest tasks leave me sorely fatigued. I suppose that my chore of driving the horses like a hired teamster has become a blessing of sorts, although I railed against the idea at first, but it means I do not have to walk this eternal distance to California. I try to hide my weakness from the children, of course, but Americus must certainly notice. He has said nothing.*

*Even the few comforts we encounter seem denied to us. At one of the river crossings behind us, there was a well-built ferry with a proprietor willing to take us across. But we couldn't pay the nine dollars it cost to take the wagon over nor the fifty cents charged for each horse, so we were obliged to drive upstream until we came to a place where we could ford. What I wouldn't have given to step onto that strong boat and let it carry me across!*

*The most difficult cross to bear is this: The farther we travel and the more I see of this continent, the more I realize that, barring a miracle, I will almost certainly never see you again in this lifetime. The distance is simply too great, so much greater than I ever imagined. It breaks my heart in two, and I have shed rivers of tears over the thought in private. I search my soul, wondering if there is any way I could ever return home, but it seems completely impossible from every viewpoint.*

*Sometimes I wonder if I have made thoughtless decisions about my life. But who could have guessed that my loving Americus would want to come West—and that he would become the utter stranger he is out here? Who could have predicted that this pilgrimage would be so much more difficult for us than for so many others? Day after day after day we plod along this tedious way. The horses recuperated somewhat while the oxen borrowed from the train pulled our wagon and offered them pleasant relief. However the last water we came across was alkaline—deadly for the animals to drink—so we had to lead them away, which was no easy task. Now the old water in our kegs is getting low, and we are not certain how far it is to the next river.*

*The only landmarks are the everlasting trail ruts stretching on forever and the many graves alongside, marked by either a pile of stones or a rude plank headboard. Sometimes I stop the horses and gather a handful of sage flowers to place on the permanent resting place of someone's sweet child.*

*Often we see an antelope racing across the plateau or calmly watching from afar, and my mouth waters for antelope steak, which we've found is quite delicious, thanks to gifts of meat our fellow travelers have given us. But Americus seems disinclined to hunt even if we did have a gun, so my yearnings are in vain.*

*As I face the task of another day, I am filled with wonder and amazement about how anyone survives out here, and it comes to mind that the Indians who live here must possess enormous amounts of skill and cleverness. It requires uncanny ability and patience even to kill a rabbit or devise a way to heat some water. Despite my fear of these native peoples whose ways seem so foreign to me, I am awed at their ability simply to stay alive in this harsh place.*

*Mother, I shan't post this letter, filled as it is with the desolate truth. Our situation is truly unspeakable. Yet if the horses can't pull us from this place, and we perish amid this parched and scrubby sagebrush, I know that my heart will be joined forever with yours in eternity. Your great love brings me solace.*

*Your affectionate daughter,*

*Mary*

# CHAPTER 13

# AMERICUS

Americus trudged beside the horses, wondering how much farther his sore feet would carry him. They chafed inside his worn-out boots and hurt where a hole in the leather exposed his foot to the rocky ground. He wished now he'd gone barefoot like the children all those hundreds of miles. Their soles were so calloused that they hardly felt the stones underfoot, although Mary was always fussing over them, dressing a cut or padding a bruise.

He scanned the sweeping horizon. No sign of the Big Sandy yet. That was one river that was probably aptly named. It was peculiar how the map showed it closer than it seemed on this infinite trail. He gave Blackey's flank a slap to hurry him, ignoring the cloud of dust that rose from the animal's dirty hide. The horse quickened its pace for a moment, but then dropped back to its flagging walk.

"Father?" Cephas was running up behind him. The boy was constantly underfoot, staring at him with those deep-set eyes. "I can see the river up ahead. See the little dark line way over there?"

Americus looked where his son pointed. Sure enough, if he squinted he could see a thin winding line slicing its way across the plains miles ahead. He wished he had Cephas's eyesight. He'd started to depend on the boy's clear vision and attention to detail.

"Hmm." It was his only answer. Cephas stood there a moment as if hoping for something more. But when his father silently began trudging ahead again, he turned back to join his sisters.

Americus shook his head. Why hadn't he answered his son? Why in the world couldn't he just act himself? Back home he would have praised Cephas for his sharp eyes that saw everything. He would have thanked the boy for watering the horses this morning, a job he should have done himself, and smiled inwardly at Cephas's look of pleasure. There were times like today when Americus could see his own behavior clearly enough to be embarrassed by it. He was as surly as the bison that roamed these plains, gruff and irritable, but he was helpless to change. Even with his physician's training, he'd encountered nothing like his own symptoms, especially the bleak melancholia that seeped into him like ink into a blotter. He wished there were a medicine he could mix up and swallow that would chase away this darkness. Most times, though, he didn't even care.

He wanted to explain away his hostility and seeming laziness to Mary. It wasn't laziness. Something else was wrong. He wondered if he had lost his reason, if he was becoming slightly deranged. Once he had told Mary that he would go to the ends of the earth for her, and he'd meant it. Now it was too hard even to plod toward the slim streak of the river. What was the point in miring themselves even deeper in this hopeless mess?

At night in the wagon, lying next to Mary, he felt none of his old urging to reach out and touch her, to share their deepest intimacy, even if the children hadn't been curled up next to them. Now he just turned his back, remote and cold as the arctic, and fell into a troubled sleep without even squeezing her hand.

In the past when life seemed overwhelming and fatiguing, he'd been able to cast off the feeling and in a few weeks regain his good humor and vitality. This time it would be as difficult as digging himself out of a grave.

Mary stopped the horses to rest.

"Americus, you're limping. Is something troubling you?"

He sank onto the wagon tongue, silent for a moment before he answered. "Just a hole in my boot, that's all."

"Perhaps you could patch it when we halt for the night. Will we reach the Big Sandy by then?"

"I'm not certain, Mary. It's a ways off yet."

They sat for a few minutes, and then with effort he pushed himself to his feet again. He felt as heavy as the wagon itself, as though it were liquid lead that ran in his veins instead of blood. "Let's go."

A hawk glided overhead on the breeze. It reminded him of the raptors that hunted the home place, their watchful eyes searching for mice in the green fields. He wished he were back there now, at Coldspring Farm he fondly called it. His brother David lived there yet. Americus wondered what David would say about the way this journey had gone sour as quickly and surely as warm milk, for David had helped him plan and prepare for the thrilling undertaking and would probably make the trip himself someday.

He should have stayed where he was with his life picture-perfect and orderly. But a man couldn't ignore the perpetual rumors about gold and wealth and opportunity in California. Even though his medical practice was thriving, years of treating bilious disorders and aches and pains got a bit dull. It made a man want to see those far-off, golden lands for himself.

Well, he was seeing them for himself, all right. On days like this he could admit it was all a dreadful mistake. And there was no sensible alternative but to try to outlast the trail.

# CHAPTER 14

# SARAH

Sarah stood at the top of the steep, gravelly bank that flanked yet another river. She looked at the battered wagon below and held Celia in her arms. The little girl's arms encircled her neck like a too-tight scarf. Sarah remembered when her sister's fine curly hair gleamed gold in the sunlight and smelled of Mother's rose soap. Now the fresh little-girl scent was gone, and her dull, matted hair held the odor of trail dust and old smoke. She was limp and grimy, but Sarah held her close.

Ceely felt lighter than she had when they started from home. Her torn gray dress hung on her small body, and her arms didn't fill up the sleeves anymore. Her cheeks were no longer chubby, and her small hands looked as though they had never been washed, even though Mother scrubbed them each morning. Insect bites were scattered up and down her legs and arms. They were raw and red from where she chafed them. A wide pink scratch ran across her cheek.

At mealtime, Sarah urged Ceely to eat. Sarah knew that her baby sister would rather go hungry than choke down even a mouthful of two-day-old beans or a charred biscuit. Sarah made a game of feeding her, distracting her with stories while she gently pushed food into her mouth. All the while they were going farther and farther from home. Sarah hated to think how each passing day took them deeper into this awful wilderness. Sometimes as she trudged along, lugging Ceely and scanning the landscape ahead, she would make believe she was a grown woman who could remove herself from this terrible trip. She would imagine using coins from her purse to buy a beautiful, fast palomino. Then she would flee back over the plains, taking Cephas and Ceely with her, never stopping until they reached Wisconsin where her grandmother and aunts would welcome them with cries of happiness.

This entire summer had been a series of plodding steps, as dull as the pendulum on a clock. She wondered how many miles she had trudged out of sheer necessity. She had stopped examining the insects she found swaying in wildflowers, or overturning stones to see ants scurry for safety. She quit imagining feathery shapes in the clouds and now wished that they would simply cover up the burning sun. She didn't run races with Cephas anymore, or show Ceely how snake grass could be popped apart into segments and then fitted back together again. Now she trudged along on calloused feet, searching only for cactus spines or sharp rocks that might jab her. She still kept watch for Indians, but the sun made her eyes squint and water.

It seemed to Sarah that no sooner had they crossed one mucky stream than there was another to ford. The big rivers were the worst with their fast, deep waters and stony bottoms. Even more terrible were the nearly perpendicular banks on either side. Sarah shuddered to see Mother drive down the rocky drop-offs. The horses' backs would disappear below the tilting wagon, and the patched-together brake would barely hold. Mother, white faced and trembling, would perch high on the wagon seat, her small feet braced so she wouldn't pitch forward under the wagon's massive iron-rimmed wheels.

Now, from where Sarah stood holding Ceely, she could see that Mother had managed to get the wagon safely down into the riverbed. The uphill bank, though, was slippery and unstable with deep gravel. As Sarah watched, the horses tried to pull the wagon up, but even straining and lunging, they made no progress. Father urged them again, but when they failed, he unhitched them, his mouth set in a straight line. Blackey and the bay, freed from their burden, scrambled up the bank.

Sarah took Ceely to where Cephas was sitting in the dirt poking at ants with a twig. She could see what needed to be done. Before Father could give her a sharp command, she slid down the bank to help unload the wagon. They had unpacked so many times that it went faster now, especially since Father had made them leave behind every single thing that wasn't an absolute necessity. She'd hidden Lucy in the trunk where he would never look, for she knew Father would demand that she abandon her beloved rag doll. As old as she was, Sarah took comfort in thinking of her at night when the coyotes howled and unseen things prowled around the wagon.

It wasn't long before the family's belongings were scattered along the river. Mother was taking the opportunity to air the quilts by spreading them over bushes along the water's edge. They looked like tents, a small village of them, soaking up the sunshine and the dry-air fragrance so different from Wisconsin's.

Father tied the long, thick rope from the horses down to the wagon, so the animals could pull from the top of the bank where the footing was solid. The late afternoon heat was suffocating. Sarah could feel both the searing sun beating down from above and the heat from the baked earth rising to meet it. Father swatted at flies as he worked. They had done this before: Father stayed with the animals urging them forward, and Mother pushed the wagon with all her might from below. Sarah often wondered why they didn't trade places, although it was true that the horses still responded best to Father. Mother, in spite of her efforts, looked like a butterfly pushing on a boulder, her slender, pastel form dwarfed by the thick oak wagon. Whenever Sarah offered to help, Mother wouldn't hear of it, saying it was far too dangerous for children to get behind that immense weight.

"Let's move, boys." Sarah heard her father urge St. Lawrence and Blackey forward, and she held her breath as the wagon inched up the bank. Mother pushed, lending her small strength to the uphill struggle. The horses' poor stringy muscles strained with the effort, the rope stretched tight, and the wagon inched upward a yard or two.

It happened in a flash, in just one second when the horses gave up and the wagon jolted backward a few feet. Sarah heard a scream before she saw Mother go down and the crushing rear wheel roll over her slim white ankle, pressing her fragile leg into the course gravel.

"Mother!" Sarah screeched, scrambling to her side. "Are you hurt?"

There was no answer. Mother's face was gray, and droplets of sweat clung to her forehead and upper lip as she lay back on the riverbank, her right leg protruding from her blue skirt. Her ankle, smeared with mud, was turning a horrifying purple color; already it was nearly twice as big as the other. Blood seeped from deep scrapes. Mother gave a series of short gasps, and she clutched her arms to her torso.

Sarah looked around for her father. Father would know what to do. Yet he was simply standing at the top of the bank, arms limp, surveying the scene as if he couldn't believe what he saw. Sarah screamed at him.

"Father! Mother needs help!"

She heard Ceely crying and Cephas also shouting. Their frightened voices awakened Father from his daze. He sprang for the wagon, grabbing the water bucket, scooping a pailful of cool water from the stream, and hurrying to Mother's side. Mother was holding back tears now and struggling to sit up, her fingers outstretched to gently probe her ankle. Father moved quickly and fluidly, as if by long habit.

"Here, Mary. Try this," he said, his voice surprisingly gentle and soothing just as Sarah remembered it from back home when he had doctored a sick neighbor. "Put your foot and ankle in this cold water for a few minutes. It will make it feel better. Then we'll see if it's broken." His long, slim fingers lifted her foot into the dripping pail and carefully washed away the blood and dirt. Mary looked at him in surprise but said nothing, her face still gray. Sarah felt a lump rise in her throat. Broken! What if Mother's ankle were broken! She wouldn't be able to walk for months, and how could it ever heal properly out here in the wilderness where so much depended on her?

Cephas and Ceely were sliding down the gravelly bank now. Cephas held Ceely's hand so she wouldn't fall. They knelt beside Mother. Cephas's eyes were big and dark in his pale face, and Ceely was still sobbing. Sarah took a long breath and pulled the little girl onto her lap.

"Don't cry, Ceely. Mother's ankle got hurt, but it's going to be all right. Everything is going to be all right." It surprised her that saying the words to Celia seemed to comfort everyone else, too. Even Mother opened her eyes and lifted the corner of her apron to wipe her face. She tried for a smile.

"Sarah's right, Celia. I'm going to be all right. We even

have a doctor in the family!" Her false cheer didn't fool Sarah, but Ceely stopped sobbing. Father's fingers were cautiously pressing on Mother's yellow and purple skin, slowly turning her ankle this way and that until Mother caught her lip in her teeth. At last Father straightened up.

"Well, Mary, it's not broken. It's just been badly bruised. The soft gravel saved you. You mustn't walk on it for a few days, though."

The verdict was like a warm breeze that blew over Sarah, taking with it the cold possibility of a broken bone. Cephas let out a huge sigh, as if he'd been holding his breath all the while. Her brother was a quiet boy, but Sarah knew he fretted and worried just as she did.

Sarah looked at the scene. Suddenly it was as if she were outside the family circle looking in as a stranger might. She saw Mother, pained and pinch faced, holding her useless ankle in her hands, unable to move from the damp gravel. Her skirt, rumpled and dirty, was bunched up around her knees. Sarah couldn't remember Mother ever allowing her ankles to show, and now her legs were exposed up to the knee. She didn't seem to notice. Father looked as though he had used up all his energy. His eyes were dull again, and his slender fingers hung over his bony knees as he sat heavily on the river bank, as if Mother's injury were one burden too many.

She saw Ceely, one hand clinging to Cephas's, the other curled up by her face as she sucked her thumb, her dusty face streaked with tears. Cephas himself was still pale, and Sarah could see him quivering slightly, though not from the river's breeze. Nearby the wagon tilted in the gravel.

Mother had told her earlier today that one of the rivers on this journey was called the Malad, and that the word sounded like the French word for "sick." Sarah wondered if perhaps this was the one, even though Mother had said it was far ahead. She imagined that the river might hold some terrible power to grab passing travelers and turn them into invalids right there on its banks. Maybe some mysterious spirit hid in the undergrowth and waited to engulf passers-by with misfortune. Sarah shuddered at the thought. Mother would say that it was heathenish to think about evil spirits. Yet today, stuck in this malevolent drainage, anything seemed possible.

Sarah stood up so suddenly that Cephas and Ceely looked at her in surprise. She'd better stop thinking about evil spirits or she would scare herself again. Besides, something needed to be done to improve the situation. She grabbed the dipper from the wagon and waded to the middle of the stream, scooping a cupful of clear water for Mother to drink. Then she fetched a clean cloth and wet it in the river, warming it in her hand so Mother could wash her face. She would build a camp-fire to make some coffee. By now it was late in the day, and the air would soon lose its heat. They might as well have some warmth and light—and some smoke to drive away the insects. Cephas and Ceely were hungry, too, she could tell. At least they were in a sheltered spot, out of sight of anyone who might be studying the landscape for lone travelers.

"Cephas, let's find some sticks to build a fire, all right? We'll cook a few beans and make some coffee."

"That's a good idea, dear," Mother's voice wavered, but she was trying to smile again. "I'll watch Celia while you two look for sagebrush stalks. Don't go far, though."

Cephas rose, eager to help. His tattered shirt hung open, showing his bony ribs, but the legs that stuck out beneath his worn pants were sturdy. Cephas had a knack for finding things, and he would return with the best wood, perhaps a shredded piece that would catch a spark immediately and burst into flame. Sometimes he returned from wood gathering with other treasures, too: a broken arrowhead, a black stone polished smooth by running water, and once, a cast-iron frypan that had jostled free from an earlier wagon.

Before them the riverbank rose steeply. The dusky land above it stretched on forever to the west. The undergrowth stirred in a light evening breeze, and the rippling stream bubbled on as before, as it had done for centuries, as if nothing had happened today at all.

# CHAPTER 15

## MARY

*Summer, 1856*
*somewhere on the Great Plains*

*My dear sister,*

*I am writing in haste in hopes of using the last of the evening's light. If darkness falls, I must write by firelight, and the smoke makes my eyes smart so.*

*Before we go another mile on this horrible trail, dear sister, I must write and warn you never to come West, even if your good husband insists it is the proper thing to do. You may as well swallow arsenic as to undertake this treacherous journey, for it is nearly suicide. Do everything in your power to avoid it!*

*Please do not worry Mother with my hardships, but you must know the truth. A westward journey is nothing at all like the entertaining campout I was promised. The reality is much different, filled with backbreaking work and daily threats to our lives. The constant dangers are overwhelmingly real and frightening. Every day I wonder whether the children will perish—indeed, whether Americus and I will perish! But it is the children about whom I fret the most. Although their health has been good (I am so thankful for that!) my poor little Celia cries constantly from misery caused by all number of things—bites of insects, sunburn, cold nights, the hair-raising howls of coyotes and wolves, the unmercifully hot sun. She is less resistant to thirst and hunger than the rest of us, and her tiny soft feet are now tough and calloused—although not tough enough to keep out thorns. Cephas plods along willingly, but his face is so thin under its grime that I wonder if his health is faltering. The children must walk all day now. Our two remaining horses have all but failed, and the children's weight in the wagon would only add to their burden.*

*And we're often hungry, having fed most of our flour to the horses. I fret constantly about where we shall get our next provisions, and try to stretch our scanty supplies as well as I am able. But I must be realistic and face the grim question: Will we starve to death?*

*Now I must set my mind toward getting to California on one foot. The wagon rolled over my right ankle at a difficult stream crossing a few days ago, and although Americus says it is not broken, it is nearly impossible for me to walk. For now I am hobbling around using a sturdy stick for a crutch and depending upon Sarah to do most of the chores.*

*My dear Sarah has been a great help to me, but she despises every second of this undertaking! She is nearly a woman now, with womanly fears of being overcome by Indians, and she sleeps poorly, worrying about encountering them. Although she says nothing, I can see the misery in her eyes and her constant longing to flee home to her school chums. She spends these long days lugging Celia along the trail, gathering the disgusting "buffalo chips" we must use for cook fires, and helping me with the multitudes of chores.*

*I am weary to the bone every day and cannot imagine what is making me so dreadfully fatigued. My own weariness renders me helpless to accomplish many of the tasks that need to be done each day, although I do my best to take proper care of the children.*

*Americus is still acting strangely. Did Mother tell you? His behavior is utterly unfathomable, and if you were here you would never recognize him. He looks and acts like (shall I say it?) a madman. I often wonder if I am married to a man who has lost his reason. Occasionally I see glimpses of my gentle husband, but most times he is a stranger quarreling with others and failing to cope with the challenges of this journey. If I were to admit the truth, dear sister, I would tell you that I am sorely tempted to take the children and flee, despite my marriage vows that tie me forever to Americus.*

*But . . . where would I go? How would I get there? I feel as though I am being pulled along against my will and better judgment, like a twig in a swift current. I've begged Americus to turn back, to end this foolhardy journey, all to no avail.*

*I think you should know that most of the women I've encountered out here are faring poorly. Many have lost a beloved child along the way, which is, I believe, the most terrible heartache a mother can endure. (I thank Almighty God daily for sparing my own children thus far.) Others are expecting to be confined with childbirth along the trail, and I cannot imagine anything more frightening. Still others are so ill they must lie in their jostling wagons all day—a trial that can, at worst, kill a person, and at the least, set one's very nerves ajar! So far we've encountered travelers with cholera, mountain fever, and all sorts of maladies that sometimes claim a person overnight. Indeed, one woman I met seemed perfectly strong and robust in the evening, but she passed into heaven during the night.*

*Even the smallest inconveniences seem designed to bring on misery out here, although I try not to complain. Amid all the other strains it seems a trifle, but I do so miss drinking coffee made with clean water. Here, I drink it because I must, only to find disgusting mud and silt in the bottom of my tin cup. Straining doesn't seem to help much, although it does get rid of the larger pieces of insects, twigs and leaves. My morning coffee is such a chore now, and if I have to eat one more bite of horrid campfire beans, I shall surely scream!*

*There is one saving grace to this journey, and that is the absolute grandeur of this unfamiliar landscape. I cannot begin to describe to you the beauty of God's West, so different from our lovely Wisconsin. The first time I saw the far-off mountains near South Pass, I was struck with awe at their majesty. I simply could not fathom their lofty heights, timbered slopes, green foothills, and peaks that glowed pink when the sun set. The rocky tops seem to scrape the sky, which is as vast and beautiful as the boundless plains we are crossing.*

*And I cannot describe the streams that cross our path. Although they are difficult for the wagon—and treacherous for me, since I am the driver and am often in danger of being swept away—there is a small part of me, when I am safely on their sidelines, that loves their beauty. The wet rocks beneath the clear water are as multicolored as an artist's pallet, and the ripples sparkle engagingly in the sunlight. They bring sustenance to us all—water and grass for the horses, and the blessed opportunity for us to replenish our drinking water and to bathe—a rare opportunity out here. Sometimes I sit on the bank of one stream or another and let its peace seep into my soul.*

*We have encountered mile after mile of sagebrush, an odd sort of branchy bush that seems to grow out of sheer rocky soil without water. When we burn its stalks for fuel, the smoke holds a wild fragrance as unusual as this untamed country we travel.*

*Wildlife abounds at every place along this road. There have been rabbits—large ones—and deerlike antelope that run at tremendous speeds, and hundreds of buffalo. The buffalo are astounding. They travel in gigantic undulating masses and seem unafraid of us, although I am afraid of them! Each bull must weigh as much as two or three horses put together, and they snort frightfully and mill about, trampling whatever is underfoot. People say the meat is good to eat, but I can't attest to that, since we haven't had our rifle for most of the journey.*

*But lest my descriptions of the landscape and wildlife lure you into thinking about undertaking such a journey yourselves, please heed my desperate warnings. This is not a lark or a simple camping adventure, that is for certain. It is a fight for our very lives, and I wonder if we will win?*

> *Don't come. Don't come!*
> *Your loving sister,*
>
> *Mary*

# CHAPTER 16

# AMERICUS

Americus looked out over the landscape. This enormous continent seemed like an enemy as dangerous as any of the world's great armies. It stretched beyond him as far as he could see with no hint of civilization except for the trail itself. Who knew how much farther it was to safety? One measly inch on the map could mean days of travel—and there were plenty of inches to go.

Reaching the top of South Pass seemed like a long-ago miracle, but they had traveled many days since then—he wasn't sure how many—and still there was no change in the countryside. No hint of a far-off trading post or fort. No enticing glimmer of a lake surrounded by lush grazing. Not even a distant shade tree under which to rest. This bare high plateau looked exactly like the countryside they traversed yesterday—and last week for that matter: miles of sloping plains domed by the reaching sky, miles of sagebrush and cracked red soil, miles of dusty trail fading into the immeasurable distance.

Americus felt sure that they must be nearing the place where Mormon settlers were building small scattered settlements, but the view ahead said otherwise. He could no longer trust the guide book, he knew that much. And the map—was the map accurate? He thought it showed this section of the trail winding between the Green River and Ham's Fork.

He wished Mary were stronger. It seemed as though she had less stamina every day, although she said little and continued to do her part. He felt unsettled watching her do the work hired hands should do. Sarah and Cephas were overworked, too. They were constantly hauling water and caring for the horses, or watching Celia and carrying her for miles on end, or scrounging for buffalo chips and sage branches, or packing and unpacking the wagon. The journey was beginning to tell upon them, just as it had taken its toll on him and Mary.

This shortage of provisions was becoming serious. His stomach felt sick half the time from emptiness. He let Mary fret about food, but when supplies were so low everyone was going hungry, it made a man nervous. Nervous and weak.

The horses were a miracle. He couldn't fathom how they survived from day to day. At least the landscape was fairly flat, and even the rivers here had low banks and, in some cases, fairly shallow water. He hitched Blackey and St. Lawrence to the wagon every day, and every day he expected one or the other of them to give up and die, but so far they were making slow progress. Slow, that was the problem. At this rate, they wouldn't be in California—if they made it at all—before the dangerous snowfalls blocked the Sierra Nevada.

The bay stumbled. Mary stopped the horses to rest.

"Americus, why are there are no other travelers out here? Shouldn't we be encountering horsemen and a few wagon trains or those Mormon travelers with their handcarts everyone was talking about back on the Missouri?"

How pale she was, he thought. Poor Mary. She kept up a brave front, but she was worn to the bone, any idiot could see that. Some women were meant for the trail's hardships, built with thick bones and strong wills, but Mary was like a flower—delicate and beautiful, and easily harmed. She sat down to rest whenever she could and her face was a terrible shade of white, as gray-white as the wagon's canvas top. Even her clothes, which back home had always been clean and pressed, were beyond repair. Her apron was dirty and torn and her blue dress tattered. Worst of all, she seemed not to care. Her beautiful hair was knotted and dull and pulled back from her face haphazardly, stuck there with hairpins that stayed in for days at a time. He could tell she had frequent headaches, and her ankle was still swollen and sore.

"I don't know, Mary." It was possible they had taken a wrong cutoff, but he wasn't about to say that aloud. Besides, a person could see so far in every direction that surely it wasn't possible to get disoriented. From the last rise he had spotted a winding depression that seemed to be another river—perhaps the Ham's Fork or the one of those sluggish no-name tributaries. It was nearer than he thought. He hoped there was water in it; the horses could use a good long drink. "I keep thinking we certainly must be nearing the first of those spread-out Mormon settlements, and yet . . . ."

It seemed forever but they finally approached the low slit in the landscape. A small river, but a deep one, flowed through it. Americus noted with relief that there was a bridge of sorts across it, yet as they approached he began to have misgivings. Whoever had hauled the logs and sticks to make this structure didn't know much about bridge building. Americus surveyed its rickety construction and wondered if it would hold the wagon.

They had to try it. He saw no other choice, given how deep the water was and the condition of the horses. There was no possibility that they could pull the load through the muck below. To add more miles traveling upstream to look for a shallower crossing wasn't practical either.

Mary was talking to him again from the wagon seat.

"I don't think it's going to hold, Americus. It's too frail."

"There's no other choice, Mary. We have to cross it."

"But what if it . . ." she stopped herself, ever mindful of the listening children. "Will you go across on foot and see if it's safe first? What if . . . ."

He looked up at her and nodded. What if it collapsed, Mary was asking. Then she would fall into the water along with a 2,000-pound wagon and two thrashing horses.

"Try to get the horses across fast, Mary. It's our only hope. I'll give you the signal, and when the horses reach the bridge, give the reins a sharp, quick slap so they'll know to move as fast as they are able." He started across, not looking back. The rude structure creaked even under his slight weight. It was risky, terribly risky. But then, so was getting stuck in the mud below trying to ford. That could be a fatal error, too.

When he reached the far shore, he turned and looked back. Mary had started the children across holding hands. He waited until they reached him safely and then, taking a quick breath, he gave Mary the signal. The horses stepped onto the bridge as she snapped the reins. The wagon bumped onto the wood, and the structure groaned and wobbled.

Americus shouted at the horses and the startled creatures sensed the danger. They pulled, fast, with every ounce of their remaining strength. The wagon lumbered across, its wheels thundering on the rough surface. As they dashed to safety, the bridge crumbled behind the wagon. With a crash, the supports toppled and fell into the muddy water. Americus stared as the logs and pilings landed in a jumbled heap.

Mary clasped her trembling hands and said a prayer of

thanks. When she climbed down from the wagon seat, her knees buckled and she caught herself on the front wheel. Sarah and Cephas looked wide eyed at the current, carrying with it scraps and debris.

Americus sat on the dirt. His knees, too, were trembling. He knew he should have driven across himself and spared Mary the danger. Out here, though, he didn't know why he did the things he did—or didn't do. As he sat, he noticed a grave beside the road, piled high with stones so the wolves wouldn't dig it up. Someone had died crossing that perilous stream, no doubt. Americus had seen countless graves along the way, but the sight of this one shot straight to his core. This one could have been Mary's.

# CHAPTER 17

# MARY

Settlers ahead! The words rang like music in Mary's head. She could feel the lure of civilization, even though it would be but a small oasis in this colossal wilderness. How could the continent she had once studied in her textbooks seem as vast as the universe itself? "Crossing the continent" had seemed, long ago, a possible undertaking, something that might be done in a few weeks or even a summer. By now they had been traveling for months—and still they were hundreds of miles from California.

But the two riders they'd encountered this morning—the first in days—estimated it was only 40 miles to the first of the widespread Mormon settlements, and the horses had crawled a good distance since then.

Mary knew of the persecuted people who had immigrated to this distant land they called Zion. Maybe this afternoon they'd reach the little town she pictured in her mind. There would be houses—real homes! They would be small, of course, and probably made of stones and logs, but they would have footpaths meandering between them for neighborly visits. There would be gardens of fresh carrots and squash and potatoes, and friendly women with sunbonnets plucking weeds from between the neat rows. They would be happy to see visitors, even someone as trail-worn and shabby as Mary, and would be eager to trade their garden wares for one of Mary's extra blankets or pair of stockings.

Little Celia, sitting on Mary's lap for a rest as her mother drove, suddenly gave a squeal.

"Horsey! I see horsey!"

Mary looked where Celia pointed her grubby finger. Two red cows lifted their heads from grazing and stared at the passing wagon.

"Those are cattle, you silly goose," Sarah chided her from the ground below.

Americus stopped the team and stared at the two healthy beasts.

"They're obviously not trail animals," he commented. "Look how well fed they are. There must be someone living around here. Mormon settlers, I'll wager."

Mary squinted ahead, looking for the town, but saw only more of the primitive trail winding into the dry, scrubby forest ahead, roughly following a small river. Bushy, short evergreens dotted the valley floor and partly covered the high brown hills rising to the north. Dried golden grasses baked in the hot sun, intermingled with sagebrush giving off its sweet smell. The air was arid, but the aridity was a comfort of sorts. It meant there would be no huddling under leaking canvas in a downpour or slogging through mud and cold puddles. Americus clucked to the horses, and the wagon jerked into motion again.

They rounded a curve, the wagon jouncing over an exposed tree root intersecting the trail. No one spoke for a few minutes, and then Mary saw a primitive shelter of sticks and mud. It was in a small clearing beside an old juniper and was surrounded by dead grass blowing in the wind. A creek, nearly dried up, trickled toward the river. Mary recoiled, fear rising up in her like swarming ants, certain they had stumbled upon an Indian village. But then she saw a woman waving from the trampled earth surrounding the structure, her yellow braids carelessly wound around her head and her long pink skirt blowing in the breeze. Two young boys, towheaded and dirty, retreated behind her, and a third looked out from a doorway so low that the child had to duck his head to walk out.

Americus raised his hand in an indifferent greeting and began to stride past, barely glancing at the woman as he kept to the trail.

"Whoa, boys!" Mary spoke firmly to the horses. Here was the first female companion she had seen for ages, and she meant to stop and visit. Americus could go on if he wanted! But this friendly woman must have a house somewhere nearby, since this was obviously her cow shed. Perhaps she even had some vegetables to trade or a cup of tea and conversation to share. Americus looked at Mary in surprise but said nothing.

Mary smoothed her hair, tucking the brittle strands into her bun as she labored to the ground favoring her sore ankle. She straightened her soiled apron and pulled her blue skirt down to hide her legs. What was happening to her? Back home she never would have dreamed of going calling in such a state. She wondered if she had soot on her face and if the woman could see she wasn't wearing shoes. Not that it mattered out here. The woman herself was barefoot, and her threadbare dress hung in wilted tatters around her ankles. Her apron lifted over her protruding abdomen. Dark stains discolored the fabric under her sleeves, and her hands were covered with dirt and red scratches.

She was a young woman, perhaps twenty-five years old. Crooked teeth stuck out from her small mouth when she smiled, but her clear blue eyes were beautiful, steady, and friendly, lined with long blonde lashes. Her face was gaunt, as if she hadn't eaten a good meal for months. The little boys, all smaller than Cephas, were skinny too, although they looked healthy enough. They stared at Mary as she hobbled toward them, using her stick for a crutch.

"Greetings," Mary smiled at the woman. "I'm Mary Powers." She looked around to introduce Americus and the children, but they were still back at the wagon.

"I'm so glad you stopped! For a moment, I thought you were going to drive right on by, and I am so hungry for company. I'm Mrs. Newburg. Florence Newburg. Do come in and take some tea with me."

She led the way to the cow shed. Mary stopped in confusion. This wasn't an animal shelter at all: It was this woman's home! There was no neat cabin with china teacups. No stacked wood or grassy path or welcome garden vegetables. This primitive structure, set as it was on the hard-packed earth, had dried-mud-and-stick walls that were barely as tall as Mary. Sagging pine boughs spread over the top were intended to be a roof. It was small as a chicken coop, and it looked to Mary as though a hard rain or a good wind storm would reduce it to a pile of mucky branches. After crouching through the low doorway, Mary could see the clouds drifting by through great gaps above her that undoubtedly let in rain and hail and snow as well as today's sunlight.

The dirt floor, though, was swept clean, and there was a small campfire encircled by rounded stones at one end of the enclosure. Smoke rose through the holes in the roof. Along one wall stood a small table made of irregular poles and a there were a couple of rickety three-legged stools. Scant bedding lay folded on hay in the corners, and a blackened teakettle sat on the hot coals.

"My children are here with me, of course, but there are no other women—or men either—nearby. My husband lives in the valley with his other wife." She set two mismatched tin cups on the table. "As much as I wish you could stay the night here with me, you'd best go on a few miles to Brother Barnum's," the woman was saying. "He and Sister Barnum have a log home that is somewhat comfortable, and, as you can see, I don't have much to offer you in the way of comfort. But I do have advice for any woman coming to live here in Zion with her man." Her voice took on an angry tone and her eyes snapped.

Mary looked up, startled. The woman assumed that she, too, was of the Mormon faith coming to settle in the Promised Land. Mary started to correct her and then thought the better of it. She wouldn't lie, but perhaps it was best to say nothing for now. If the woman thought she were a fellow Mormon, what harm was there in that? She took the battered cup filled with steaming tea that was offered to her.

"Thank you. Are you in need of a blanket for the children? I have one I can spare." Mary guided the topic in a new direction. Her pity for this brave young mother was overwhelming her. The bare ground around this dreadful shelter was packed hard and littered with the effects of everyday living, but Mary had seen no other sign of civilization at all. She glanced at a limp flour sack on the floor near the fire, and saw a rifle lying next to it—Mrs. Newburg's means of killing meat and protecting the children, she supposed.

She heard her voice continuing. "I do have a few sewing pins, too, if you're in need." The thought of shiny silver sewing pins suddenly seemed ludicrous, like a pair of satin shoes or a feathered hat would seem out here.

"I'd be so glad for a blanket, but I don't need any pins,

thank you." The woman looked down. "I don't have much to exchange, though."

"There's no need to trade. The blanket I have is an extra that I've kept tucked away in the wagon until I encountered someone who needed it." Mary's thoughts flashed to Americus demanding she leave it behind that day along the Sweetwater, and her own certainty that they would need it.

She took a sip of hot tea. Its sweet, soothing flavor surprised her. Mrs. Newburg noted her expression of pleasure.

"It's wild mint, the tea is. That's it! That's what I can give you in exchange for your blanket. I've enough dried to last for the rest of your trip. My husband was supposed to visit and bring some bedding for my comfort when I'm confined soon," she glanced at her rounded apron, "but he hasn't come yet and I'm feeling unsettled about how the children and I will make do. A blanket would be a great help." Her roughened hands unconsciously rubbed her swaying back.

"Will you have help when your time comes?"

"I'm hoping so. I plan to send Abbot for one of the neighbor women," she said, gesturing to her oldest son, a bright-looking boy of perhaps five or six. "It's just a few miles, and I'm certain he can make it without getting lost."

Mary smiled at the youngster, trying not to let her misgivings show. She couldn't help picturing this small child, alone and frightened amid these thick junipers and low pines, confronted by a snarling cougar twice his size. Getting lost was only one of the many hazards that could befall a child in this wilderness. "You're certainly fortunate to have such good, strong boys," she said. "I'm sure Abbot is equal to the task."

Mary couldn't imagine sending Cephas off on such an errand, but this young woman was living under far worse conditions than her own. Alone and nearly deserted, she would have her baby within a week or two if Mary wasn't mistaken. She would give birth to it here in this clearing lying on her hard bed of hay staring at the sky through her crude roof. There would be no midwife with hot water and comfort, probably not even her husband. The thought made Mary draw a sharp breath.

Seated on her wobbly stool, Mary visited a while longer, bringing Mrs. Newburg news of the trail and the things happening back home. Those events seemed years behind her, not months. Part of her mind was on Americus and how long he would tolerate waiting for her as she sat sipping tea. Fearing his annoyance, she rose to leave long before she was ready to say good-bye. Mrs. Newburg helped her fill her big apron pockets with fragrant dried mint, and together they strolled to the wagon, Mary leaning heavily on her makeshift crutch. Sarah, Cephas, and Celia were inside the wagon. To her surprise, Americus was stretched out on the bed sleeping—not, as she had expected, impatiently waiting.

Mary lifted the heavy blanket from its storage place, and handed it to her new friend with a smile. She desperately wanted to share food with this hungry family, too, but there were barely enough beans left to feed her own children.

Impulsively, she reached out and took Mrs. Newburg's hand and looked into her light blue eyes. "God bless you. And bless your little ones, too. You'll be in my prayers." Mrs. Newburg smiled at her, her eyes filling with tears, but she didn't speak.

Mary climbed onto the wagon seat. How could she possibly leave when this lonely woman was in such dire circumstances? But there was no choice out here. The coming of winter with its inevitable storms forced her back on the trail as surely as if she had been at gunpoint. With a last good-bye, she gave the horses the signal and they started up with a jerk. She would let her family ride inside for a few minutes. The wagon creaked as it jostled over a broad stone. Mary stared ahead, the events of the past hour running through her mind.

This western country never fully came clean with all of its secrets. Instead, it revealed them to her one at a time. She felt betrayed each time, taken by surprise by some new undeniable fact that appeared to her like a ghost from the future. Perhaps it was best that they were doled out to her one by one agonizing one, for she certainly couldn't endure knowing them all at once. Today she knew without a doubt that life on the frontier would never be as she hoped. She wondered if she'd best begin taming her eternal optimism and start expecting the worst, hoping that, in comparison, reality would look better. Maybe when she imagined her own little house in California, she should cease envisioning a tight cabin with bedsteads, clean rag rugs on a smooth board floor, and a cloth-covered dinner table large enough for her family. She'd best conjure up rain dripping through a primitive roof, packed dirt beneath her feet, and hay on the dank ground for bedding. Perhaps then, something about the western frontier would surprise her pleasantly. This wilderness journey had taken its toll, but it was giving something back, too, teaching her its lessons. It still stunned her, but she'd learned in no uncertain terms out here that depending on Americus meant trouble, not feminine deference. Of necessity she was learning to do a man's work, despite her small size and inexperience. Just yesterday, she'd taken that disgusting tar bucket that swung from the wagon's underside and spread tar on the leaky cracks that had opened in the wagon box.

Persistence and faith and new skills—those were the things that shaped one's destiny in ways that crocheting lace doilies in a polished parlor didn't. And patience. Patience that brought a speck of inner peace. Perhaps that was what she sought most: forbearance to outlast this ordeal and Americus's dismaying ways. Patience to smile for her children and cook more beans when she wanted only to turn around and race back to civilization.

Americus hadn't wanted to stop here at this small, scattered settlement. The trouble was, Mary insisted. Blackey was in dire shape, and the provisions were virtually gone. So here they were, stuck in this place for too long while they deceived these good Mormon people who called themselves Brother and Sister Barnum.

He wondered if the children would blunder and reveal the truth. One slip from Celia and all the care he and Mary had taken to pretend to be devout Mormon followers would be for naught.

He wasn't used to deception, nor was Mary, who was just as strict about absolute honesty. To be living a lie unsettled his midsection. That's what this hellish trail had done. First it took away his will and his strength, and now it was robbing him of his moral convictions, too. He and Mary were actually willing to pretend to be something they weren't in order to be readily accepted here. Americus wondered if the Lord would forgive them, in light of their desperation and hunger. The folks from their congregation back home would throw them out in anger if they knew.

He shook his head to clear the cloudiness that hovered

over his brain. His sluggish thoughts made him feel as though he were walking through fog so dense he couldn't see clearly ahead or behind. He felt slow, too, as if his ability to react and respond were buried deep within, and his natural energetic quickness had turned to methodical plodding. It was almost as though something in this western air entered his veins and slowed every movement, every thought. He must concentrate so he and Mary would not be found out as imposters.

These few resourceful Mormons scratching out a new existence in this harsh land were hard-pressed to provide even for their own broods of children. There was, as yet, little bounty to share with emigrating trail families starved for sustenance. But Americus had been told that the settlers would greet fellow Mormons with open arms and hearts, and would offer their very lives, if necessary, to welcome their brethren to this promised land. Being desperate for food, rest, grass for the horses, and just about everything else, Americus could see he had no choice but to force his innate honesty down inside and act as though he were a newly arrived Mormon looking for a place to settle. He hadn't actually lied about it, just failed to correct the settlers' natural assumptions. It was working, all right. Already Brother Barnum had welcomed the weary family into his home until they recuperated. At this moment, Blackey and the bay were out to pasture, grazing the luxurious golden grass that grew between the sage, and taking long drinks of clear, fresh stream water. The children, well fed at last, were playing hide-and-seek with some of the Mormon children who seemed to be everywhere he looked, running and screeching behind each bushy juniper. Mary was sitting in the Barnums's log cabin, her sore ankle propped up on a handmade wooden stool, talking in her engaging way to the black-eyed Sister Barnum. Americus could see them through the open doorway.

This would be a prosperous settlement someday, but for now it was hardly underway. Brother Barnum seemed to be a leader in the small valley, and he had several grown sons with families of their own. They were tall, strong, vigorous men who could cultivate fields, haul rocks and stumps, dig wells, and build thick-walled log homes with their bare hands. There were women, too, many of them. Americus had seen the rumors in reality now. He hoped he hadn't looked astounded the first time one of the young men introduced the two young women standing by his sides as his wives. It seemed a strange and foreign custom to his way of thinking, but who was he to judge? So far he had seen only unfailing generosity and kindness from these people.

"There's a nice spot for your farm not far from here." Americus realized Brother Barnum was addressing him, and he tried to focus on what the man was saying. "You could put up a cabin before winter with a little help from my boys and me. And the hunting is adequate to get you through this first winter. Next year you could get some planting done."

"Yes," Americus replied. He felt his shoulders tighten with the deception. "Maybe we could take a look at it."

An unspeakable fatigue washed over him, as strong as the guilt he felt at his own dishonesty. He needed to get away from this fine man who stood offering him a new life without even a suspicion that he was being deluded. Americus kept his gaze on Mary, certain he couldn't look Brother Barnum in the eye or remain talking to him one moment more.

Mary hobbled out of the doorway with her companion. They stood together in the woman's garden, a hard little patch of earth laboriously freed of choking weeds. There were sickly rows of vegetables baking in the August sun, but it looked as though there would be a harvest of sorts. Someone had been hauling water to nourish whatever was growing. Americus could see the women talking in low voices. Every now and then, the Mormon woman would dart her eyes toward Brother Barnum, and then go on talking low in Mary's ear, her words indistinguishable. Mary tilted her head, looking closely at the other women, her forehead etched into thoughtful, serious lines. Americus had seen that look many times. When Mary wore it with him, he felt as though every word he uttered was important.

"I've asked Luke, one of my sons, to look after that brake on your wagon," Brother Barnum was going on. "He'll repair it for you. You'll need your wagon for hauling logs and stones for your cabin."

"I'd be grateful if he would," Americus replied. "I didn't have the proper tools in the wagon to fix it well myself." Another half-truth, he thought, correcting it in his mind: no tools, no inclination, no strength, and no will. He wished Mary would rescue him from this blasted conversation that got worse with each passing minute. He could smell meat cooking, a hearty aroma that drifted by in savory wafts, and he felt hungry for the first time in weeks.

A group of children scampered close. Celia was among them, tagging along with a chewed-on carrot in her hand. When they stopped, it slipped from her grasp, and she bent to pick it up. Taking another bite from the end, she squinted up at Americus.

"They have two mamas, Papa," she said, pointing to the other children, perplexity furrowing her face. "Two." And she held up two fingers on her free hand.

"Yes, Celia. Now it's time for your afternoon nap, child. Come with me." Americus picked up his daughter and with a nod to Brother Barnum, strode toward the wagon waiting in the shade of a low pine. Let Barnum think he was doing woman's work by taking Celia off for her rest, but he couldn't risk any more discussion on the topic of multiple mothers. And besides, the child had saved him from more of that nerve-jangling conversation. Slung over his shoulder, she began to protest, but he ignored her—and the odd look Mary shot him from the garden.

They'd stay here for a few more days to let the horses recuperate, and he'd continue to act interested in the farm site Brother Barnum had in mind. But when the horses could travel better and Mary had been able to trade her buttons and thread for some fresh greens, onions, potatoes, and more beans, they would leave, saying they had to buy supplies in Salt Lake before they got settled. Americus knew Mary would do whatever it took to make things fair. She would produce something of value from the wagon to pay for anything they took, something he might not even know was there, like the flower seeds she had hidden in a crack in the wagon boards, or the sewing pins she had produced from nowhere, or that baffling gold coin.

The shorter this deception, the better. It made a man weary. He laid Celia, still sniffling, on the Rising Sun quilt and then stretched out at her feet, watching the shadows of the pine branches dance on the wagon cover.

S arah didn't care what Father and Mother said. She knew
they were never going to make it to California. There
were too many dangers, too many miles to go. Already the poor
horses had returned to their bony, fly-bitten condition, and the
look in their horse eyes was enough to make Sarah cry. At least
they had rested at the Mormon settlement, but that was behind
them now, and they were tired again. Mother had begged Father to trade the horses for oxen, but he hadn't even tried.
When Mother made an attempt herself, Brother Barnum
glanced at her strangely and said he'd talk it over with the Doctor. Nothing came of it.

St. Lawrence looked at Sarah as though she had betrayed
him, even when she offered him a few bites from her own scant
dinner plate. And Blackey, whom she loved more each day,
stared at her with his big, dark eyes pleading for help. He was
begging her to let him rest, to lead him to the green pastures
Mother was always reading about in the Psalms, to let him lie
down beside those still waters. She stroked his soft nose and
talked to him, telling him he could outlast the trail.

But it was a lie she was whispering to Blackey! California seemed as far off as heaven right now. All she could do was

bring him extra drinks of water and stay out of the wagon so he wouldn't have to pull her weight.

Now they were on the banks of the Bear River, staring down at its deep cut and the steep climb up the other side. Sarah felt dull as she looked at it. Not again! She wished she could just grow wings and fly across. She didn't know how she could stand another treacherous climb out of the river bottom. It was in a place like this where Mother had hurt her ankle. Sarah could tell it still hurt, even though Mother made light of it and said it was healing nicely. The swelling was mostly gone, and although Mother still limped, she didn't need to use her walking stick anymore.

Sarah wished Father hadn't mentioned the name of this wide, rapid stream out loud. The Bear. It was certain there were bears around somewhere. Every time Sarah thought about bears, she imagined their long claws that could rip a whole log apart in seconds and their big yellow teeth.

"We can cross here," Mother was saying to Father. "The down slope isn't too bad and the water's not too deep. It's the uphill that will be hard. We'll have to unload and block the wheels with boulders while we urge the horses up."

Father's shoulders sagged.

"Come on, Ceely. Let's slide down together and see the pretty water." Sarah said, thinking that at least she could spare Mother the chore of watching Celia. The little girl looked pathetic again today. Sarah had braided her hair a few days ago, but by now whole strands had blown loose and tangled into snarls. Her small pink fingernails and toenails were black, and her knees were scabby from where she had fallen time and again. Sarah lifted her up and carried her to the bottom of the slope.

In the driver's seat, Mother braced her feet and clucked to the horses. The wagon tipped to the side as it lurched down the bank to the river. Thank goodness for Brother Barnum's son who had fixed the wagon brake, although Sarah thought it still looked crooked.

"Get in the wagon so we can ford the river, children." Mother said. Sarah hated river crossings but did as she was told. When they were all sitting on the bed, Mother clucked again and the wagon bumped its way over the rocks, tipping and splashing across the frightening current. Sarah hid her head under the quilt. She made believe she was playing a game with Ceely, but in truth she was shutting out the sight and sounds of the ford.

With a great heave, the horses hauled the wagon out of the water and stopped, exhausted again. She and Cephas jumped out, and Sarah lifted Ceely to the ground. Sarah watched as Mother secured the lines and carefully stepped down onto the gravel. Despite Father's impatience to begin the ascent, Mother had one thought in her mind, and that was to help Sarah get Celia safely up the slippery bank away from the current. The wagon could follow. Mother lifted Celia into her arms, and began to climb. Sarah and Cephas followed. The hot sun beat down on Sarah's neck, and her wool dress itched everywhere. She longed to shed it, like a mayfly shucking its skin, and leave it to blow away on the riverbank. Instead she continued to climb, taking her turn at lugging Ceely. The exertion made her heart race.

Mother, too, was breathing hard. She paused halfway up, her ankles deep in the gravel, trying to catch her breath. Then, biting her lip, Mother hoisted Celia again and continued climbing until she finally stepped, gasping, onto the level ground above.

"Mary!" Father was calling impatiently. He had already begun to drive the horses up the incline in a zigzag pattern.

The still-dripping wagon tilted dangerously. "Block the wheels!"

Still out of breath, Mother slid down the bank, favoring her ankle. It would take a good-sized boulder, Sarah thought, to prevent the wagon from slipping back into the Bear. Mother found one she could barely lift. She hefted it with all her strength and, when Father stopped the horses, she dropped it behind the left rear wheel. When he urged the horses a few more feet, she grasped it again and lunged up the incline until the horses stopped.

Sarah didn't dare go help her. Mother had told her to stay at the top and watch Ceely. Besides, Mother was right: It was dangerous. Several times, the wagon lurched backward to the place where Mother was laden down with her boulder, but each time, she was able to get out of the way.

Over and over again, the horses inched uphill and Mother moved the rock. It seemed forever before the animals heaved themselves up the last few feet and strained with all their might to bring the wagon with them. Their mouths frothed, and the bay trembled all over from the exertion. Sarah grabbed the bucket. She asked Cephas to mind Ceely while she slid down the bank to fill it with cold water for the horses.

When she got back, Mother had collapsed on the ground. Her whole body trembled and shook, and she gasped for breath. Father stood over her, an astonished look on his face.

"I had no idea you were so used up," he said.

"I'd best lie down in the wagon," was all Mother could pant. With Father's help, she staggered into the wagon. Sarah climbed in, too, and laid her hand on Mother's forehead. Mother tried to smile between gasps. Sarah took her apron corner and dried the streams of perspiration from her face.

It was unlike Mother to lie down during the day and ride

behind the tired horses if she wasn't driving. Today she slept for long hours as the wagon rattled along the trail.

When at last Father pulled the wagon into the shade of some low trees and unhitched the horses for the day, Sarah wandered up the nearby creek looking for something to tempt Mother's appetite. Sarah knew that Mother was so tired of beans it was all she could do to swallow them day after day. Perhaps if she searched she could find something different tonight. Even some dried-up berries or a wild onion would be better than nothing.

She rounded a big slab of stone. It radiated the sun's warmth, and she paused to run her hand over its rough, hot surface. She glanced ahead, hoping to see berry bushes, when her heart lurched and blood rushed to her head. A little way off, an Indian woman was standing on the bank of the stream, her back to Sarah. Oh, dear God. Here was what she had dreaded this whole journey. This was her nightmare coming true! Her knees felt as though they might collapse.

Steadying herself on the warm slab, she saw that the small woman was young, perhaps only five or six years older than Sarah herself. She was holding something in her arms, looking down at it with her full attention. Sarah could hear her speak softly, words she didn't understand, and as the woman turned slightly, Sarah saw that she cuddled a small baby in her arms. Its shock of black hair blew softly in the slight breeze.

Sarah knew she should turn and run, but a strange peace came over her. This was not what fellow travelers had described when the campfire conversations inevitably turned to talk of Indians. This was a mother, like her own mother, so engrossed with her child that she hadn't heard Sarah approach. As she watched, the woman stroked the baby's hair with her slender hand, and then softly placed her smooth cheek on the baby's forehead. Her black hair shone in the sunlight, and her skin was tawny and smooth.

Sarah stood, entranced, while her wild heartbeat slowed. She knew with certainty that those guide book writers were wrong. The native peoples along this trail were simply families living as they knew best, mothers and fathers who loved their children, as this young woman obviously loved her baby.

She took a step forward but then stopped. It occurred to her that this lone woman would be frightened by her presence. Her heart would leap, her abdomen clench, and the whirling panic Sarah had known would come over her. She would clutch her precious baby to her chest and flee, perhaps running across the creek, slipping on the underwater stones or ripping her feet on rocks and sticks as she plunged away.

Sarah watched a moment longer. Then she silently turned and crept back to the wagon. She wanted to tell Mother about her encounter, but partly she wanted to hoard the small secret to herself. It brought whole new images to her mind: pictures of Indian fathers sitting beside campfires bouncing babies on their knees, or girls like herself picking berries and braiding their hair. She wondered what it would be like to sleep in a tipi, especially in winter when snow blew cold. She knew why these people, content with their lives, would be disturbed by wagon travelers, thousands of them, rumbling through this land, leaving their debris and taking whatever was in sight.

For a minute, Sarah's old fear returned—certainly there must be an Indian encampment nearby—but she pushed it back. Perhaps at this moment, somewhere in the vicinity, an Indian girl was gathering firewood, or stirring something over a fire, or urging her small sister to eat.

# CHAPTER 20

# CEPHAS

This water tasted bad, bad, bad. Even after Mother put sugar in it, it still tasted like rusty metal, and it smelled rotten. It reminded him of the time he licked biscuit crumbs off the wagon wheel's iron rim.

Sarah said it was like soda, this fizzy water that bubbled straight from the ground here, but he spit it out the moment it touched his tongue, soaking the front of his shirt. The metal taste still stayed. He picked up a smooth pebble and popped it into his mouth. Even a dusty rock would be better.

It was astonishing to watch the water bubble up from the ground and run down over those orange-stained rocks. He'd never seen rocks that color. He stuck his finger in the small current and tried to scrape off the orange, but it wouldn't come off. It looked soft, like mud, but when he tried walking on it, it turned out to be hard and slippery. His feet swooped out from under him and he fell with a small splash, but it was so shallow he got only his pants wet.

He looked around quickly, but Father wasn't watching. Mother saw him fall—she always saw everything. Sarah, too. Sarah looked as though she wanted to laugh at him. She didn't, though. She just kept holding Celia's hand to keep her from going too deep into the creek.

He was proud of himself for finding this place. Today the trail had passed by another spring that was much bigger and showier, but this little shaded one was hidden. He had discovered it while he was looking for wild onions. He loved wild onions. Mother said he had a knack for finding treasures, and he guessed she was right. He did find a lot of treasures, like that whole bobcat skull. And the glittery rock he had hidden in the wagon so Father wouldn't find it, or the jar of preserves some wagon traveler had left behind that Mother had served with biscuits one night.

Father used to take Sarah and him looking for hawk feathers and pretty rocks back home. That was before Father got so cross. Now Cephas stayed away from him and went looking for treasures by himself.

Mother always fretted that he would go too far, but he didn't like being out of sight of the wagon. Once when he wandered off, he almost stepped on a rattlesnake. He saw it just in time to jump back. Another time he waded too deep in a river, and the sucking current tried to pull him under. He hadn't gone in rivers much since then.

He was tired of walking west! It was dull and hot, but Mother said he mustn't complain, even when his feet hurt. They were so full of thorns and cuts and scratches that he hardly noticed anymore, unless he had a deep gouge or a bad bruise. The mosquitoes bothered him most. In some places they were as thick as a snowstorm, and they made a nasty whining sound around him. If he snatched a handful of air, he ended up with several squashed in his fist. Even when he stood right in the campfire smoke, they still landed on him and stuck their long pointed biters into his skin. He had bites all over his body, like Celia. Some nights he could hardly sleep because he kept scratching them, even when Mother told him to stop.

Poor Mother was still worn out from lifting that boulder to block the wagon wheels a few days ago. Cephas could tell she was sad about this trip, too, especially about leaving all the home folks behind. Sometimes he saw her crying, like the day Father made her leave her best teapot behind. He wished he had picked it up when Father wasn't watching and hidden it back in the wagon. Father mightn't have noticed.

He wished she would read *The Pilgrim's Progress* aloud again and draw sketches like she did at the start of the trip. She couldn't sketch very well, but Cephas liked how she made up stories about her little drawings to entertain them. Now she never made up stories at all. And she never sketched.

He spit the pebble out of his mouth. He couldn't taste the bad flavor of the soda water anymore. Mother was calling. It was time to start down the trail again. Good-bye bubbling spring! Cephas looked at the sun to see how much longer this day would last. It was high overhead, and he willed it to hurry up. Sometimes these days seemed as long as weeks.

Mary heard the faint hoof beats before she saw the single rider approaching in the hot morning sun. He was galloping across the broad, flat expanse behind the wagon, coming nearer each second. Her heart began pounding louder and faster than the horse's hooves, and images crowded her mind. She'd heard the stories. Stolen children, burning wagons, whole families lying bloody on the ground.

"Children! Into the wagon!" Her voice cracked.

Mary saw Sarah grab her little sister and run for the wagon with Cephas close behind. Where had Americus gone? Mary scanned the wide horizon, shaking. There he was, a hundred yards off, bent over this stretch of the Bear, unaware of the approaching danger. She screamed and he looked up, following her pointing finger with his hollow eyes.

The rider was closer now, slowing to a trot. His horse raised a small billow of dust from the hard, dry dirt. Mary could see his dark face and black hair. She grabbed the axe—the only semblance of a weapon they had—and screamed again for Americus, who stood rooted to the riverbank.

It took her a few seconds to register that the horse had a saddle, and that the rider wore boots and trousers like the Doctor's. He held leather reins in his hand, tugging on them gently until the shiny brown mare halted a few yards away. It was then that Mary realized he was smiling.

"Hello, ma'am," he said. He had the bluest eyes Mary had ever seen, and a lean, bearded face. He was looking at her in surprise. "Did I frighten you? I'm sorry." He looked at the axe that Mary still held in her trembling arms.

Mary managed a weak smile before the earth started swirling and the rider began to disappear into a reddish blackness. She dropped the axe and grabbed the wagon wheel for support, bending at the waist and gulping in more air. After a moment, her vision cleared and she straightened again, still shaking. The stranger had jumped from the horse and was striding toward her with a look of such concern on his face that Mary felt a quick lump in her throat. It had been a long time since she'd seen a look like that.

"Are you all right, ma'am?"

"Yes, I think so. I'm very sorry about the axe. I thought you were an outlaw or a warrior."

He smiled down at her. The creases fanning out from his eyes were lined with trail dust. He looked kind, Mary thought, if it was possible to see kindness in a total stranger's face. There was a solid confidence about him, nothing arrogant or cocky, just a quiet stability and certainty of purpose. His trousers and shirt had obviously encountered downpours and muddy trails. Today they were covered with a fine layer of dust—dust so fine it might have been flour. His heavy eyebrows were still gathered in concern.

Her ears were filled with the loud hissing she always heard when she nearly fainted, but she heard the stranger asking again if she were all right. She nodded. She could feel the solid, splintery wagon wheel under her fingers, and a faint breeze, welcome as a cold drink. The baking sage and dry earth sent up their dusty, pungent fragrance.

"I'm proprietor of a sheep train about an hour's journey up the trail," he was saying. "We're a small train, only a few wagons, but our sheep make up for us in numbers." Mary saw him glance at Americus's horses and then look again, sizing up the situation. Blackey and the bay stood with drooping heads, their bony ribs making ridges and deep gullies in their hides. There was rustling inside the wagon that had been silent a moment ago, and Cephas's brown eyes peeked from behind the canvas. The rider winked at him.

"You folks having trouble?"

Mary faltered. She wasn't accustomed to lying, but she had to be careful. No wagon train would take on a desperate family with worn-out animals, no rifle, and a man who quarreled with everyone. Americus was still down by the river, his back to Mary and the children, waiting, no doubt, until the intruder was gone.

"Well, we're getting along," Mary gave him a smile that felt as empty as her flour sacks. "Goodness, you must be thirsty. Could I offer you a cold drink from the water keg?"

"Yes, please, ma'am." The man tethered his horse to the wagon. "Mind if I take a look at your bay horse over there? He's looking poorly."

"He's been a bit weak these past few days," Mary said, trying for a light tone, as she fetched the dipper. "Would a plateful of beans refresh you?"

"Thank you, no. I don't want to trouble you or use your provisions. Is that your husband by the river?"

"Yes." She was silent. Now what? Should she warn this possible rescuer that Americus wouldn't pass the time of day? That he would be cold or unresponsive, or worse, shoot angry words from his mouth like bullets? If the Doctor treated this man the way he treated everyone else, the stranger would probably ride off into the dust and lead his sheep train down the trail away from them. Mary chose her words carefully. "He's a bit troubled today. The heat, you know. And the horses are tired, although they're still able to pull the wagon."

"Ma'am, if you don't mind my saying so, that bay isn't up to pulling this wagon or anything else. The black doesn't look much better. It looks to me like you need some oxen or bigger horses."

"Yes, you're right about that. We thought we'd trade the horses for oxen when we get any opportunity at all."

"If you want my honest opinion, I don't think you'll make it another day with those animals. They're worn to the bone, ma'am, and they're going to leave you stranded long before you get to wherever you're going."

Did she dare speak her mind? Tell him about all the times the horses had wobbled in the traces or strained with every bit of their remaining strength without budging the wagon? Confess that her family had eaten nothing but beans for days, having run out of every other provision again except some coffee and a few cups of sugar and some mint tea? Suggest that Americus was losing his mind and was no more help to her than Celia's little stick doll?

She started to speak about the horses but stopped. Back home, she would have been appalled at the very thought of discussing livestock with a strange man. She felt as though her carefully cultured gentility had been stamped out somewhere along the trail, along with everything else she held dear: Sunday church services, white lace curtains framing sparkling glass windows, sweet-smelling roses over her swept-clean doorstep. Tea served from her grandmother's silver teapot, now abandoned far back on this wretched trail like a deserted orphan. Out here she was reduced to things like this horrifying conversation—so foreign and distasteful that her stomach roiled and she wondered in dismay if she was going to be sick. She could not lift her eyes from the ground, but she made herself speak, softly, mindful of the children behind the thin canvas. It might be her only chance.

"We do need help, sir. Could your train sell us some animals?"

He looked at her, a hundred questions in his clear eyes. Then he glanced at the river, where the Doctor was still bent over, acting as though something on the dull, stony bank was taking up his full attention.

"I'm Todd Curry, ma'am," he said, reaching for the brim of a hat that wasn't there, a gesture not lost on Mary. Here was a man with some upbringing and, if she wasn't mistaken, a New England accent. "And I think we can help you folks. Maybe I'll stroll down to the river and talk it over with your husband."

"I'm Mrs. Powers, and it's a pleasure to meet you, Mr. Curry. My husband isn't himself today. He's . . . a bit disturbed by our situation. But we'd appreciate your help very much." She hurried on. "We've got three children, and it's been very trying traveling alone without protection. If you could allow us to buy some oxen, and perhaps join your train . . . " Her voice faltered. She couldn't say another word, absolutely couldn't beg for anything more! She stood, her cheeks red and her eyes downcast, aware that her once-crisp apron was limp and gray despite her efforts to clean it in the river a few days ago. Her dirty bare toe stuck out from under the tattered hem of her faded calico dress, and she quickly moved her foot out of sight. She shuddered to think how her complexion must look after walking in the sun and wind all these weeks and cooking over a smoky fire, despite her diligence in wearing her sunbonnet. If her hands were any indication of what the raw elements did to skin, she could just imagine. Good thing the children were still in the wagon. Tousled and spattered, dirty and ragged, the three of them looked as though they had no mother at all. Even the wagon gave away the secrets of this trip. Once, eons ago back home, it had sported a sharp white cover that snapped in the prairie wind. But now, like the rest of them, it was diminished and faded by this unfortunate journey. It hung between the crossbows, sagging low and collecting dust and water stains in its hollows.

Mr. Curry didn't seem to notice. Mary saw him reach for the brim of his hat again, and cross the dry distance toward the river, whistling softly to announce his approach. Mary knew he expected Americus to turn and extend his hand, as any other traveler would do, but Mary was sure the Doctor would do neither. She took a step to follow, then changed her mind and shut her eyes, silently praying that Americus would be civil and that he would, for once, accept a kind offer of help. To think of traveling with a train again, of having friends and helpful companions—and the protection of guards at night! She hardly dared to let the thoughts slip into her mind. Americus could ruin it all in an instant.

But miraculously, he turned, stiff as a tin soldier, to face Mr. Curry. Mary could tell he wasn't cordial or warm—he seemed to have forgotten how!—but at least he didn't appear to be angry either. From her distance she watched him nod his head slightly in greeting, then slowly extend his hand in response to Mr. Curry's outstretched one, as if it were some great effort. She exhaled with relief, and realized she had been holding her breath.

God had heard her prayer and had answered it. Mary closed her eyes once again, this time in thanksgiving, and then took the old bucket filled with water to Mr. Curry's mare.

# CHAPTER 22

# SARAH

Sarah sat in the front of the wagon and peered out the puckered opening at the Bear River Valley. It was surrounded by low mountains turning brown in the summer heat. The sage had given way to long green grass here beside the river. Those white dots in the distance ahead were wagons, of course, the small wagon train that Mother said was going to help them. Sarah counted seven canvas tops winding slowly along the trail. They were followed by a huge flock of gray-white sheep and a few mounted shepherds.

The river looked like a silver necklace, she thought, with white wagon tops dotting its edge like beads. Overhead, the sky was deep blue. It reached down to the earth in all directions, turning lighter near the horizon. Inside the wagon, the canvas cover trapped the sunlight until even the bedding radiated its warmth. At least she was out of the glare. It was a small refuge from the brightness and the awful dust and all those insects she hated.

Part of her wanted to speed across the remaining miles and catch up with the wagons so she could find out if there was a girl her own age in one of them. Perhaps there was someone with whom she could laugh again, and whisper secrets, and swim in this beautiful river. Another part of her wanted never to arrive. It was mortifying when Father caused those unpleasant scenes as he had with the last wagon train. Then came the pitying looks and whispered comments among the women and the furtive conferences among the men.

Sarah watched Mother bathing Celia in the river. Celia didn't understand how important it was to be clean and carefully dressed when they caught up to the wagons. She protested as Mother wiped the grime from her face and thrashed her legs when her hair was gently submerged in the current.

Sarah and Mother had bathed last night by the light of the stars that twinkled down at them like little sparks from heaven. Sarah loved the cool smoothness of the water against her skin. It washed away the trail dust and soothed the scratches and cuts on her ankles and feet. She felt like a mermaid swimming there in the blackness with her braids undone for once and her hair being tugged downstream in a wavy brown cascade. The soap Mother had made didn't lather much, but it smelled of rose water, and it reminded Sarah of home.

When she and Mother were dry and dressed again, Sarah hoped Father would take Cephas bathing, but he hadn't. This morning, Mother sent Cephas off by himself, cautioning him to stay near the shore and to scrub thoroughly.

Mother dried Celia and dressed her in her only other set of clothes, which she had washed last evening and laid flat over the sagebrush to dry.

"Sarah, dear," Mother said, poking her head through the canvas. "I can't bear the thought of you wearing that old wool dress of yours when we meet our new friends. I think you're tall enough to wear one of my dresses. The brown is too ragged and dirty, but I washed the green. It's a bit short for me, so it might be just right for you."

Inside the wagon, Sarah smoothed the cool folds of green-sprigged cotton and slipped it over her head. The full skirt reached to her toes, hiding her calloused bare feet and brown chapped ankles. The bodice was too full, but Mother made tucks with a few quick basting stitches and rolled the sleeves back to make cuffs. The fabric felt as smooth as water on Sarah's skin, and the dress fit better than she imagined.

"Perfect!" Mother smiled with satisfaction. "Let's brush your hair now, and I'll show you a new way to fix it. You're old enough to wear it up like a young lady for this occasion. And you may keep the dress, Sarah. I have the other two, and you need something larger and cooler. I've been meaning to start on a new dress for you, but . . ." Her voice trailed off.

It was nice, sitting alone in the wagon with Mother, talking about clothes and how to wear their hair, almost the way it would have been back home. Mother brushed Sarah's hair one hundred strokes on each side and piled it loosely on her head, expertly securing it with hairpins. Then she handed Sarah the looking glass. Sarah gasped and smiled. Gone were the childish, stringy braids, the tight sleeves that climbed halfway to her elbows, and her ankles poking out from under itchy gray wool. Wearing her hair this way took attention away from the freckles that were scattered across her nose, too.

Mother had laid out Father's clean work shirt and his spare pants, and asked him to refresh himself in the current. But he hadn't, and right now he was napping under the wagon as usual, still in the soiled trousers and torn shirt he'd worn every day for the past few weeks. At least he had his boots on, and Mother combed his wild mass of hair while he rested. It receded from his forehead and snarled in bunches over his ears. One tuft stood straight from the center of his head.

It was dark by the time they finally caught up with the

wagon train. By then, Blackey was used to his new teammate, Mr. Curry's strong mare, who had pulled all day without faltering. The travelers had finished supper and had pitched their tents for the night. Mother's face was gray with fatigue, but she had stopped just before reaching the camp to braid Celia's hair again. Quickly she brushed the day's dirt from Cephas's trousers. Then she redid her own long, glossy hair into a simple bun at the nape of her neck. Sarah thought she looked beautiful in her pale-blue calico dress, even if it did need pressing.

As their wagon approached the small camp, Sarah's hands got clammy. The other wagons were pulled into a circle, but Sarah noted there was an opening just large enough for the Powerses to slip in. A small campfire blazed there, like a welcome lamp lighted in anticipation of their arrival. Two of the women looked up with smiles, and one of the men hallooed "There they come!" A woman with a baby on her hip was bending over the river, but she straightened and began to approach, watching carefully where she placed her feet. The fine puffs of dust raised by the horses' hooves drifted off into the cool evening air.

Sarah looked at Mother to see if she was nervous, but already Mother was smiling and looking at this group of strangers as though she had never seen such a welcome sight, just as she had done when they encountered the ox train. If anyone was an expert at gracious greetings, it was Mother. Sarah loved the way she smiled warmly and tilted her head ever so slightly as she listened to others with all her attention. Mother would look straight into their eyes, silently encouraging them to say more, as if she were trying to see beyond the words into their hearts.

"Good evening," Mr. Curry called out to Mother and Father. "Come meet these good folks. They've been eager for you to overtake us all day." He strode over and held out his hand to Father, who stared at his face and then slowly offered his own hand. "Evening, Dr. Powers."

Father didn't reply, so Mother spoke up. "Greetings, Mr. Curry. We're looking forward to meeting everyone."

Mother addressed each person cordially, repeating their names to Father as she smiled and made polite comments. She looked every bit a lady, despite her chapped face and rough hands. Sarah wondered how she could still bring forth that beautiful smile after all the hardships they'd had. Her face with its high forehead and dark eyebrows fairly shone with relief. Sarah herself only nodded politely, saying nothing, wondering if she should be seen and not heard as she'd been taught, or whether—now that she was dressed in Mother's long dress— she should speak to these people as an adult would. Cephas and Celia had climbed in the wagon and were staring out from behind the canvas.

Mr. Curry had said there were 16 travelers including the baby, but it seemed to Sarah like more. The men looked as worn and dirty as father, but they had a vigor about them that Father lacked. The women wore patched dresses and sun-faded bonnets, and they came forth and greeted Mother warm-ly. One handed her a battered cup filled with coffee. Sarah wondered how such a small thing could say so much. "Wel-come to our train," she smiled. "I'm so glad you've reached us after this long day. I'm Amelia Pearson."

"I'm happy to meet you," Mother answered.

Amelia Pearson looked into Mother's face. "Please let me know if you need anything. Mr. Curry says you've had some trials lately."

It had been Mother's doing, joining this new train. Sarah had heard her talking with Mr. Curry, making their needs known. She had also made it plain that the Powerses would be a pleasant addition to the group. She had explained away Father's cold behavior and let her own warmth outshine it. Sarah realized suddenly that Mother didn't have to act like a trail boss or a military general in order to take charge.

Mr. Curry had said that this train was made up of adults, with the exception of the one baby, a dark-eyed child sleeping on his mother's shoulder. Sarah liked the way these travelers surrounded them with generosity before ever saying a word. One of the men was helping Father pull the wagon into the reserved space and unhitch the horses, and Mrs. Pearson had gone to her cook fire to bring a warm dinner. Nearby, sheep bleated. Sarah thought it was a comforting sound, familiar from the farmyards back home. She realized that if wolves prowled around this place, it would be sheep they were after, not children. And of course, these travelers would have a guard on duty all night. Something unclenched in Sarah's middle. She sat on the dry ground with Celia, accepting a heaping plateful of bacon and biscuits from Mrs. Pearson, smiling and tilting her head just slightly as she said her thanks.

*August, 1856*

*Dear Mother,*

   *My spirits are bright tonight! Our Heavenly Father has heard my plaintive cries for help as we neared the brink of exhaustion and starvation in this harsh wilderness. He has sent a small wagon train to rescue us and help us continue our trip to warm and sunny California.*
   *Mother, you cannot imagine my fear and agitation when their leader came galloping up to the wagon this morning. I thought he was an outlaw or a warrior coming to end our travels, but the rider turned out to be the nicest gentleman, Mr. Curry, looking for lambs that had wandered away from the huge flock the group is driving West. When he discovered us stopped, alone and unable to proceed further because the horses were too weak, he offered to let us join his train. We will commence traveling with them in the morning.*
   *I will be able to sleep tonight at last. Knowing there will be a guard watching over the train, which is pulled into the customary circle for protection, is such a comfort! Now I*

*won't lie awake in the blackness (as I have done every night in recent weeks), wondering whether each rustle or peep outside the wagon is some dreadful danger.*

*It's a small train, but Mr. Curry seems so capable and generous that I know we are in good hands. He has with him two other young men, John and Joseph, whose job it is to help with the vast numbers of sheep, as well as four Spanish shepherds to keep watch over the flock.*

*And Mother, you can't imagine what a pleasure it is to have other women nearby! I did so miss having kindred souls with whom to share my burdens. This train is comprised of a few married couples along with the single men, so there are four women along, much to my delight. Already I have had a friendly chat with each of them, and each has offered me a most cordial welcome. Mrs. Pearson brought us some fried bacon with biscuits for supper. How delicious it tasted, since we've had no meat for what seems like months, and our meals of old beans have been scant, to say the least. And since there are a few milk cows along, there is a taste of sweet milk for everyone. It astounds me how delectable something as simple as good milk can be. Little Celia's eyes fairly lighted up when she saw her portion.*

*I'm sure I will have much help watching Celia, for she has charmed the women here. It will be nice for me not to have to depend upon Sarah so much to care for her. I am doing the best I can to keep up with the ever-present chores, but I am eternally fatigued. Sometimes I can hardly move for exhaustion. I can no longer walk long distances or climb uphill without becoming completely spent. It makes the journey so much more difficult, especially when I can't sleep at night. I seem unable to regain my strength.*

*Americus continues to be in such a sullen mood that*

*some days he doesn't even speak to me, not more than a few necessary words. When he addresses the children, it is to bark at them for any slight mistake they've inadvertently made. I am fearful that he will offend our rescuers so that they will leave us behind as the earlier wagon trains have done. Quite frankly, he acts like a perfect lunatic, although it is unseemly of me to say so. Sometimes he raves over the smallest of things—if the coffee tastes a bit "off" having been made with the only available water (which comes from the nearest muddy river), or my choice of Bible verses to read to the children—something I try to do even if I am deathly tired. Other times, he ignores the most pressing concerns of travel. The care of the horses has fallen to my little Cephas, who, at seven, is doing a better job of watering them and moving their picket lines than his father. This is all so frightening, Mother, and it tries my wifely patience severely. I want to shout at him, but must be ever mindful of my duty to honor and obey him—and to consider the children at all times. So I quietly try to do his work for him despite my fatigue, and depend upon Sarah and Cephas for the rest. Even Celia has become quite good at collecting fuel for our campfire.*

*But thanks to our rescuers, we are safe and protected, so I hope this letter will lift your heart. Somehow I will find a means to send it—and my earlier letters, which I have not yet had an opportunity to post.*

*Back home I never would have thought I could be so thrilled to travel with a flock of sheep! But the smell of lanolin and wool is a sweet scent to me tonight, and the continual blatting and bleating is music to my ears. Mr. Curry entertains us with stories about his western adventures, and it makes the time pass quickly and pleasantly.*

*It is so dark now that I can hardly see, and the children*

*must be sent to bed. I hope the others in the party, sleeping comfortably under the stars in their tents, will not think it is strange that we Powerses all crowd into our cramped wagon for the night. Our tent is much preferable, but it is too heavy and cumbersome for Sarah and me to manage.*

*Bless you, Mother, and God keep you safe. He has certainly watched over us today. I pray that your health is good and that your rheumatism is better in this warm weather. Give my love to each of my dear friends there in Wisconsin. Are the roses still blooming?*

*With all my heart I am your loving daughter,*

*Mary*

A horsefly buzzed around Americus's bald forehead. He swatted at it, but it got away only to find a different spot to bite. He wanted to smack it aside forever, the same way he wanted to get rid of this irritating sheep train with its busybodies and bleating animals. It was beyond him what Mary saw in traveling with a noisy group of folks who interfered with his ways. Thanks to that blasted Mr. Curry, here he was this morning with someone else's horses in his harness. Blackey and St. Lawrence were following behind the train. And it had all happened without his saying so.

He couldn't forget the way Curry had stood in the shade talking with Mary this morning. Mary had looked beautiful in her graceful, long, faded-blue dress. Her smooth brown hair gleamed today, and her small chin lifted a bit as she looked up at the sheepman, earnestly making some point or another. Mary was as faithful and trustworthy as could be, and Curry seemed a complete gentleman, but he'd felt a sharp chill as he watched them standing there together. Curry was tall and muscular and had the looks of a stage actor with his dark wavy hair and blue eyes. His manner suggested culture and refinement with his easy laugh and engaging way of telling stories.

Americus felt awkward and gangly in his presence.

The thick smell of sheep filled his nostrils. At least at the moment those annoying animals weren't near enough to disturb the day with their continual noise, even if they were up ahead fouling the morning air.

The new horses stopped at a sharp dip in the road. Americus clicked his tongue at them, as he would have done with his own horses to instruct them to go ahead, but these animals paid no heed. One tried to turn off to the left while the other snorted back a step, causing the wagon to jerk. Americus spoke to them in a low, steady voice. This time they stepped off, jolting the wagon along behind them. It was, after all, a good thing he was driving today—another of Curry's suggestions—to make sure these horses were predictable and manageable. Mary was walking with the three other women. She had plenty of help carrying Celia, but her ankle would be swollen again by the time they stopped at the next creek, and she would be so fatigued she would need to rest in the wagon.

Americus swatted at the horsefly. He had to admit that it was nice to be able to drive without stopping every hundred feet to rest the horses. These draft animals clipped right along, easily keeping up with the wagon ahead. Far larger and heavier than Blackey and the bay, they had huge feet and muscles that rippled under their broad flanks. He could see the muscles that drove their strong legs, too, like thick hams swelling beneath their tough hides.

The dust was bad here where the trail meandered far from the river bottom. It roiled up under the wagons thicker than fog and sifted its way into everything: bedding, dishes, supplies. A man's hat hanging from a nail inside the wagon would collect a brimful in half a day. Even the coffee had grit in it, and a person's face, shielded beneath a bandana, would be lined with muddy streaks at day's end.

Americus had seen places where earlier families tried to avoid chewing on the dust kicked up ahead of them by fanning out so they rumbled across the land in 50 different parallel trails. Old camping places lined the road, burned-out camp-fires, and places where the glittering streams had been turned to muck by oxen and ironclad wheels. Furniture was left behind, and dead, rotting oxen, or someone's jars of pickles, too heavy to carry any farther. Like Mary's ridiculous silver teapot that he'd insisted they leave behind back on the Sweetwater. It was beyond him why she thought she'd need a sterling teapot in California.

The trail was turning rougher. Curry said there were hundreds of miles to go, through deserts so long and dry that plenty of emigrants had perished crossing them. The Sierra Nevada awaited, too, mountains with such lofty altitude that it was said the snow never melted from some of their razor peaks, but they were so far off he couldn't think about them now.

He was tired again, so tired he couldn't keep his eyes open. The horses would be all right if he dozed on the seat. They simply followed the others, seeming not to notice the flies that buzzed around their heads, or the baking sun that beat down on their tough backs—or that the trail was getting steeper and rockier with each passing hour.

# CHAPTER 25

## TODD CURRY

Todd Curry leaned back against his wagon wheel and looked up at the vivid sky. This broad, beautiful Bear River Valley was awe-inspiring country. He thought he could spend his life in this fertile valley. Profuse grass lined the winding river and promised perfect farmland nearby. Above it, low evergreen-covered ridges rose from the bottomland turning smoky-blue as they unfolded into the distance. He loved the carved gullies that cut the ridges, each holding its own lure. Occasionally, gigantic boulders were strewn down their slopes as though tossed there by the very hand of God.

Leaving the farm had been rough, and the day he'd said good-bye to Mamie's grave he thought he would die himself right there on the little rise behind their cabin. Leaving her behind made him feel as though he'd sliced his heart in half. He'd tried to keep the farm going for a year after she died, but he couldn't escape the harsh fact that his wife lay beneath the soil not a hundred yards from their home. He wondered constantly if the old country physician could have done something—anything—differently to save her life. In the end, leaving seemed the only way to escape the dreams that haunted him and the constant reminders of Mamie's gentle spirit that were everywhere in the cabin.

Surprisingly, out here on the trail, he felt like a new man. Not that he would ever forget Mamie, but this was a different life. It was all his own. Today, sitting where the wagons had halted for the midday meal, he couldn't remember the last time he felt so quiet inside, as though the breeze and the wild landscape soothed a sore place in his soul, maybe even cured it forever.

He bit into another biscuit. It was odd how delicious plain food tasted out here in the fresh air, even his own biscuits that were burned on the bottom more often than not.

"Curry, are you eating more black biscuits?" It was John, one of his two partners in the sheep train, wandering by and sizing up the condition of things. Todd's biscuits had become the joke of the trip, although his knack for baking over a campfire was slowly improving.

Todd grinned. "They're not half bad. Want one?" John was a good man, smart and funny and kind like his brother, Joseph, their third partner. They were Irish, although the accent had nearly faded from their speech. John was younger than the others with white-blonde hair that made his lean face seem even more tanned; of the three of them he was the most driven. He was pushing this train—and the sheep—along at a good pace, a pace that challenged them all. Fall snowstorms weren't too far off.

"Probably give me indigestion. I've never seen such poor lookin' excuses for biscuits," the younger man joked back. "Let's be on our way."

Todd stood, ready to move out. When he'd joined up with this little train, he'd felt strange being the only single man with a wagon. At first, watching the other men care for their wives, he'd had to wander off occasionally to collect himself, but as the trip grew more difficult, he came to appreciate being alone. It was easier, much easier. It freed him up to help the others—Hal Johnson, who nearly broke his leg when his horse spooked early in the journey, and Mrs. Brill, who buried a whole family before leaving home with her new husband. Now there was this new family, the Powerses. It was odd, the way the husband acted. His wife, though, had a graciousness he hadn't seen since he started out. She was beautiful, too. Powers was a fortunate man, but he didn't seem to realize it. In fact, he didn't seem to acknowledge much of anything, least of all the fact that those expensive horses of his were completely unsuited to pulling a covered wagon. It seemed incredible that anyone would set out on the trail with such animals—and even more incredible that they had lasted this long. Todd wondered if he had even noticed the crack in his wagon tongue. No man in his right mind would let that go unattended.

"John." Todd walked over to the other man and lowered his voice. "What do you and Joseph think of Dr. Powers?"

"He's an odd one, all right. Seems a bit daft. We'll need to keep an eye on him until we can figure him out."

"He doesn't say much."

"Well, keep your eyes open. Make sure they stay with us this afternoon, and we'll talk again tonight. That poor woman of his . . . and the children."

Todd's wagon was second to last today, just in front of the Powerses'. As he approached it, he could see Mrs. Powers putting away her kettle, and she smiled his way. She looked stronger than when he'd discovered them stranded two days ago. The deep shadows under her eyes were fading, and her smile seemed refreshed now, although her face was still too pale under her lightly tanned skin.

"How are those horses of mine doing?" he asked. He already knew the answer. His animals were strong and in good shape. He'd made sure of that, every step of the way.

"They are delightful creatures!" she answered, although he noticed she gave their high broad flanks a wide berth. "Gentle and diligent, and so strong. They're much better suited for pulling this load."

"Yes, they're good fellows, those tough old boys. Let me know if you're needing anything else."

"Thank you. Thank you so much."

"John just gave the signal to get back on the road. Where's your husband?"

She glanced about. "He was here a few moments ago. I'm sure he can't have gone far."

"We'd better find him. John is our time clock, and he doesn't like to be held up."

A furrow wrinkled Mrs. Powers's forehead, as she scrutinized the brown and forest-green hills and peered into the wagon. "I can't imagine where he is." An instant later her eyes widened, and her work-coarsened hand covered her mouth as if to prevent herself from voicing the thought. "Cephas, go see if Blackey and the bay are still back with the livestock."

Todd felt uneasiness creep under his skin. Would the man just go riding off somewhere without telling anyone? Didn't he know the dangers out there? Todd smiled with a confidence he didn't feel.

"Don't concern yourself, ma'am. We'll find him. I'll help you look." He'd have a word with John and hold up the train for a few minutes.

He was turning to leave when he saw her boy running up from behind the wagons, his eyes wide.

"Blackey's gone, Mother."

She slumped against the wagon wheel, her eyes dark in her face, and pulled her tattered handkerchief from her pocket. She looked fragile there, hardly taller than the wheel, with her small hands clutching that bit of lacy fabric. He took a step toward her, but then stopped himself.

"He's probably just gone for a ride by himself and didn't know how soon we'd be leaving," he said, his voice hiding his misgivings. "But we ordinarily don't take long midday stops. This is first-rate travel time."

"It's unlike him to leave without telling me. I'm certain he'll be back soon. Do you think we'll have to start up before he comes?" she asked, her voice breaking slightly before she got control of it. "If that happens, I . . . I'm not certain he could find us." She hesitated. "And I'm not certain I can manage your team. I've never driven such large, spirited horses before." She hesitated again. "And I've noticed that the crack in the wagon tongue looks worse."

"These horses are easy to drive; they're far more responsive than that worn-out team of yours," he replied. "I can show you what to do. But my partners and I won't leave with a man missing. As for the tongue, I think we can fix it with a solid splint and some strong leather strapping that should hold it for the time being. Joseph is an expert at repairing things. I'll get him and we'll do it now. It won't take long."

He went in search of his partner. No one would be happy about the delay, but having a cracked tongue in the nearby steep hills could mean disaster. Anger at Americus Powers simmered beneath his outward calm. The man didn't deserve his wife and those beautiful children. How long had he left the wooden tongue near the breaking point? And where could he have gone?

Todd lifted tools from his supply box and headed for Joseph's dinner spot. With a little luck, they could be on the road in less than an hour, tongue mended temporarily. Maybe by then Powers would show up, unless he got scalped in the meantime.

Damn these blasted dry gullies. They all looked alike. Up here away from the grassy river bottom, each one was strewn with the same gray-green sage, the same shapeless evergreens. They made a man yearn for Wisconsin, where overgrown hills weren't always blocking the view, and where, if a person got a little confused about his directions, there was always a familiar landmark to set him straight.

He'd been gone from the wagons too long, but what did they expect him to do? Sit there with the rest of them during the midday meal, enduring that endless drivel, trying to force down more of those disgusting beans? He was irritated by the constant bleating of the sheep up ahead, and it was a huge effort to answer John and Joseph and the others when they asked how his family was faring.

When he spied Blackey grazing behind a clump of undergrowth, he had been propelled toward the faithful, familiar animal. He'd just take a short ride, he told himself, and leave all this hellish commotion behind for a while.

He gave Blackey free rein and let his mind wander. Todd Curry—was that his name?—kept coming by the wagon, trying to strike up a conversation. He was congenial enough, but

Americus didn't care to talk. It was as if the man were sizing him up, measuring him against some strict code of wagon travel like one measured the height of corn stalks in relation to the passing summer. He had a way of squinting his eyes that made Americus feel as though Curry could see all the way to his soul.

Let Mary do the talking. She always did. That woman could talk to anyone, anywhere, under any circumstances. She'd tilt her head and listen with all her attention, making perfectly timed comments, and her listener would be mesmerized. Just as he himself had been mesmerized by Mary's charm and beauty from the day he met her. He still had trouble believing she had married him. For that matter, he still marveled that he'd had the courage to ask if he could walk her home from church that first time, so long ago.

"It would be my pleasure, Dr. Powers," she had replied, smiling in response to his request. Americus remembered how she took his arm with one gloved hand and held her pastel, flowing organdy skirt out of the dust with the other. She looked straight into his eyes with an interest so sincere that he forgot his shyness. "It's a lovely day for a walk."

"I enjoyed your organ music today." It was his carefully planned remark to start the conversation.

"Thank you. I relish playing for the services, except when I miss the A flat, the way I did today playing 'Rock of Ages.'" She laughed. "Did you notice?"

He smiled. All he had noticed was her slender profile in the mottled light from the stained glass window and her long, graceful fingers moving over the keys. But he liked a woman who could poke fun at herself.

Out here, though, nothing held him spellbound—not Mary, not this trip he'd wanted so badly, not his son and daughters. Blackey's hooves made a lulling rhythm, and the sun was warm on his back. He turned the horse westward. Maybe he could meet the wagons down the trail a bit, later in the afternoon. That way he wouldn't have to turn back, not when he was so relaxed. The coveted silence was welcome. Blackey was stronger than he thought, and his pace steady. It was remarkable what a couple of days of good grass and water—and no pulling—could do. He knew he hadn't been caring for the horses the way he should, but was it Cephas or Todd Curry who had been feeding and watering them?

He thought again about what odd country this was. He'd never seen such landscape before, living in Wisconsin and before that, back East. These arid foothills seemed like tall strangers watching his every move. He missed the familiar prairie sky. Here, the blue was intersected with the pointed tops of evergreens as if shot through with arrows. It was always uphill or down, too, never just the gentle land he was used to. Even the birds were different, flitting from bush to bush, calling out in strange voices, their flight and colors as unidentifiable as the plants underfoot. It made a man feel far from home.

The others would be angry if he didn't return right away, but he wouldn't be bullied into behaving like them, a bunch of docile animals following their leader. He hadn't asked to be a part of this train. He'd follow someone else's command only if it suited him. Right now it suited him to keep riding.

Mary could drive the wagon. She cowered from the massive work horses Curry had insisted they borrow, but her fear was ridiculous. Those animals wouldn't hurt anyone, unless their gigantic hooves inadvertently crushed whatever they stepped on. After his own horses, they felt as powerful as one of those threshing machines back home. Driving them was usually easy. For the most part, they just plodded along following the wagon ahead. Even with her small size, Mary could handle them just fine.

Americus ran his hand over his dry mouth. He should have thought to bring his canteen. The creeks that trickled down these gulches had dried up. The sky was sapphire blue, and the blinding sun was hot now. The strong rays were a burning reminder that he was at the mercy of this land and its raw elements. He was at the mercy of a lot of things out here.

He pulled on the reins. Blackey halted willingly as Americus considered the land ahead. More damned hills. He thought he had turned west, but he should have reached the trail again by now.

He must have dozed a little while Blackey meandered along. Maybe that's why he wasn't certain how long he'd been riding or how many gullies they'd crossed. Whatever the case, he needed a good long nap.

A sound off to his left pulled at his attention like a nagging voice. It sounded like the faint, far-off bleating of sheep. Yes, it was sheep. Blackey turned toward it of his own accord, and Americus gave him the reins.

M ary slid from beneath the quilts, careful not to awaken Americus and the children. She hadn't slept for more than a few minutes. The Doctor's solitary ride into the gullies had set her on edge, and she couldn't shrug off the anxiety. Sleep was impossible in the cramped wagon anyway; she could barely move, crushed as she was between Celia and the Doctor. In the darkness her worst fears forced their way into her mind, circling there like waiting vultures.

It was better to get up than to lie fretting. Dawn would come soon. She could build up last night's fire without awakening anyone in camp and huddle as close as her skirts would allow until she began to get warm. By then someone else might arise, and the day begin. The others always looked mildly surprised to find her already up, but despite her fatigue, Mary liked the early-morning hours she spent alone. Sometimes, if the night guard wandered off to check the animals, she could brush her matted hair instead of pinning it up still tangled. Getting rid of the stubborn, brittle snarls made her hair feel almost normal again, a reminder of home. It was as if straightening out her hair helped straighten her mind, too, and she felt as though she could think more clearly.

She'd never anticipated how important her own clear thinking would be out here. Instead of riding along on a well-planned pilgrimage to California, she was continually working out solutions, pondering illusive answers. She knew that Americus was no longer able to get them through. His actions of late made no sense, and protesting only made him more obstinate. The load was on her shoulders now; she had to find the strength to carry it. The unfamiliar skills were coming to her, like a difficult music passage practiced over and over, but she knew now that survival meant more than physically beating the rigors of the trail. She could also simply outlast them with good grace and new friends and borrowed horses.

She tried to regain her energy by taking long, sweet afternoon naps in the wagon when she and Celia could spread out on the quilts. The naps helped, but she was still curiously weak. Thankfully, adding her weight to the animals' load didn't seem to faze Mr. Curry's big horses at all. The Doctor obligingly drove for a few hours each afternoon when she couldn't go another inch without lying down. She slept soundly despite the wagon's jolting and swaying, its squeaking wheel, and the noise of the iron rims on the unforgiving hard-packed ground.

Mary quietly placed more dry twigs on the fire and poked the red coals with a stick. Sparks, bright as stars, flew into the dark night air and went out. Welcome flames warmed her hands and face as she moved the half-filled kettle onto the embers. Holding her skirts, she turned her chilled back to the fire and breathed in the fragrance of wood smoke.

She made a point these days of finding small pleasures and making them large in her mind: It helped her cope with the onslaught of problems that pulled her spirits down. A quick laugh with Amelia Pearson. Celia's soft skin as the little girl nestled close seeking Mary's love and protection. A dramatic vista, or a silver ribbon of water. She taught herself to notice the delicious fragrance of pine needles baking in the sun and the acrid smell of new raindrops on parched ground. Some days she carried a bit of sagebrush in her hand, rolling the fragrant leaves between her fingers to release their pungent odor.

There were a thousand blessings in each day, if only one could notice them. Out here it was easy to center one's attention on the frightening difficulties. It was much harder to see the silver linings edging this journey's dark clouds.

The water bubbled in the kettle, and Mary filled her tin cup, dropping in a few mint leaves and nestling it close. Mr. Curry had showed her the map last night. He came to the Powerses' wagon to let the Doctor know their exact location, but Americus was napping so he showed Mary instead. Her spirits plummeted when she realized they were still hundreds of miles from the California settlements. The long trail ahead wound through a desert and the dreaded Sierra Nevada Mountains. The very thought made her courage fail. It was inevitable they couldn't reach the threatening peaks until late in the season, which, according to the guide book, was highly dangerous. Travelers could get snowed in on the wrong side of the passes without shelter or food. Mary shuddered and inched nearer to the fire.

Pale light brightened the eastern sky. There was a rustling from the wagon. Celia's small face emerged from the canvas. Mary put her finger to her lips, so the little girl reached out her arms to Mary instead.

"I'm cold, Mother," she whispered as Mary lifted her from the wagon.

"I know, Celia. Let me hold you by the fire, and you'll soon get warm." She sat on a large rock near the flames, pulling her long skirts over the child's legs and feet for warmth. At least there was one use for her skirts! They were always catching on things and tripping her and getting in the way.

Celia snuggled close and sucked her thumb. She was usually up earlier than the others, like a baby wanting sustenance and attention in the night. Americus said she was infantile, but Mary knew better. The little girl was only responding to this journey's uncertainties and hardships as any small child would. Mary cherished the times Celia cuddled on her lap before dawn, drowsing as she got warm. She offered a silent prayer of thanks. Her children were well. She had heard terrible stories about other children dying of cholera and mountain fever and accidents out here. Sometimes she prayed that God would hold her family in the hollow of His hand, and she could almost imagine being nestled safely in His protective palm, the wagon guided by His gentle fingers.

There was something stiff in Celia's pocket. Mary pulled out the stick doll. Sarah had redrawn its face with charcoal and taken time to sew a little red skirt and trousers from scraps. The result was a charming toy. Celia reached out and grasped it in her delicate hand. She seldom let it out of her sight, even when she was sleeping. Mary marveled that such a simple thing could bring so much comfort and security into her daughter's small world.

Over the eastern horizon the sky was a brilliant orange. A few long black clouds scudded through it, their edges gilded. Overhead, the colors were muted, a pale yellow, then pink, and finally light blue. Mary silently added thanks for the sunrise to her prayers. Here was evidence that if she looked for glimpses of the perfect and the sublime, she could find them in the most treacherous situations. One had only to reach deep inside and find the strength.

Celia was drowsing now. Her curly hair was nestled

against Mary's arm. Mary looked down at her daughter's complexion, tanned and freckled but still smooth and beautiful. Three mosquito bites made pink bumps on her forehead, and some of last night's dinner was encrusted beside her mouth. She slept with a peace Mary wished she herself could feel just once on this journey.

The camp was stirring. Amelia Pearson climbed down from her wagon, smoothing her frizzed brown hair with one hand and adjusting her skirts over her short, stocky body with the other. Mary waved and smiled. Amelia waved back before she put her apron over her dress and began to build up her fire to make biscuits and bacon. It wasn't long before its fragrance wafted over the camp. Mary's mouth watered as she lifted Celia into the wagon and covered her with a blanket. She pulled last night's beans from the grub box.

# CHAPTER 28

# SARAH

This pretty Bear River valley seemed to loop around forever, but Sarah didn't mind. There was grass in the bottomland for Blackey and St. Lawrence, and a whole river full of water for them to drink. Now that they weren't pulling the wagon anymore, they were stronger and their bones didn't poke out so much. Sarah thought Blackey knew how to say thank-you with his eyes.

The valley narrowed here, and above it the hills rose steeply. It seemed to Sarah that whoever had discovered this route wanted to reach California by the shortest possible way, no matter how dangerous. In places the trail climbed straight through the gulches. She hid her eyes when the animals labored up those places. The men had to hitch several teams to one wagon and whip the poor beasts to make them haul their burden to the top. Sometimes the whips gashed their flanks until they bled.

Mr. Curry didn't whip his horses, though.

They had seen three bears as they traveled this Bear River country. Sarah had leaped into the wagon the first time, even though the big animal was only a black speck down the river. The second bear was closer, but it turned and shuffled away before Sarah could even start for the wagon. Mr. Curry told her they were shy animals that would almost always run from people, so after that she wasn't so afraid. She watched the third bear splash in the shallows across the river before it caught her scent and ambled off.

Traveling with the sheep train was nicer than she had imagined, even though there weren't any other children—just that one baby. There was plenty of food and company and protection. Yesterday, one of the lambs had died along the trail, so Mr. Curry brought them a tender roast. Mother rubbed it with salt and pepper, and then cooked it over the open fire. Sarah thought she had never tasted anything so delicious, especially after all those beans. When they got to California, she was never going to eat another bean!

In the long, cool evenings—if Mother allowed—Sarah and Cephas followed the flock's bleating until they found John and Joseph and the shepherds. Sarah loved to listen to the shepherds' Spanish that flowed like rapid music from their tongues. If she listened closely, she could sometimes understand a word or two. Other evenings she and Cephas stayed in camp, where Mr. Curry told stories of his trail adventures. Sarah noticed that Mr. Curry had tried to be friendly with Father, but now he was simply polite.

It was nice after supper because she had a rest from watching Ceely. When the dishes were washed and put away, Mother kept Ceely with her and prepared her for bed. Sarah didn't complain to Mother, but watching her little sister was sometimes so tiresome! When they traveled close to the river, Sarah had to be alert so that Ceely didn't fall into the current. It was impossible to let up her watchful guard, even for a moment. Added to that, there were always sharp things to step on, or insects that stung, or the dull oxen's lumbering hooves that could squash Ceely's delicate feet. At least the little girl was becoming more sensible about staying away from campfires and not putting things into her mouth. And now, thanks to Mr. Curry's horses, she could ride in the wagon, so Sarah didn't have to carry her so much.

Mother didn't ask Sarah to watch Ceely all the time, but her grateful looks let Sarah know how much it helped. Poor Mother had so many other things to worry about. This was one way Sarah could lift her burden. Her little sister was attached to her now, too, in a way she hadn't been before. Even when she was sleeping, she snuggled close to Sarah in the night. Sarah liked her warmth and closeness, but sometimes Ceely nearly drove her to distraction with her elbows that felt like darning needles.

"Sarah, Cephas!" It was Joseph carrying something white in his arms. "See what I found!"

At first Sarah thought it was another hurt lamb, but as Joseph got closer, she could see it was too small.

"What is it?"

"Snow! I was high in one of those shaded gullies scouting ahead, and I found a patch left over from last winter. I brought some back."

He scooped off handfuls and gave one to each shepherd, who gathered around. They began flicking bits of it at each other, running and dodging like the boys in the schoolyard back home. Then he offered one to Cephas and another to Sarah. Sarah broke hers in half and packed two snowballs, one for herself and one for Celia.

"Do you remember snow, Ceely? Put some on your tongue and feel how cold it is."

It was a novelty to walk along the trail in the hot sun nibbling on an icy snowball. She loved the coldness on her tongue and the fresh outdoors taste of it. Ceely's melted down her arm until it dripped water off her elbow. Sarah held it for her when it got too cold.

It reminded her of the way it had been before, back when she had enjoyed showing Ceely new curiosities.

# CHAPTER 29

# MARY

Mary lugged the dirty clothing to the water's edge, stepping carefully through the mud and tall grass. The undergrowth was so thick here she couldn't see the uneven ground where she could turn her still-tender ankle, so she moved slowly, studying the riverbank for the most suitable place to scrub clothes. The moist smell of the stream was a welcome relief after trail dust, but Mary hated the way her bare feet sank into the dark mud as if she were wallowing in molasses. It squeezed through her toes and dirtied the hem of her dress.

So this was the Malad, which she thought they had crossed days ago. Mary could scarcely believe Mr. Curry when he showed her the hairlike line on the map and the wagons' proximity to it. They were farther from California than she thought. It was discouraging, but it didn't provoke panic in her as it would have done earlier. Mr. Curry and his partners were so capable that the train moved along at a good, steady pace every day. At last, Mary felt they were making progress toward the end of this interminable journey.

A warm wind ruffled the tall, wide-bladed grass, cooling her skin and blowing her hair off her hot neck. It would be suppertime in an hour or so, and the heat of the afternoon was wan-ing. Mary stopped for a moment and closed her eyes. Surely she had the strength to wash clothes for a mere hour. She tried to put the chore out of her mind and center her thoughts on the beauty of this spot. Wild roses grew here. They were finished blooming, and Mary knew that their fragile, simple flowers were nothing like the showy roses back home, but their small red thorns and jagged leaves and newly forming rose hips were a sweet reminder of Wisconsin. She could hear the gentle sound of the water rippling and insects chirping in the undergrowth as if calling to each other. Out in the stream a fish jumped.

Patches of cattail and an odd thistle-headed plant lay ahead, but at last she saw a small muddy bar where she could do her scrubbing. There was nowhere to lay the clean wet clothes to dry, for the light wind would blow them into the muck here. She'd have to haul the heavy load back to the wagon and stretch one of the Doctor's ropes for a clothesline.

Despite the breeze, it was quiet in the bottomland beneath the chalky riverbanks that rose vertically in places like the walls of an adobe fort. The murky, slow water got deep quickly as it flowed by, green-brown against the hazy sky. In the distance, shadowed hills turned blue and gold in the late afternoon sun. Mary sighed and turned to her chore. Finally she had persuaded the Doctor to let her wash his old pants; she meant to scrub the filthy fabric until her muscles gave out. She'd have to be careful, though; the cloth was so worn and tattered that it was in danger of turning to nothing but shreds in her hands and floating off down the Malad like pieces of autumn leaves. She leaned over the water, wetting the hem of her dress as she worked. There was so much silt she wondered if the river would wash her clothes clean or simply add its own mud to the dirty cloth.

Downstream, Mr. Curry stepped from the undergrowth

with a fishing pole. He was too far off for a greeting, but when he saw her he waved and then cast his hook toward the center of the stream. Mary waved back. He was her lifeline right now, as steady as the eternal hills. He made certain each day that Mary and the children lacked for nothing, all the while treating Americus with deference. Mr. Curry somehow recognized that Americus needed to be acknowledged as head of his family, although Mary quietly took the responsibility. He unobtrusively presented her with the things she needed—a skinned grouse, grease for the wagon wheels, help with keeping an eye on Cephas. Mary wondered for a shocking instant how it would feel to be held in his strong, safe arms.

She gasped aloud at her shameful thoughts. Of course he could never be more than a friend as long as Americus was her husband. But she was so weary of the Doctor's stony, cold back and unpleasant moods. She wondered if God would condemn her for wondering.

By the time the sun set behind the hills, Mary's hands were red and stiff, and her arms were sore from scrubbing. Using every bit of her strength, she lifted the heavy load of wet clothing and made her way back to the wagon. Her dress, wet to the knees where she had leaned over the current, slapped cold against her legs.

Americus was asleep. Sarah stood beside the cook fire, watching Celia. The ground was carefully scraped bare around the fire, and the blaze was small—precautions they always took in this tinder-dry land. Cephas had gathered a pile of thin sticks for fuel. Now he was engrossed in pulling apart a cattail, letting the downy seeds float away on the breeze by handfuls.

"Sarah and Cephas, whatever would I do without you?" Mary smiled. She deposited her load on the clean grass. "We'll be able to have supper much sooner, thanks to your help." First, she had to sit down for a moment. Her back ached, and the usual deadening fatigue had overtaken her body.

"Father was shivering, so he got under the quilts in the wagon, Mother." Sarah looked perplexed. "But it was so hot out here—and even hotter in the wagon. I don't see how he could be cold."

A stone seemed to settle in Mary's stomach. Shivering on a hot day like this could mean only one thing.

"I'll look in on him in a moment, Sarah. It does seem peculiar, doesn't it? Did he say anything to you?"

"No. He acted as though it were as cold as January."

Mary frantically searched her memory. What had Tessie told her about fevers on the trail? Mountain fever, she called it. No one knew what caused it, but it infected plenty of travelers, some of whom recovered—and some of whom didn't.

Mary filled the coffeepot with water and put it on the coals. Then she took a cool, wet cloth and climbed into the wagon. The Doctor was awake, the heaviest quilt pulled up to his chin. His eyes looked glassy.

"Are you ill, Americus?"

"It's fever, Mary. I need a cold drink."

She nursed him through the evening with sips of river water and admonished the children to play quietly. Mr. Curry came by and cared for the horses, leading them to the river to drink and pouring grain from a sack for them, looking them over as they ate for any signs of distress—a rankling burr, a spot rubbed raw, a limp. He carried water for Mary's breakfast and checked the splinted wagon tongue.

It was getting dark when Mary pulled him aside.

"I think the Doctor has mountain fever, Mr. Curry."

His eyebrows shot up. "How do you know?"

"He said so himself. And he's lying in the wagon shivering under every bit of our bedding."

The man looked sober. "Mountain fever is no trifle, Mrs. Powers."

"No. Do you know a remedy? Anything at all?"

"My wife, Mamie, used to make some sort of a tea for fevers. I'll ask John and Joseph. They might know of something. In the meantime, you and the children should quarantine him in the wagon. I'll set up your tent for you to sleep in."

It was late by the time Mary got the children to bed and hung the wet clothes on a rope to dry. Her head pounded. She realized she hadn't eaten when she fed the children and urged Americus to take a few bites. Now she was too tired to move. She'd just have a cupful of cold coffee and wait until breakfast. She wanted to write to Mother, though; the process brought her such solace.

She drew out her pen and paper and went to sit on the wagon tongue. It was then that she noticed three golden-brown biscuits, carefully balanced on the wheel hub on an unfamiliar clean cloth. Mary gathered them into her hands and smelled their buttery aroma. It could only have been Mr. Curry who noticed her fatigued distraction tonight and left this welcome, nourishing gift. She looked around for him, but he and John and Joseph were already asleep in their bedrolls by their fire. Mary swallowed the lump in her throat. These biscuits, a bit brown on the bottom but perfect in every other way, nurtured her soul even more than they fortified her thin, hungry body. To have someone take care of her! To have someone notice that she hadn't eaten! The warm knowledge seeped into her soul as she bit into one, catching the crumbs in her hand.

*Dear Mother (and my sisters, too),*

*It is late, and I am sorely fatigued, so I will just scribble a bit tonight and finish tomorrow. It has been a day of mixed events. Americus has taken sick, almost certainly with mountain fever. He is quarantined, shivering and shaking in the wagon for the night, and we shall see what morning brings. One of our companions, Joseph, remembered a recipe his mother used to make to treat fever—a tea of herbs. Amongst us all, we had nearly all of the necessary ingredients. I brewed a cup for the Doctor tonight and hope he will be recovered in the morning. The children and I will sleep in the tent, which Mr. Curry kindly set up for us so that we might keep the Doctor isolated.*

*Mr. Curry has been a true blessing; he has assisted us by every possible means. Our wagon is now pulled by his powerful horses, and we are finally making good progress toward California. We have adequate food, ready water, and his attentive concern. He even brought some warm biscuits for my supper tonight, one of which I saved for my little Celia's breakfast. I shall be eternally grateful to him for his kind deeds. How can I ever adequately express my gratitude? Already he has saved our lives many times over, if truth be told.*

*I must go lie down, for dawn comes early, but I shall complete this later when I've had an opportunity to rest. We have so much farther to travel; I must save my strength.*

*Your loving daughter and sister,*

*Mary*

# CHAPTER 30

# AMERICUS

Why was it so blasted cold in this wagon? The sun sizzled in the sky, and the quilts were heaped on top of him, but his rigid body quaked like an aspen. How many days had he been lying here with this tortuous fever? The bugs, too—those biting black fleas that infested the quilts no matter how often Mary washed and aired them—made a man miserable.

Sleep came and went along with people's voices which wafted in and out of his brain like summer breezes, floating and drifting somewhere above him. It was odd, the way his brain felt detached with this fever. Todd Curry poked his dark head in the end of the wagon. Americus spoke to him in a haze. No, he didn't feel too warm—he was cold. And he was perfectly capable of driving his own wagon across this morning's stream, whichever one it was. He just had to find the energy to get up. Give a man a minute. A minute to rest.

"Americus." It was Mary now. He tried to sit up, but her tender hands pushed him down and tilted his feverish head. Water trickled onto his chin, and he gulped, opening his eyes and seeing her in faded brown dress and a soot-streaked apron. "Americus, are you worse?"

He tried to answer, but fatigue stole his voice and blanked out his mind.

He heard a man's voice from somewhere nearby. "He can't drive, Mary—he's too sick. I'll take your wagon across. You can ride inside with him and Celia. Cephas and Sarah need to cross on horseback. We'll be on the far bank in no time."

"None of us can swim," Americus heard her answer. "Except Cephas and Sarah."

"No need to swim," the man's voice answered easily. "You'll be in the wagon."

"But if it capsizes . . ."

Americus didn't hear the answer, and then he dozed again, until the wagon made its lurching start, as though it were reluctant to face the ordeal ahead. The ironclad wheels struck the stones on the river bank and then in the shallows. Next to him, Mary was wrapping her Bible and her letters in a flour sack and tying them high overhead in the bows. Celia's voice piped up, "Mother, put my stick man up?"

Americus struggled to sit up and look out the front. Was he seeing things, or were there eight oxen hitched to the wagon instead of the usual horses? He must have slept a long time, because most of the wagons were already on the far side of the stream, dark water stains high on the weathered wagon boxes. Todd Curry sat in Mary's accustomed spot on the wagon seat, and Joseph was on a drenched horse tethered to the upstream side of the wagon, his clothing wet to the waist. Americus fell back. The water's rushing grew louder, and there was a shout as Curry nosed the oxen into the current.

A man could almost enjoy being ferried across like this if it weren't for the creases in Mary's forehead and Curry's white knuckles on the reins and the rush of too much water. Somewhere in the haze, men were shouting. "Pull 'er around, Curry! You're drifting too far!"

"Watch the boulders there."

"You're taking on water; hurry it up."

Mary gave a little gasp and pulled her feet up under her.

His mind drifted as the wagon jerked and swayed. He was a child back on his father's farm in the East—a tall, skinny boy of twelve. The raft he made that summer between chores floated on the duck pond, but his mother wouldn't let him unmoor it until he learned to swim. He tried to master the skill but couldn't keep himself afloat and soon learned to despise the feel of cold water washing over his head, pushing its way into his mouth and nose. He thrashed his arms and legs as he'd been instructed, but his body sank anyway. The raft sat there, tied up, until one day his parents rode to town for supplies, leaving him and his brothers alone. He sneaked away, untied the rope, and pushed himself back and forth across the pond several exhilarating times before mooring again and hiding the pole in the reeds.

"Ho! Boulder!" There was a jarring lurch from the downstream side, and the wagon tipped. Americus watched his feet fly up and heard Mary scream and grab for Celia. An icy slosh of river water doused his head. He saw Curry grab for the supports and nearly pitch into the stream. Mary's Bible catapulted to the bed. She grabbed it and stuffed it in her apron pocket, still clutching Celia with her other hand. For a few seconds, it seemed as if the wagon would keep tipping, flipping onto its side and dumping them and their whole life into the surging stream. But just as suddenly it righted itself, and the oxen worked steadily against the current, pulling with all their worth toward the opposite shore.

There was a jolt from underneath. Americus knew the wheels had finally reached the riverbed on the other side. He could see Mary frantically pulling things off the wagon floor and piling them on the quilt. Poor Mary had trouble if a little mud got in the wagon. Water in the bedding and beans would seem catastrophic to her.

But they'd made it across this stream—which one was it?—thanks to Curry and his friends.

The wagon had stopped now; he could hear the water inside slowly draining to the ground. The sun still shone on the wagon top, and he wasn't cold any longer. Now he felt as though his blasted skin was burning up. He kicked his way out of the damp quilt, feeling his bare feet hit the fresh air.

# CHAPTER 31

# TODD CURRY

Todd Curry circled his wagon, checking. Plow, tied on securely. Tar bucket gone from its place underneath and tucked into the wagon bed for the rough road ahead. Grub box lashed down. The treacherous trail made him appreciate the level plains behind them. Here it was all up and down with brakes and chains and locked wheels. He'd better check Mrs. Powers's wagon, too.

He was quiet as he circled the other wagon, cinching their axe tighter, checking the brake repair. Powers was asleep inside. He'd just as soon the man slept through his inspection.

"Mr. Curry?" Cephas's small face poked through the puckered back of the wagon cover.

"What is it, Cephas? What are you doing in the wagon? It's quarantined."

"I feel sick, too."

Uneasy, Todd looked closely at the boy.

"Hmmm. Where do you feel sick? Is it your belly?"

"It's all of me. And I'm cold, too."

Todd looked again. Cephas's eyes were large and glazed, and his color was off. He always looked peaked, but today his skin was gray with muted dark lines underscoring his eyes.

Todd reached up to feel the boy's forehead, keenly aware of the doctor's deep breathing on the other side of the canvas. Cephas's skin was hot.

"I'll find your mother, Cephas. Do you know where she went? She'll know how to fix you all up, and you'll be good as new." Mountain fever. Could be.

Mrs. Powers was probably down in the ravine washing the breakfast cups with the slight trickle of water there. He strode toward its steep edge and looked over. There she was, sitting behind a silvery-green bush, her back to him. He paused as she doubled over, and then stopped altogether when he realized she was crying. This trip was excruciating for women, who gave up hearth and home and loved ones for their husbands' perplexing drive to go West. Today she had good reason to cry. Mountain fever could kill, although he'd seen it touch down so lightly that it could be gone the next day, too.

As he watched, she pushed herself to her feet and went to the stream, dipped her cupped hands into the current, splashed her face, and dried it on her apron. Todd waited a moment. She would be embarrassed if she knew he had seen her. Then he scrambled down toward her, eyes on the ground as if he'd been too preoccupied with his footing to notice what she'd been up to.

"Cephas is looking a little poorly this morning," he said as he got near.

"I know." Her face was blanched and her eyes a telltale pink. "I'm so worried. He was restless all night."

"Keep him quiet today. Chances are he'll be all right by tomorrow," Todd said quietly. "Once we're over the rough spots, he should be able to sleep in the wagon." He searched for something to say that would bring a small speck of comfort to her. Joseph, who had scouted this stretch, said they were in for a hard day of it, with plenty of steep descents.

"You don't suppose . . ." She rubbed her bare toe in the mud, not caring if he saw her lack of shoes, her bruised and calloused feet. "It's most likely mountain fever, isn't it."

"It could be, but perhaps not. We'll watch him carefully—you can stay with him all day if need be. I'm sure he'll be alright." His voice was strong, but his stomach felt as though someone was cinching a rope around it. He went on, hoping his next words would give her some encouragement. "When you folks get to California, all the hardships of this trip will be over for good."

She stared at him, as if trying to decipher a code written somewhere on his face. When she spoke, her voice was low and frightened.

"You folks? What do you mean by 'you folks,' Mr. Curry?"

Oh, dear God. Dr. Powers hadn't told her. Todd had asked him to, days ago, before the fever hit, and then assumed he had.

"Mrs. Powers." He could feel his jaw twitch in anger. Americus Powers was more than just odd. He was an undeserving coward. "Didn't Dr. Powers tell you? I asked him if he would. John and Joseph and the sheep and I aren't going to California. The place we want to raise sheep is only two weeks' journey from here; that's where we intend to establish our operation. There's water there, and I'm confident the railroad will come through in a few years. . . . We won't be able to travel with you much longer. I'm sorry. I thought you knew."

"Oh, it can't be true!"

"We'll find a way for you to get safely to California. We'll find another train for you to join or . . . "

"I'm going back home, Mr. Curry." Her voice was abrupt,

flat, and there was an odd light in her eyes. "I'm taking the children and going back. Americus can go to California if he likes, but we're going back."

"Mrs. Powers, that's absurd! You'd die in a matter of days out here by yourselves!" Could she be serious? He'd heard stories of women who hated the trip West so much they'd set the family wagon on fire and started a solitary trip east on horseback.

"Please." Her voice climbed several notches. "I . . . I can't bear the thought of traveling without . . . traveling alone again. I just want to turn around and go home."

"Mrs. Powers! You mustn't think such thoughts. Your only hope is to make it safely to California." He was speaking louder than he should, but his tone seemed to be getting through her near hysteria. "It's not so very far now. You've come the long half of the trip. You can make it now."

She looked at him a moment longer, steadily. He could almost see her determined effort to rein in the shock as she took a deep breath and pressed her pale lips together until her mouth was a straight, firm slash across her face. Her eyes were black in her thin white face as she nodded to acknowledge his words, but the gracious smile was gone and her hands were clenched by her sides like small stones. She nodded her head at him, then turned away, gathered her skirts and started back to camp. Todd watched her climb the steep bank, favoring her sore ankle. He sank down by the trickle of water, scooped up a handful of pebbles and tossed them one by one down the ravine. They bounced from rock to rock like his thoughts, ricocheting here and there.

"Curry!" It was John, calling from the rim. "There you are. I looked all over creation for you." Todd scrambled to the rim to meet him.

"Think we can get the wagons through all those steep places today?" John asked.

"I wish we could just pluck 'em up and set 'em down again ten miles farther on."

"So do I . . . I've been thinking. How about trying that first ravine with my wagon, since mine is the most expendable. Then we'll take the Powerses' outfit down."

"Sounds fine to me. Their brake isn't in good shape; it's been repaired somewhere along the trail. I think it'll make it all right, though. By the way, their little boy is sick. Feverish."

"Feverish . . ." The other man looked at Todd. "Mountain feverish, you mean?"

"Well, it stands to reason. He doesn't look good to me. Mrs. Powers is there now seeing to him." As he spoke, he could see her detach herself from the wagons and hurry toward them. She carried the weather-beaten wooden bucket, which Todd had filled for her earlier; now it swung empty in her hand. "Here she comes. You can ask her yourself. I don't know if I'd mention mountain fever, though. She's already plenty worried."

"You seem to know a lot about her, Curry." The tone was low and mild, not accusing, and Todd glanced at John's face to see if he meant anything by the comment, but John was already walking toward Mrs. Powers to take her bucket and fill it for her. "Curry here says your son is a little peaked this morning."

"Yes. He's feverish. Along with Americus, who's still feeling ill. They're buried under all our quilts shivering so badly the whole wagon shakes. I'm so worried. It's an oven in there."

"I'll fill your bucket and come around to have a look," Todd heard John say. "Maybe we can brew up some more of those herbs for Cephas."

Todd headed back to his own wagon. How had this trip gotten so complicated with fevers and rough road and a woman he couldn't stand to see suffer? John's offhand comment bothered him, too. It wouldn't do to let improper thoughts get started about him and Mrs. Powers. He'd better be more careful not to be seen with her, but it was hard to help while keeping a prudent distance all the time.

Dr. Powers wasn't recovering as he should. The thought bothered Todd like a needle pricking his skin. The man was emaciated. He never ate, even when Mrs. Powers tried to tempt his appetite or force a few mouthfuls down him. His bones stuck out from under his transparent skin, and his face was skeletal. Mountain fever had killed many a stronger man.

With a sigh, he returned to camp and hitched the team to his wagon, then started hitching the spare horses to Mrs. Powers's wagon. He could hear her inside, talking softly as she sponged Cephas with river water. The doctor's deep breathing had quieted, and Todd could imagine him lying there, watching insects land on the canvas, their shadows larger than their bodies in the slanting morning sun. Or maybe he was watching Mrs. Powers's face, drawn and pinched but still beautiful, as she tended to Cephas.

Something bright on the ground caught his attention as he rounded the back of their wagon, and he looked down to see Celia's stick doll, dressed in a scrap of red gingham, staring up at him with its arms outstretched in the dust. Beside it was a matching stick pony, obviously more of Sarah's handiwork. Todd bent and picked them up. Sarah had collected a bunch of matted lichen for a mane and tail. Todd held them in his hand for a moment and then silently slipped them under the wagon cover.

Mary had expected the worst, but instead Cephas was already overcoming the fever. His eyes lost their glassiness, and although his face was still pale and hollow eyed, he fidgeted until she gave him permission to step down from the wagon for a few moments. She closed her eyes in thankfulness. If only Americus could do the same, she could breathe again.

She realized she was thirsty. Water was scarce now that they had entered what Mr. Curry called the Great Basin, a gigantic dry bowl filled with dust and sand that stretched hundreds of miles ahead. The name didn't let on about the steep granite canyons they encountered nor the odd rock formations that stuck up like gray castles on the landscape. Huge rounded mounds of them piled up to form low mountains where a few hardy evergreens clung to the cracks. The trail wound through the route of least resistance, but even so the wheels scraped along granite outcrops and slid screeching down unforgiving steep pitches.

Still, there was striking beauty to this unusual landscape that looked like some drab ancient city. They were camped at the base of a granite spire that lifted a hundred feet or more above them. Sitting on a boulder as big and flat as a rocky throne, she spent a few minutes with Sarah imagining shapes in the stones—huge loaves of bread, a herd of buffalo, an elegant hotel. Sarah laid her head on Mary's shoulder, glad for the respite from walking and dull chores.

Thank goodness Mr. Curry was there to drive her wagon in the terrible places that made her stomach clench in alarm. Where the trail dropped off to a steep decline, he would set the brakes and tie one end of his thick rope around the wagon's axle, looping the other end around a sturdy tree or a boulder. Then John and Joseph would pull back on the rope with all their might as the wagon descended. With sheer brawn, the two of them prevented the massive wheels from hurtling down the gulches and running over the horses.

In a few short days, though, Mr. Curry and his companions would reach their destination, and what would she do then? The thought flooded her with dread. Maybe she should just fling herself from the top of one of these stony cliffs! She shook her head to banish the thought. What a strange idea to enter her mind!

She busied herself by building a small fire and feeding the children and tending to Americus. Long evening shadows fell across the quiet camp as she scrubbed the supper plates and dried them with an old flour sack. The bedding needed attention, too, but there wasn't enough water here to wash it. Instead, she took the Rising Sun quilt, which Americus had kicked aside in the day's heat, behind the towering stone steeple to shake it out.

"Mrs. Powers." It was Mr. Curry. "I came to tell you something."

She looked at him and tucked a stray wisp of hair into her coiled braid. His forehead was furrowed.

"I want you to know that I won't—we won't—desert you

out here," he went on. "I know you're troubled about being left alone when we reach our destination, but I would never allow that to happen."

She tried to smile. "Thank you."

"We'll find a new wagon train to take you in," he added. "You can stay with us until one comes through."

"Thank you," she said again. "You . . . you don't know how much that means to me."

Their eyes locked, and for a moment they held the gaze. Neither spoke. Mary yearned to reach out to him in gratitude. Her mouth went dry. She took a step toward him, then stopped and lowered her eyes, thanking God for this man who had offered her so much.

Mr. Curry was still looking at her, and she raised her eyes.

"You know, Mrs. Powers, I'll always be your friend, no matter where you are." He smiled.

"Yes," she answered. "And I'll never forget all your kindness."

"We'd best be getting back."

Mary watched him disappear and took time to calm her shaking hands. She smoothed her hair and took a deep breath. Then she pulled the old quilt around her shoulders, sat on an outcropping, and pulled her pen and paper from her pocket.

*Dearest Mother,*

*Ere I lay down for the night, I must tell you that—much to my dismay—Mr. Curry and the boys will not be traveling with us much longer, as they have nearly reached the destination they scouted on an earlier trip. Mr. Curry has promised they will not desert me and my little family, especially since Americus is so poorly. There are so many*

*wagon trains traveling westward that Mr. Curry assures me
we will find one sooner or later that can take us in. But I am
sorely grieved that we must leave our cherished friends.*

*I long desperately to hear from you, and the thought of
your letters quite possibly waiting to greet me in California
gives me strength to carry on. And I do need strength, given
the events of the past week! A few days ago, my little Cephas
contracted mountain fever soon after Americus did. I thought
I would perish from worry, but to my vast relief, our
Heavenly Father gave him the strength to overcome the chills
and weakness rather quickly. He must still ride in the wagon
but he is eating again and looking less peaked. I am nursing
him with herbs and feeding him nourishing tidbits that John
and Joseph and Mr. Curry bring me, and Amelia Pearson has
helped Sarah watch Celia while I am so distracted. Their
kindness and generosity have no end.*

*Americus, though, is still causing us all great concern.
He is so weak that he is in grave danger. Mother, he can
barely lift his head, and sometimes his words make no sense at
all. He is so thin that he is truly nothing but bones. I have
nursed him day and night until I am ready to collapse, and all
the while we have been pushing, pushing, pushing onward.
Never in my life have I feared the arrival of autumn, but
here the very thought of it fills me with dread.*

*Sarah, Cephas, and Celia went this evening with John
and Joseph to see the shepherds, who are "watching their flock
by night." Cephas hasn't the strength to stay long, but he
begged to leave the campsite for a short time, and I suppose
the fresh air will do him good. John gave him a quantity of
jerked meat today and some cheese. Cephas ate what he could,
which seemed to give him some strength, and then saved the
rest for me, bless his little heart. It tasted so sweet and tender!*

*Even Celia relished it more than you can imagine.*

*We are pushing ahead toward a river bearing the name "Humboldt." Mr. Curry's guide book shows we are to follow it for a very long way before reaching the desert we must traverse and, after that, the dreaded Sierra Nevada. I will continue to write you, Mother, even though there will be no way to post my epistle until—if—we reach the sunny valleys of California.*

*Please share this with my sisters and know that in my absence I send my love to you all,*

*Mary*

# CHAPTER 33

## SARAH

Tears ran down Sarah's face as she picked her way beside the wagon avoiding sharp stones. Inside, Father was talking nonsense while Mother tried to make him comfortable. Sarah had watched her brew a blend of herbs over this morning's fire to bring Father's fever down. But the deep creases in her mother's forehead told her all she needed to know. Father was so skinny and weak. The mountain fever had taken hold of him like a vicious dog. Mother could soothe and nurse him all day, but it wouldn't do any good.

She was so thankful that Cephas was better! Today he was walking for a few minutes until he got too tired. Sarah wondered how long they could keep plodding through this hot country while the wagons kept up their steady, deadening pace.

No matter how she tried, she couldn't stop the tears. Father might be difficult, yet the thought of his death was worse than anything. She wiped her cheeks with her grimy handkerchief, but that didn't keep her eyes from feeling red and swollen. How shameful it was to be crying right out in the open where everyone could see!

She turned when she heard Cephas call her and waited until he caught up. His bony chest was heaving and he gulped big breaths of air. He stopped short at the sight of her streaked face.

"What's wrong, Sarah?"

"It's Father. I'm afraid he's going to die."

"Can't Mother fix him like she fixed me?"

"She's tried and tried but she just can't. Father was too weak in the first place, she says."

"But, Sarah, I don't want Father to die!" Cephas's own eyes filled with tears, and he glanced around as he brushed them away. Mr. Curry was riding toward them.

"Morning, Sarah, Cephas." The man smiled as he rode up beside them. "Everything all right?"

"Everything except Father," answered Sarah. "He's talking nonsense in the wagon, and Mother says he's burning up with fever. Oh, Mr. Curry, is he going to die?"

He looked at her blotchy face and seemed to search for the right words. "I'm not sure what will happen, Sarah. I think he'll pull through. But your father hasn't been eating much for a long time and he's lost a lot of stamina out here on the trail. That weakens a body, so a disease has a better chance."

"Can't we find a doctor somewhere?"

"I wondered about that, too, Sarah. I don't know where we'd find a doctor out here. Your mother is trying some new herbs today, though."

One last desperate question burst from Sarah before she could stop it. "What if Mother catches the fever, too?"

"No sign of that, Sarah." Mr. Curry answered, his voice firm. "Your mother is stronger than she looks, and she'd certainly be ill by now. Now, I have an idea. Why don't the two of you take this good horse of mine and ride her for the day? She's big enough to carry you both, and it'll give you a rest from all that walking. Give those sore feet a chance to heal, too. How about it?"

Sarah looked into the man's blue eyes in surprise. "You mean it, Mr. Curry? You'd let us ride your horse?"

"I do, Sarah. This past week has been hard on you two, with your father sick and your mother so distracted. You've shown your worth, all right. I noticed all the times you cooked beans and coffee, Sarah. And Cephas, I never knew a boy who could do such a good job of watering horses and finding firewood. Now, you climb on Sadie here and catch up with the wagons before your mother gets worried about you."

He stepped down and held the reins while Sarah and then Cephas climbed onto the brown horse's back. Up here Sarah could see forever, it seemed. It was like being on the top of a hill, looking out over the land below. Sitting on the Sadie's warm back with Cephas's tousled hair under her chin and her sore feet dangling in the breeze made the day seem like a holiday. Mr. Curry handed them each a long strip of jerked meat, and they set off toward the wagons savoring the salty flavor on their tongues and the mare's gentle rocking.

# CHAPTER 34

# MARY

Mary rested a moment longer perched on the wheel hub. The early morning air smelled of pine and wood smoke and coffee as dawn lightened the sky in the east. She stood up, purposely stretching herself as tall as she could, and pulled her shoulders back. Perhaps by forcing her body to carry out the day's duties she could make her mind follow, dragging it from its trampled state and prodding it upright, insisting that it take charge of whatever these next hours would bring. If it meant saying a last good-bye to her husband or severing her connection to Mr. Curry, she needed to be strong enough.

She marveled at how she could act so composed and calm outwardly yet feel so near despair inside. She could carry on a pleasant conversation with one half of her mind while the other half was stunned into silence by harsh reality, or swallow the lump in her throat and paste a smile on her lips for the children when inside she felt as shriveled as a dead leaf.

She checked on Celia to be certain she was still asleep in the tent with Sarah and Cephas, and pulled the beans out of the fire. Then she started off for a secluded spot not far from camp where she could be alone.

How her mind yearned to be free of its constant fretting! She'd lain awake again, wondering if the Doctor would recover.

Even if he survived this terrible fever, how could he ever return to his old livelihood? There seemed no possibility that her husband could ever be a physician again.

She worried constantly about the children, too. This demanding journey had changed them forever. They had "seen the elephant," as the saying went, meaning that they had stared risk and treachery in the face. What effect would it have on them? Her poor Sarah was so serious now—of necessity a second mother to Celia. She wondered if Sarah would benefit from Mary's new boldness and budding leadership—and if her example would cause Sarah to develop those traits herself. Would young gold seekers someday find such qualities appealing? Or would they feel a strong, independent, capable girl was an undesirable marriage partner and look instead for someone who knew how to defer to her husband's wishes?

Mary sighed as she picked her way through the undergrowth. The children would suffer long effects from being battered by the West's outdoor elements and deprived of healthful food. Not to mention being the recipients of everyone's charity! These past weeks, the children had watched their parents accept far more than they had given, despite Mary's desperate efforts to make things right. She was afraid her lesson that it was better to give than to receive was being erased along with all the other manners and refinements she had worked to instill in them.

She sat down on a lichen-covered log. It was sheltered here, and private, and she savored the rare moment alone. She took a long breath and stretched her arms, feeling the cool breeze on her wrists and hands. Behind her a bird began to chirp as if all were right with the world.

How would she have spent such a moment back home? Walking by the creek, perhaps, or playing the small pump organ in Mother's parlor. Every time she visited, she had filled the little house with music, some contemporary, some classical, some of her own composition. She missed it terribly out here where the only musical sounds were coyotes howling at the moon, or an occasional jangly banjo beside someone's campfire, or the ripple of silvery tones that delighted Celia when she threw a fistful of pebbles into a stream. Music touched Mary's soul in a way nothing else could.

Her soul. It was as battered as the rest of her, but she still thought of it as a great internal river, drawn off by the daily grind of chores and drudgery—and replenished by faith and small comforts, triumphs, love, and music.

She rested her hands on the trunk of a partially fallen tree that leaned out over her lap, feeling its rough bark and pausing on tufts of lichen. Slowing she began fingering the spellbinding notes of Handel's "Largo," a few slow chords at first, and then a few more. She knew the glorious music by heart and she could almost hear its grand echo here in this forest—the crescendos and decrescendos, the sweet high notes interwoven with the rich, deeper background. Her fingers, dirty and chapped but nimble nonetheless, flowed over the bark, and her body leaned forward with concentration. The huge hollow silence seemed to resonate with the harmonious chords as she played on and on, the music rising and swelling to a grand crescendo that reverberated through the rocks and trees until it faded away to a gentle, soft closure.

When she opened her eyes, she sat motionless in the morning light, her hands resting on the bark. Her inner river was flowing strong and full again. She could almost feel its power surging through her like the current of the Bear itself, or the Malad, or the Sweetwater, or any of these mighty and invincible western streams. Now, surely, she could carry on.

# CHAPTER 35

# TODD CURRY

Todd scanned the trail ahead. He was the first to admit his tracking skills weren't good, but no one could overlook the signs here: fresh ox dung and new hoof prints amid several sets of wagon wheel tracks. There must be a small ox train ahead, perhaps the help Mrs. Powers needed to get to California. He knew he should be thankful, but he felt utterly joyless about it for some reason.

Americus Powers's fever had finally broken and the man was lucid if terribly weak. Mrs. Powers's faithful nursing and all those herbs she gave him pulled him through, but the man was completely emaciated now. His skin looked like parchment stretched over sticks, and his eyes were sunken into his skull as though taking a distant and removed view of the world. Todd wondered what kind of a man Powers really was. His wife said he was smart and kind and gentle, but it was hard to believe. Todd had seen only irritability and rash decisions and anger.

At least the man's horses were finally recovering, especially the one named Blackey, an astounding animal, although completely unsuited for pulling such a load. He seemed intelligent to Todd, and dogged and devoted in an almost humanlike way. Powers must have paid plenty for such an animal.

Todd was glad the poor beast had regained some strength while his own horses shouldered the burden. It had taken plenty of rest and Bear River grasses, but even the bay, which had been nearly dead that day when Todd first came across the Powers family, was much stronger now.

Todd went to check the Powerses' brake repair and found the doctor sitting up on the bedding. Mrs. Powers had tied back the cover so the sunshine could reach him. Todd tried talking to him for a minute or two before he realized the man wouldn't answer, but it was encouraging, at least, to see him sitting up. Given another day or two, it was possible he would be able to walk a little. Good thing. There wasn't a wagon train anywhere that would invite a traveler with mountain fever into its midst, even as an act of charity. It was simply too dangerous.

"Move 'em out!" Joseph gave the signal. Todd saw Mrs. Powers secure the canvas cover back into place and climb up to the wagon seat. If she was embarrassed after their quiet encounter yesterday, she showed no sign. He wasn't sure what had prompted him to seek her out. All he knew was that he had wanted to reassure her that they would never desert her. It seemed as natural as the wind in the trees.

This stretch of the trail was bad. It seemed to Todd that it took on a life of its own here, almost as if it were a difficult personality to be reckoned with. It was no longer a monotonous track across the plains, where outlasting its distance was tougher than conquering its impediments. Here it twisted and dove and offered up obstacles almost too daunting to face. Mrs. Powers's horses would need every speck of their new flesh and muscle to get through to the Humboldt.

Just ahead he could see the trail enter a narrow canyon where a tumbling stream squeezed between stone cliffs. They rose dramatically on both sides, reminding Todd of the weather-beaten sides of an indomitable fort. As hard as it was to get the wagons through a place like this, he was awed by its grandeur. This West never failed to satisfy his yearning for wild places and beauty.

The trail went directly up the streambed. He splashed through the cold water urging the horses over the slippery rock bottom. Behind him, he could hear John bringing Mrs. Powers's wagon. Todd's feet and legs ached, but before the cold became unbearable the canyon widened out and there was room to drive the wagons along the north bank. Thankfully the shepherds were taking the sheep around a longer route. He could hardly imagine the stench of wet wool and the thunderous bleating of a few hundred panicked sheep refusing to be pushed through a place like this.

Todd was in the lead when the group rounded a bend and saw a stalled ox train. One of the wagons was hung up in the water, tipped crazily as if awaiting permission to flip on its side. A quick assessment told Todd it was as he had predicted: There were six wagons pulled by a typical number of overused cattle. As he drew near, one of the men—an imposing gentleman so tall that Todd's own six-foot frame seemed small—approached, his hand outstretched in greeting.

"Greetings. My name's Whitesides, Major Whitesides. Most folks call me 'Major.'"

Whitesides. The name didn't fit, Todd thought, as he held out his own hand. The man looked as though he had been in the sun and wind his entire life. He was solidly built with a bushy dark beard and a bald forehead so shiny that Todd had a hard time not staring at it. The man stood straight while his eyes flickered past Todd to the slowly advancing wagons beyond. He acted as though taking charge came naturally to him.

"Need help?" Todd asked. "It looks like one of your wagons is mired."

"We did fall into a hole," the Major replied. "We may have broken a wheel, but the water's too roiled up to see. If you folks could lend another hand, we might be able to free it without unloading."

It was a backbreaking mucky job to dislodge the wagon, wedged as it was behind a nasty boulder. It wasn't until late afternoon that multiple oxen, levered planks, and ingenuity lifted the wheel—unbroken, as it turned out—out of the hole with a giant heave, and the two trains were able to continue their slow progress toward the canyon's mouth. Where the sheer walls opened onto a flat plateau, they stopped for the night.

Todd's muscles were sore, and he'd taken a bad gash on his shin. He sat on his wagon tongue for a moment, watching the sunset before beginning the evening's chores. Overhead, a lone eagle soared high, a black silhouette against the deep purple sky. The August nights came earlier and earlier, provoking in him a slight uneasiness. A cool breeze blew down the canyon ruffling the wagons' canvas tops. Warm as the day had been, a campfire might feel good tonight.

The Powers family would do well to arrange to travel with the Major. The man and his party seemed a strong, competent lot. Protocol demanded that Todd leave the arrangements to Dr. Powers, but unless Todd was terribly wrong, Americus would never look the Major in the eye and ask for help. Mrs. Powers would be the one to take action, to do a man's job and ask for the charity she hated to accept.

He unhitched and led the horses to the stream. Mrs. Powers's two girls were there filling their old bucket. Todd watched little Celia run to a smooth stone slab and pull a piece of chalky rock from her pocket. In the evening's dim light, she was soon engrossed in drawing lines and stick figures on the flat surface.

"I have something I want to show you, Sarah," Todd said to the older girl, letting the horses drink for a moment. "Tonight might be the last opportunity. Wait a minute while I get it."

Todd strode to his wagon and secured the horses, then took a muslin-wrapped bundle from his knapsack and returned to the girl.

As he unwound the muslin in the fading evening light, Sarah clapped her hand over her mouth. Her eyes opened wide. "It's Mother's silver teapot! Wherever did you get it? We left it behind weeks ago."

So. He was right: This was Mrs. Powers's heirloom, the one she'd had to abandon near the banks of the Sweetwater.

"I thought it was, Sarah. Those engraved initials . . ."

"Where did you find it?"

"Another family I met way back on the trail saw its value and picked it up. They offered it to me in exchange for a couple of sheep. I thought it might be worth something out West. Now I'd like to give it back to your mother. I was hoping you could surprise her with it when you get to California."

"If Father finds it, he'll make us leave it behind again."

"Not to deceive your father, Sarah, but it's small enough to hide fairly easily."

"I can put it with my rag doll, Lucy. She's hidden inside my old wool dress in the bottom of the trunk where no one ever looks."

"Your mother'll get plenty of pleasure having it in your new home."

"She will, Mr. Curry. Thank you."

He wrapped the heirloom again in its protective cloth and handed it to the girl. It felt good to set one small thing right in Mrs. Powers's world—a world that had no certainties, only worry and doubt and a long, long trail ahead.

# CHAPTER 36

# MARY

There they were, her hoarded dried strawberries, tucked away in the wagon's back corner, wrapped in a light cloth— a preserved bit of home, the last vestige of her Wisconsin garden that made her chest ache. Mary untied the string and breathed in their sweet fragrance.

What a distance these treasured stowaways had traveled with no one but Mary knowing they were there! She remembered the day she packed them into the waiting wagon. Americus was loading the trunk when she slipped them into a hidden cranny without his noticing. She wasn't sure why she didn't tell him about her little stashes. It was as if she needed to be in control of some small portion of this trip, no matter how insignificant. It brought her comfort to know about the sewing needles and pins pressed into slits in the floorboards—hadn't she used them for trading more than once?—along with the seeds for her California garden. There were her buttons, too, and even the daguerreotype of her parents slipped inside the trunk's lining. After Americus insisted that she abandon her teapot that terrible day, Mary guarded her small secrets with care.

If she worked quickly, she could make the strawberry dumpling before Americus returned. Yesterday he had climbed down from the wagon for the first time since he took sick and sat on a rock by the fire until he tired. Today he'd gone for a little walk to try to get some strength back in his legs. She didn't want to answer his questions about where she got the berries, what she was making, or for whom it was intended, because she meant to share it with Mr. Curry and the boys as a meager but devout thanks and a sad good-bye.

She stewed the berries and mixed up a light dough with a few cupfuls of Amelia Pearson's flour, using the bottle to roll it out on the wagon seat. Then she deftly spread the strawberries over the dough, rolled it up, sewed her creation into a cloth and boiled it in water. While it cooked she used the juice that was left to make a sauce.

Stooped over the fire, loneliness settled over her like a shadow, and her head started its familiar aching. Mr. Curry and John and Joseph would be gone soon. The thought brought back the empty feeling she remembered from childhood when she tormented herself by imagining how it would feel if there were no safe, steady God in charge of the universe. The sky overhead lost its sheltering protection then and became a wide, open, calculating space that stretched in icy blackness to eternity. She felt alone to her core at those times and as frightened as if she'd suddenly been orphaned.

Some days, the immense wildness of this western landscape made her cautiously thank God for its beauty; today it felt huge and hollow and devoid of any warmth. The air around her reverberated with its silence. If not for the friendly bubbling of her cook pot and the sweet smell of strawberries that wafted through the wood smoke, she could have screamed. What would they all do, she wondered, if she simply sat on a rock and screamed? Screamed until her voice gave out in protest and frustration and fear.

She shook her head. Mr. Curry said that the folks in the new wagon train were nice enough, even if there weren't any women among them. They were willing to let the Powerses join them. Americus rightly should have done the negotiating, and when he ventured out of the wagon they left plenty of opportunities for him to speak, however briefly, to the Major. It didn't take long for Mary to realize that the Doctor actually thought they could reach California on their own. By his way of reasoning—could she call it reasoning?—two worn-out horses, one skeletal man, an exhausted woman, and three children could conquer the long desert and then the deadly Sierra Nevada like a victorious army. Finally she and Mr. Curry had cornered him into meeting with the Major. The Doctor stood with the three of them, shifting from foot to foot, looking as though he wanted to sink into the very earth.

"To the Sacramento River, then?" Mr. Curry had spoken up, Mary knew, to spare her from the actual negotiations. "You'll see them over the Sierras and into the river valley beyond."

"That'll be our contract." The Major looked curiously at the three of them: Mary with her clear eyes looking at him as if she were an equal partner in the arrangement, her odd husband who was so standoffish that the Major didn't yet know his first name, and the handsome sheepman with some mysterious interest in a family he didn't belong to. "We'll combine our goods into your wagon, if that's agreeable. It's sturdier than mine, and we can get along easier without the extra one."

"That's fine, Major." Mary had recoiled at the thought of sharing their privacy with an utter stranger, but if this man could see them through, hauling his supplies seemed a small price to pay.

Now, as she bent over the fire, her back ached, but the dumpling was big and light and fluffy, oozing ruby-red juice.

"Cephas, run over to Mr. Curry's wagon, won't you, and invite him and John and Joseph to come share our dumpling? Hurry now, while it's still warm."

When they arrived a few minutes later, Mr. Curry gave her a long glance trying to discern her spirits, but she was determined not to dampen this last occasion by showing distress. She sliced the sweet dumpling and passed small portions to Americus and the children, saving the larger servings for her guests, who sat around her fire savoring the rare treat.

"Remember the time we tried to make dumplings?" Mr. Curry asked John. Mary knew he was entertaining them, trying to keep her mind off the upcoming separation. "They were so hard even the butcher knife wouldn't cut them."

"Yup. The dogs couldn't bite into them either, remember?"

"I'll wager they're still back there on that river bank, hard as rocks in the grass where we left them."

Americus sat staring into the fire. Mary noticed his tin plate was scraped clean. Now that the fever was gone he was ravenous, although his mind seemed as far away as ever. She hoped eating would bring on new vitality; so far it hadn't helped.

It was dark when Mr. Curry stood up and thanked her. She looked at his tall figure in the fire's orange glow, realizing with terrible finality that tomorrow she would be off to the Humboldt without him. She felt like a ship leaving port for the dark and endless ocean.

He was speaking, looking courteously at the Doctor but sending his words straight to Mary. "You know our route parallels yours for a couple of days more. We might even share another camping spot, so we'll be in the neighborhood if you need anything."

The Doctor stared back at him without answering. Mary

smiled, unable to speak past the lump in her throat. She felt Sarah looking at her curiously. The girl was probably wondering where Mary's usual gracious reply had gone, but Mr. Curry understood. He tousled Cephas's hair and smiled at Sarah and Celia, gave Mary an encouraging nod, and then he was gone.

The night's cold blackness pressed in on the campfire's glow. Out in the darkness, a coyote howled. Mary moved into the shadows and tilted her head to the heavens to keep her brimming eyes from spilling tears.

# CHAPTER 37

# AMERICUS

Why couldn't that fool Todd Curry just let a man travel by himself in peace? Here they were saddled with more people, just when he thought he and Mary could finally go their way alone. He'd stood there feeling like a bug on a pin while Curry made a contract with those new travelers that would last all the way to the Sacramento River.

At least they were getting rid of the man himself with his handsome looks and charming manners, although Americus had to admit he'd become accustomed to the man's considerate ways. All those irritating sheep would be gone, too. Finally he would be free of their blatting and bleating and the way they nipped off the grass so short no horse behind them could find a speck to eat. Good riddance to them and to those shepherds who couldn't even speak English.

He wanted to hitch Blackey and St. Lawrence to the wagon right now and hightail it south, away from the disruptions, noise, and strangers that got under his skin as surely as a cloud of biting flies. He'd tried that earlier this morning, though, but Curry and his friend put an angry stop to it.

"Powers, are you a madman or a confounded fool?" Joseph demanded.

"I'm wondering the same thing." Curry locked his gaze on Americus, his customary courtesy gone. "Here's your chance to travel with good people who can get you through this mess alive, and you're trying to take off on your own."

"Might as well cut your family's throats now, since they're sure to get cut out there somewhere if you try it alone," Joseph observed dryly. "Don't think for one minute we're going to let you take those children and go sashaying off toward certain death."

"Try it yourself if you like, Powers, but Mrs. Powers and your young ones will stay right here with us."

Americus looked at the two of them, standing there glaring at him, arms folded across their brawny chests, breath coming fast. What business was it of theirs how he traveled? Still, he hadn't the energy for a fight; already he wondered how much longer his legs would hold him. Maybe he could travel with the Major for a while and break off after Curry and his friends were long gone.

He wasn't prepared to have the Major pile all his belongings into their wagon, though, and then sit in the driver's seat smug as could be. Actually, the man was a gentleman about it, offering the reins first to Americus and then to Mary, but Mary told him they'd be grateful if he would drive. Grateful indeed. Americus felt as misplaced as he had when Curry first took the reins.

They started off with Blackey and the bay in the harness once again. The horses were filled out, if not frisky, after their long respite. Mary rode inside with Celia, but Americus walked for a mile or two before climbing aboard. The wagon lurched from side to side at every rock and root, straining up bad inclines, tipping its way down. Mary untied the canvas cover and rolled it back. She looked especially peaked today and kept surreptitiously wiping her nose with her handkerchief.

He pulled the guide book from its place. He hadn't looked at it for a long time, but they should reach the headwaters of the Humboldt shortly, if Curry was correct. Off in the distance, mountains rose to a showy peak, and underfoot the ground was becoming a mire of springs. A rivulet circled through them. Americus wondered if perhaps they had reached the bare beginnings of the great river sooner than anticipated. What a novelty that would be. Usually he thought he had their location pinpointed only to find out it would require two or three more days to reach it.

The Major was quiet sitting up there on the driver's seat. Once this morning he turned around to survey the wagon's crowded interior and opened his mouth as if to say something, but apparently thought the better of it. Now he was hunched over in the heat of the day, the sun beating on his hat with ferocious intensity. Wet stains reached down his solid back, but he drove the horses steadily even where the ground was soft and uncertain.

Mary had her back to Americus as she half-heartedly played a counting game with Celia. If he were Mary, he'd be out of this wagon in a flash, walking in the fresh air instead of sitting on this sweltering bedding. But something happened to her back there on the Bear—or was it the Malad?—that took the starch right out of her. He could understand. He himself felt as though a stiff wind had blown through him and swept away his vitality. His bones felt lightweight, and his muscles had shriveled and shrunk until picking up a stick of firewood was an effort.

The wagon stopped. Americus felt the wheels settle into the mud as the Major cracked his whip, but the load was mired. Americus stepped down from the wagon, surprised when his knees gave way. He hit the mucky ground with outstretched hands.

"We should have kept to higher ground," the Major commented, choosing to ignore the incident. "Help me push while we turn the horses west."

Americus leaned into the wheel. He'd pushed so much on this journey that his shoulder fit the task perfectly, except now he felt like a skinny child lending his puny weight to a massive undertaking. The Major, arms and shoulders bulging and cheeks puffed, leaned his substantial might on the back of the wagon while Mary guided the animals to dryer ground. Miraculously, the wheels slurped their way out of the wet mud. At least they wouldn't have to lug everything out of the wagon—including the Major's considerable pile of bedding— and then load it all back in again. It made a man tired just thinking about it.

Birds buzzed at each other from the cattails and reeds. There were wildlife prints in the mud, too, everywhere he looked. He'd seen enough of them by now to recognize the feline look of bobcat prints and the slightly larger tracks of coyotes, and the long, slender ones of skunk. There were the sharp pointed hoof prints of antelope and deer, too, and plenty of bird tracks winding through the rushes and disappearing in the puddles and pools that warmed in the midday sun.

The other wagons avoided the mire, forging their own way on drier ground. Maybe he could tolerate this arrangement with the Major and his small group of men for a little while after all. Americus knew his body wasn't up to pushing a 2,000-pound wagon out of mud alone or attending to all that needed to be done.

The guide book said they could count on good grass for the stretch ahead. A bigger problem was water. Many of the surrounding springs were said to be alkaline or even boiling hot. The other men—Potts, Smith, Barnard—seemed unconcerned, though. Americus climbed back into the wagon and reclined against the Major's belongings. They smelled like old smoke and sweat and dust, a rank contradiction to the clean scent of crushed green undergrowth and fresh mud drifting on the air. They occupied his wagon, a taunting reminder of his own inadequacy.

He needed a nap, a long nap, like Mary. He turned to look at her where she had fallen asleep on the bedding with a pink-cheeked Celia sprawled beside her. She looked exhausted today, and the skin around her eyes was puffy. Impulsively he reached out to touch the fraying hem of her old blue dress.

A mighty gulf lay between them now, and he felt powerless to overcome it. Yet she had saved his life from the fever; Curry had told him that much. He had hazy recollections of Mary bending over him, covering or uncovering him, dribbling that awful herb concoction into his mouth, cooling his forehead, once even singing to him. Could that have been mere duty? Surely there must be a remnant of affection left for him, a speck of love hidden somewhere beneath her newly capable exterior.

# CHAPTER 38

# SARAH

From across the campsite, Sarah saw Ceely wander too close to Blackey's hind legs and fasten her eyes on a round pebble just behind his hooves.

"Ceely, stop!"

The little girl flashed out her hand for the stone just as Blackey stepped back, putting his full weight on her small fingers.

Celia screamed, and Blackey startled and stepped forward. As Sarah ran to her sister, Ceely pulled her hand from the dirt and popped her fingers into her mouth with a wail.

"Let me see, Ceely," Sarah bent down pulling the little girl close. Gently she pried the fingers from Ceely's mouth and studied them. They were red but not bleeding or bent in an unnatural direction. "Can you wiggle them? Try."

Ceely obediently bent each small finger, still gulping air and sobbing. Sarah turned, relieved, to study the depression in the dirt. It was deep sand scattered with a few small stones; Blackey's hoof had pressed Ceely's fingers down into the forgiving softness. If the sand had been a rock instead . . . .

"I told you to stay away from the horses, Ceely. I told you a hundred times."

Mother hurried from behind the wagon, out of breath and limping. "I heard Celia cry out." She looked at her little daughter's blotchy, tear-streaked face and then at Sarah's pale one. "What happened, girls?"

Sarah explained, wondering if Mother would say Sarah had been careless about watching Ceely. Instead, Mother smoothed back the little girl's hair. "You were very fortunate, Celia. Blackey could have broken your fingers, and it would have been your own fault. How many times has Sarah told you to stay away from those big hooves?"

Thinking about it that night in the wagon's dark stillness, Sarah knew she had found what Mother called "the silver lining" to the horrible dirty sand that plagued them that day. Mother told her to watch for it: some small event that turned a trial into a blessing of sorts, like a fringe of silver around a day's darkest cloud. Tonight the sandy soil seemed like a friend that had protected her sister's delicate fingers.

After slogging through 6 or 8 inches of it all day, though, it hadn't seemed so friendly. For the poor horses, it was torture. Sarah had patted their hot necks and helped Cephas water them, but already they were weakening again from the hard work of keeping the wagon moving. St. Lawrence faltered on yesterday's small pass.

Sarah awoke thirsty. The Humboldt's water tasted foul, even after it was boiled. She and Cephas held their noses while they drank it and tried to teach Ceely to do the same, but the little girl couldn't manage to plug her nostrils and swallow at the same time.

She scrambled out of the wagon. Mother already had the fire going. Coffee perked in its black pot sending its aroma into the chilly morning air.

"Would you like some?" Mother asked quietly. Father

didn't like them to drink coffee—he said it was bad for children—but Mother understood how hard it was to drink the awful Humboldt water without something to disguise its flavor and hide its color. Even Mother's mint tea couldn't cover up the terrible taste. Thank goodness the coffee supply was holding out. Sarah took the cup Mother offered her and sat on the ground near the fire.

She shivered. It was cold here. They were near a place called Emigrant Pass, so the altitude was probably high, and it was nearly September. That would account for the morning chill. At least it turned warm during the day, especially where the trail left the river and cut off across the dry countryside between river bends. The cutoffs saved miles, Sarah knew, but it was much nicer to follow the water. She and Cephas could wade then. Sometimes they found hidden springs where, if the water was good, all kinds of bullfrogs and snails and other little creatures lived. Sarah liked them, all but the snakes. She didn't think people were meant to like snakes.

The man who was the leader of this small wagon train wandered by. Cephas called him Mr. Major, but his real name was Major Whitesides. He or Mother drove the wagon while Father rode or walked. He was pleasant enough, and he looked big and strong, but Sarah didn't think he was nearly as able as Mr. Curry. She missed Mr. Curry. She had even cried to herself when they had to say good-bye to him. Mother cried, too. Sarah could tell by the way her eyes looked, but no one else noticed.

She missed John and Joseph, too, and the shepherds. She even missed the sheep. She had liked how feebleminded they were and how they relied upon the shepherds to keep them from poking their silly heads into danger.

Two of the men in this party didn't seem to care for children much. They wouldn't even say good morning to her and

Cephas, but Mr. Smith, Major Whitesides, Mr. Potts, and Mr. Barnard were cordial at least. One of the others—Sarah couldn't remember his name—had a nice little donkey that ran free. Ceely didn't like its loud braying, so she stayed away from it, but Cephas loved to lead him to where the best grasses grew.

It was time to help Mother pack the wagon. The sun was up, and soon the Major would give the signal to get back on the trail.

# CHAPTER 39

# MARY

Mary stared at the Major's mountain of belongings dumped on her Rising Sun quilt exactly where she wanted to sit. His tin plate encrusted with old food topped the strewn mound of sweat-stained clothing and dirty bedding. A bag of flour leaked its precious contents through a small hole. She ought to feel grateful, she knew; this man had promised to see them across the dangerous Sierras. Still, the invasion of privacy felt like another hardship. She perched on top of the trunk instead, but the hard surface magnified each jolt and sent jarring blows up her spine. She rubbed the back of her neck.

"The Doctor's horses are doing relatively well, aren't they, Major?" she said, making an effort at conversation. Although standoffish, the man was driving the wagon straight to California at a good steady pace.

He turned from the driver's seat to glance at her.

"I was thinking they could use another rest, ma'am. The bigger one keeps stumbling."

"Well, yes, he does, but he's much improved from his condition back on the plains."

"These horses aren't built for pulling so much weight, Mrs. Powers." It was said flatly. "If my own animals weren't so near collapse, I'd use them instead. But they can't manage another mile just now."

"Well, we seem to be covering some good distance. I hope I'll be able to walk a while this afternoon to spare the horses my weight."

"Or you can drive and I'll walk."

The trail wound along the Humboldt for a hundred miles more before their party's turn-off to Rabbit Hole Springs. She couldn't imagine how many steps that was, how often a person had to place one foot in front of the other to cover that distance. Her heart beat fast at the thought of the road ahead. The upcoming desert—a relatively short but difficult stretch, according to the Major—seemed bad enough, but the mountains! Mountains were as foreign and ominous to her as a distant planet. Children and weak horses and deep snow and jagged slopes were a combination that filled her with utter dread. It was common knowledge that others had met their fate in the rugged, icy canyons of the Sierra Nevada.

Mary pressed her fingers to her temples. She shifted her body, tucking her bulky skirts under her to create some padding on the hard trunk. When the wheels lifted over a rock and crashed down again, she stood with a sigh and shifted the Major's bag of flour so she could sit on the bedding.

*Dear Mother!*

*I am in a state of anxiety at the thought of crossing the approaching desert (which takes about two days, we're told), harsh and dangerous as it is reported to be. I have a few vessels to fill with water for the children, but the animals must have water, too. The sand is said to be so deep that it slows progress considerably. Travelers have perished there from thirst and heat.*

*If we are fortunate enough to succeed at crossing the desert, we must then face the high, wild mountains and the possibility that deadly snowfalls will catch us there. Despite my constant prayers for strength, I cannot force from my mind a picture of my dear children freezing to death in a dreadful mountain gulch—and Americus and me following suit.*

*Americus! Mother, I am so vexed at him, and yet I should be rejoicing. He has overcome the mountain fever, much to everyone's surprise. Although he is still weak, he is eating well and is sometimes able to walk again alongside the wagon. Unfortunately, his state of mind has not improved, and so, of necessity, I have been forced to continue taking charge of this journey.*

*You would be astounded to see me command the lead, Mother, for I've come to realize that I must do so if we are to survive. Your gentle daughter, who learned your lessons of acquiescence and humble submission so well, is busy planning and trading and negotiating with the best of the trail's men.*

*Speaking of the best of the trail's men, Mother, I suffered great sorrow when we had to say farewell to Mr. Curry. He took us under his protective wing and made me believe we could complete this ill-conceived journey. For his generosity, kindness, and chivalry, I will be eternally grateful.*

*Now we are in the company of a man we simply call "Major" and his comrades, with whom Mr. Curry and I contracted the remainder of our trip. We are in good hands, although I will admit that my efforts to form a congenial partnership have thus far fallen short. I can only hope they will honor their promise to see us though to the Sacramento River, which, they tell me, is only 15 days' travel beyond our Rabbit Hole Springs cutoff. It has been my sorry experience that 15 days often turns into 30 or more here in this wilderness.*

*We must change our planned route of travel and take another road that the Major has chosen. It crosses the mountains far north of where Americus intended to cross. We have no other choice, although Americus is not pleased. Where the Major goes, we shall go.*

*The desert lies directly ahead. Travelers we have met along the way advise us to cross the first stretch at night to avoid the suffocating, intolerable heat, so we shall heed their advice—I have already spoken with the Major about it. Even so, we will be mere mortal specks upon that alarming landscape. I fear that the very ink with which I write will dry up, and then what would I do? My letters to you are my ties to civilization, my bridge to home.*

*With all my love,*

*Mary*

# CHAPTER 40

## MAJOR WHITESIDES

They were seven days down the Humboldt, and still the Major wasn't certain how to size up Americus Powers. This afternoon, driving the doctor's worn-out team, he pondered the fact that Powers wouldn't converse with him, wouldn't even pass the time of day.

"Morning, Dr. Powers," he'd offered again today, his use of the title "Dr." an attempt to warm the man up. "How do you think your bay will fare today?" Americus had looked his way with a slight shrug of his shoulders.

So far the Major knew nothing about the man except that he was a physician—and a strange one. He didn't want to imagine being doctored by a man as sickly and surly as this, one who simply plodded along, mile after mile, his gaze on the ground, his mind somewhere else. It was hard to tell if Powers was grateful for the help or resentful of it.

The Doctor had sputtered when the Major informed him of the route they were taking, turning off from the Humboldt at Lassen Meadows instead of continuing south to the Carson River as Powers had planned to do. He seemed to accept it now, though maybe he was angry about the forced change. Some men could hold a grudge forever.

His wife and children were a different story. The Major wondered what Mrs. Powers saw in that old scarecrow when she herself was so pleasant and pretty. He made a point to keep his distance despite her friendly overtures; he didn't need a woman's tongue distracting him from getting through to California. He wondered why she couldn't walk more than a few steps before she resorted to riding in the wagon. In his experience, travelers stayed out of their wagons as much as they could to avoid the constant, unpredictable motion. If he tried to ride in the back as she did, his stomach would be riled up in no time.

He liked the children, too, especially that little Cephas. What a good fellow he was, always tagging along full of questions. His father hardly answered his inquiries, so Cephas had started following the Major instead, watching as the man went about his trail work. The child was smart and quick and mostly quiet except when his intense curiosity made questions bubble forth by the dozen. The Major couldn't put a name to it, but Cephas had a keen awareness of his surroundings. It was as if his senses were sharper or he paid childlike attention to details adults missed. More than once he pointed out something the Major had overlooked.

"Mr. Major? See that place where the river turns? I bet we could catch some good fish there." Sure enough, there would be a good fishing hole, just as the boy suspected.

He shifted on the hard seat. He'd have to stop the wagon soon on the pretense of resting the horses to relieve himself, which was a whole new challenge with a woman along. Before the Powers family showed up, he hadn't even bothered to stand behind a bush. Now, ridiculously, he felt humiliated to go wandering off by himself; anyone could tell what he was doing. The best he could do was duck behind Smith's wagon and make quick work of it. He didn't like having his personal belongings spread out for the world to see in Mrs. Powers's wagon, either.

Normally he was easygoing, but this whole journey was starting to wear on him. He was irked at this continent that stretched out before his disbelieving eyes week after week. His back hurt, and his lips were cracked from the alkaline dust that collected on his face as though drawn there by a magnet. He'd always prided himself on his strength, too, but now the toil and inadequate food and lack of good water ate away at his physical power. Supplies were dwindling, making the Humboldt seem as endless as the Great Plains had been.

Right now his whole being was centered on reaching Lassen Meadows, maybe four or five days down the trail. He wasn't betting on any meadows, though, not in this arid country. He'd be happy to find a little fresh water and some sparse grass. Turning off from the main trail there, they would leave the Humboldt behind. A couple of weeks of rough travel after that might be enough to see them to the California river valleys—if the animals held out.

The animals. That was another thing that bothered him about Americus Powers. Why would anyone choose such horses for a trip like this? The one called St. Lawrence was stumbling regularly now. This morning the poor animal was even leaning against the black one for support when they stopped to rest. He couldn't understand how Powers had made it this far. By all rights, these beautiful examples of horseflesh should have fallen to the ground and died a long ways back.

He glanced around to make certain his handful of men was still behind him. They were good fellows, mostly younger than he, and single. Barnard and Potts and Smith knew how to travel this country, even if they were getting tired. Their minds were set on California, its gold, its rich soil. A few of them had grumbled about adding a woman and children to the group, but mostly they were simply resigned to conquering this trail.

The Major wiped his face with his free hand. The only thing to do was press on, sore hands on the reins, tired muscles hunched toward the west, and his mind on the promise of California. Keep the wagon moving, his men near, and his sun-scorched eyes on the horizon.

# CHAPTER 41

# CEPHAS

Cephas knew where he was without asking. This big flat place must be where they left the river for the meadows. Wagons from other trains were stopped here, scattered about any old place they chose. Cephas watched two strange men scything thick grass.

"Mr. Major, what are those men doing?"

"Cutting and drying grass to take with them across the desert."

"Take with them? How?"

"I suppose they'll pile it in their wagons."

"Will we do that?"

"There's no grass in a desert, sonny. What would the animals eat if we didn't?"

"Can I watch you?"

"You can help, how about that? After we cut it, we'll need someone strong to help spread it in the sun to dry for a spell. Think you can manage?"

"Yes, sir. Can I explore the river bank before we start?"

"Ask your mother."

Cephas felt safe here. It was almost like a little town, there were so many wagons and people. He paused to watch two boys playing tag. One of their wagons had words painted on the canvas. Cephas tried to figure out what they said. Back home Mother was teaching him to read, but out here he didn't have lessons. Dogs roamed from wagon to wagon, and the stock animals were scattered, grazing. Mother told him not to wander too far, and he wouldn't, of course—he wasn't a baby like Celia. She had to stay near the wagon every minute unless Sarah took her for a walk.

He headed straight for the river. He knew enough to stay out of the current ever since that time he almost got pulled under. Besides he didn't like this river except for wading along its shallow edges. It was warm and murky and smelly.

He stopped, feeling the sandy mud ooze between his toes. The air was hot, but a light breeze lifted the hair off his sweaty forehead. He wondered what creatures lived here. He crouched down, imagining himself a mouse or a vole, small enough to hide under a stone.

Something dark was partly buried in the muck a few steps ahead. It looked like an old wagon hub. Cephas stood up sloshed through the shallows to get a closer look. His pants were getting wet, but he didn't care. He tugged on its exposed end. It wasn't a wheel hub at all, but a wooden keg. An old water keg, covered with mud but good and solid. Wouldn't that bring a smile to Mother's face!

He pulled it dripping from the water and rolled it into the shallows, rinsing it off and checking for holes. Setting it upright, he saw that the iron rings around it were rusty but strong. There were no leaks that he could see. He tried lifting it, but the sodden wood slipped and fell to the ground, just missing his bare toes. Now his shirt was all muddy. He laid it on its side and began rolling it toward the wagons.

Mother must be napping with Celia. Father and Mr.

Major were gone. Cephas rolled the keg close to the wagon and set it upright in the dust. He felt like a hunter bringing home a prize kill to his starving people.

Mother poked her head out of the wagon when she heard him.

"What have you got there, Cephas? Oh, my heavens! It's a water keg!"

"I found it down by the river."

"You found it? Just simply found it? Does it belong to someone?"

"No. It was almost buried in the mud. It's been there for a long time, but it doesn't have any leaks."

"Cephas, those sharp eyes of yours! This will help so much when we cross the desert."

He loved it when Mother smiled the way she used to. He wrapped his arms around himself. These days she was almost always distracted with work—looking at the map again, or talking with the men about the next day's route, or greasing the harness. Cephas skipped off. Now maybe Blackey and St. Lawrence and that nice little donkey could have water in the desert.

He could see Mr. Major now, swinging a blade to cut the long grass. Mr. Smith was there, too. Cephas wanted to sink down in the warm, good-smelling cuttings and spread them out to bake in the sun. He would make sure there was enough hay to fill the wagon to up to the sky.

Rabbit Hole Springs. The name connoted things Mary never thought she would readily anticipate: a desolate, muddy watering hole where nothing but rabbits made up the population. Out here, though, she looked forward to these unlikely milestones as if she were a world traveler awaiting Paris.

This inhospitable country looked like the plains all over again; it was the same rocky dirt interspersed with sagebrush—rabbit brush, the Major called it—and two wobbling ruts leading off into the sun-baked and lonely distance.

She was trying to walk today, at least a short distance, to spare St. Lawrence and Blackey her weight, but already she could hardly drag her feet along. It didn't feel like September. The sun beat down with unmerciful strength, making her dress stick to her as if glued there. She lifted her heavy hair off the back of her neck and adjusted the hairpins to make it ride higher, but it sagged low again.

At least the nights were cooler. Mary couldn't decide whether that was cause for relief or concern. Cold nights might mean snow in the Sierras that could strand travelers on the wrong slopes. It was hard to imagine a snowstorm today, though. Winter seemed as far off as Antarctica at the moment.

She stopped to rest. Whatever had robbed her stamina wasn't going away. If Americus were himself, he would give her some sort of remedy to boost her strength. As it was, though, he seemed like the one who needed such a cure.

When the Major glanced back, she signaled for him to stop the wagon so she could get in. Moving around inside the wagon required agility now that Mr. Smith had piled some of his belongings next to the Major's. The men filled Mr. Smith's wagon with cut grass back at Lassen Meadows. Mary almost would have preferred mounds of sweet-smelling hay in her wagon instead of the men's sweaty things, but at least they had moved them off the quilt so she could lie down.

She must have dozed because Cephas's shout outside the wagon startled her.

"There it is!"

"What do you see, sonny?" It was the Major hollering back.

"That place where there's water and rabbits."

At last. Mary sat up on the quilt rubbing her hands over her face as if to scrub away the dust and perspiration. Now they could stop to rest the horses before tackling the desert directly ahead. She peered around the Major's broad back to see the springs. "Springs" was such a lovely word. It brought to mind shaded, mossy, cool places where cold water bubbled from the ground into clear pools. Mary knew better than to expect that, but she didn't see anything ahead at all, just a small depression that seemed nothing more than a dent in the land.

Cephas was hurrying on, hoping, Mary supposed, to see scores of rabbits clustered around the watering hole. Sarah trudged behind him carrying Celia piggyback. The wagons creaked on, stirring up dust and following the two thin tracks that led to this welcome place, however dismaying it might turn out to be. She lay back down to wait.

"Whoa." The Major's low voice stopped the horses immediately; they needed no persuasion. Mary climbed down to survey the water. It was larger than the wet hole she'd imagined, but just as bleak. At least she could strain a good amount of drinking water to store in the kegs. Already Americus and several of the other men were crouching beside it cupping their hands and splashing water into their mouths. Sarah was flinging handfuls at Cephas. Mary hurried to collect her drinking water before the mud was riled. There were rabbit prints, but the hares Cephas saw had fled.

There would be no bathing here, not with all these men. Mary sighed. Back home, most people bathed once a week, but Mary made the effort to wash two or three times a week. Out here, others thought you were daft if you took time to bathe more than absolutely necessary, so Mary called it swimming if there was a river nearby. She furtively washed her body while hiding in the current. Certainly there was nowhere to bathe in tomorrow's desert, so she would have to endure her own unpleasant sticky skin for a few more days.

"Cephas, would you collect sage stalks for me, please? I need to bake some bread for the desert crossing." She sat on the wagon tongue for a moment. Bread making was such an arduous task these days, but they must have sustenance to cross the grueling stretch ahead; there would be no fuel for fires out there. "Bread" was a word she used loosely here on the trail. Her odd, flat campfire loaves were nothing like the beautiful, golden-brown loaves she made back home. Thank goodness the Major allowed her to use his flour, though, or there would be no bread at all.

By nightfall, Mary could think of nothing except collapsing into the wagon again, but there would be little rest tonight. They would start the desert crossing shortly, traveling under the cool night sky. The fresh bread was stored, the horses were well watered, and every container Mary could muster was filled with water, including her tin pail and both water kegs. She even filled the old bottle she used as a rolling pin out here, and then hid it away in the wagon.

Patting Blackey's nose in apology, Mary crawled into the wagon with the children. The trapped air was still smothering, but it cooled as the wagons began moving and the first stars came out.

Mary was still awake when the wagons inched up a slight grade and stopped on a bluff. The men gathered in a group, looking and pointing, so she crawled out of the wagon while the children slumbered. Below her was the desert stretched out flat and barren in the moonlight. It looked strangely peaceful, intersected with the silent black rock formation that would serve as their guide. The scene seemed surreal, like a picture in a book. Stars, millions of them, sparkled overhead.

"Doesn't look so bad from here," Mr. Potts commented.

"No, but you can bet it'll be a long haul across," Smith answered. "I doubt if we can do it in less than a night and two full days."

She had feared this place for so long. Now that they were here, a strange tranquility settled over her. Daylight would come before they were halfway across, and with it, tomorrow's stifling heat. But tonight, overlooking this scene that took her breath with its stark beauty, she could appreciate its serenity.

Later, back in the wagon, Mary lay between the children and listened to the sound of sand under the wheels. She could almost imagine that its soft swishing was gentle waves sloshing against the sides of a boat. The wagon bed undulated gently like a vessel sailing through water. This soft ride meant heavy pulling for the horses, though. She wondered if St. Lawrence could last. Holding Celia near, she closed her eyes and prayed for safe passage.

His returning strength had seen him through the night, and he was surprised at how strong he still felt. With only the light from the moon and stars, he labored into the desert with the rest of them, pushing through sand so deep in places it climbed up his ankles. Even in the darkness, Americus could see the horses' muscles straining beneath their hides. St. Lawrence foamed at the mouth as they crawled along at a dangerously slow pace.

The Major called a halt just before dawn when they reached the campfires set by the two men assigned to scout ahead. The fires shone across the sand like beacons marking this small desert spring of dark, warm water. Eagerly the animals approached the watering hole, sniffed, sniffed again, and then backed off. Americus didn't protest when he saw Sarah slip from the wagon and offer Blackey and the bay a few handfuls of dried grass and a hoarded drink from a bucket.

The men ate a hasty breakfast and sprawled on the sand for a catnap. Americus leaned back against the wheel spokes and let his head nod. It seemed only a moment before the camp began stirring again, each man disheveled and gray faced, to prepare for the rest of the crossing. Already the sun was rising, white hot and blinding.

As the wagons ground along, he put one foot ahead of the other, sometimes pointlessly counting his own steps, slogging through the sand as the sun scorched the top of his head, his face, his bare hands. St. Lawrence was so weak that he didn't dare ride.

Americus spotted the boiling spring ahead, but Cephas was the first to reach the little cloud of steam spouting from the monotonous sand. The boy knelt at its side and peered into the water, too mesmerized even to call out for the others.

The wagons stopped. Americus stood back a few feet as the others gathered around the small bubbling formation. Mary got out of the wagon and stared into its depths with a slight gasp, and even the Major sauntered over. Curious to see what held their attention, Americus drew closer. To his surprise, he saw that the spring glimmered with thousands of shiny silver flecks that clung to its sides. The sand that churned up from the bottom flashed and sparkled, too, like a brilliant pool of glittering gems.

Mary smiled. "It's the silver lining to this desert, quite literally, Cephas," she said quietly. "Do you see how it triumphs over this wasteland?"

"Maybe it's God's way of telling us we will, too," the unexpected words came from the Major. "Triumph, I mean."

"I believe you're right, Major." Americus surprised himself and everyone else by speaking up. "I believe we will." He could feel Mary's astonished look at him and the others' curious glances.

The Major knelt and tested the water for drinking, but shook his head and spit his mouthful on the ground.

As they started up again, Americus saw that the sand was no longer dull and gray. Instead it glinted with millions of shiny flecks. It could almost blind a man with its glare. The surface was crusted over so that his feet and the horses' hooves cracked through to the softer sand underneath, but the footing was more solid. What other surprises did this unlikely country hold?

The sun was overhead when the bay began wobbling. Blackey was worn out, too, but he wasn't as bad off as the bay. Ahead, the land shimmered in the intense sunlight, distorting the Doctor's sense of distance. He'd heard about desert travelers encountering mirages; today he believed it. It did look as if a large, flat lake lay awaiting them, yet he wasn't about to be tricked into thinking there was a pool of water in the wavering distance.

The bay halted of its own accord, head drooping, sides heaving. Americus saw Sarah take him the bucket again. Celia cried through cracked lips, so Mary gave her another small drink.

"Powers, have you got a drink in your wagon?" It was Potts, with Barnard at his side. "We've both run out of water."

"Ask my wife," he said shortly. He knew what the answer would be. Mary would decide how much life-sustaining water the children would need and then give away whatever was left, even her last ounce, if she thought it would help someone in need. Thank God for Cephas's 10-gallon keg.

"I'm nearly out myself," the Major commented, watching Mary dole out careful portions from the second keg.

"We'll reach good water later this afternoon," Potts stated. "The map shows another desert spring."

"Then, by all means, help yourselves," Mary invited. "Keep your strength up."

They dragged on through the heat. The animals couldn't be expected to pull much longer. Rotting carcasses from earlier parties dotted the trail on both sides. Their stiffened forms sent up a putrid stench. Americus wondered how many of their own horses and cattle would succumb. The Major's remaining oxen looked especially poor.

Americus peered ahead looking for something to indicate the end of this expanse. He saw nothing, but the others thought they could reach the desert's far edge by nightfall unless the animals failed.

As the afternoon wore on, they approached the rare spot where the map indicated water.

"There has to be a spring here somewhere," the Major said, looking about in frustration. "Cephas, boy, don't wander too far but see if you can find us some water, all right? Barnard, Smith, you go search, too, will you?"

Americus sank onto the wagon tongue. His legs felt like sticks and his stomach was half sick. He could tell his lips were cracked and bleeding like Celia's. Every drop was gone from the kegs, and he was parched.

A light hand touched his shoulder. He turned to see Mary offering him a dose of water in his tin cup. She winked at him and silently put her finger to her lips. She must have a secret stash somewhere. Trust Mary to keep them safe.

# CHAPTER 44

## SARAH

Mother said the desert was nearly behind them. To Sarah, it looked as if it had no end. All she could see were shimmering heat waves and more sand—and dead cattle and horses. She put her dusty hand over her nose to block out the stench and trudged on beside the wagon.

Some of the Major's own animals had died, adding to the hundreds of stiff, bloated bodies strewn across this desert. A traveler here could almost jump from one carcass to the next and never touch the sand.

She needed a drink. Not a sip from Mother's hoard, but a real drink, a long one. Her tongue felt as if it was covered with powder, and her whole body yearned for water and a cool breeze. The desert's air surrounded her like unbearable heat from a blazing fire. She walked in the shade of the wagon like Father and Cephas, but even out of the sunlight she felt as though she couldn't breathe. Poor Mother on the driver's seat had only her sunbonnet for protection. Celia rode inside.

Blackey and St. Lawrence couldn't escape the sun, and they had the added burden of pulling the wagon. Blackey was holding up somewhat, but not St. Lawrence. Sarah's throat closed when she looked at him. His head and ears drooped, and even swishing his tail seemed like too much work. He stumbled even when there was nothing to stumble on.

"Whoa!" The shout from Mr. Potts startled Sarah. Usually only Major Whitesides gave that command.

Mr. Potts jumped from his driver's seat and ran yelling toward the other wagons, pointing to the east. Sarah heard the word "Indians." As the others clustered around him, Sarah looked where he was pointing. She wished someone had a spyglass, but no one did. She squinted her eyes, trying to see through the heat waves, and then her body froze.

A group of mounted Indians was circling behind them. Sarah could hardly make out their dark shapes in the distance, but there were a lot of them—60 or 70, she guessed. They were galloping closer, their images wavering in the desert heat.

"Circle the wagons! Get your guns." The Major led the wagons into a tight oval. Just as fast, the men grabbed their rifles and took cover beneath the wheels. Sarah and Cephas scrambled into the wagon. Sarah grabbed Celia and threw the quilt over her head. She caught a glimpse of Mother's face, deathly still and white. Then she turned and looked out the back. The Indians were approaching quickly, as if they had no intention of stopping. Sarah cinched up the opening in the wagon cover and dove under the quilt with Celia.

It was only a moment until the dark heat smothered her. Ceely began to cry.

"Can't breathe, Sarah!"

Sarah didn't want to poke her face out and let Ceely do the same, but Ceely was right. It was impossible to breathe under here. Her heart was pounding. She pushed the quilt back. Cephas was at her feet, trying to squirm behind the trunk. Mother sat frozen on the driver's seat, her head turned to stare at the approaching warriors. Father was nowhere to be seen.

Sarah strained to hear hoof beats, but there were none. Even the men were quiet now as they waited with grim, pointed rifles. Heavy silence pressed in on Sarah's ears. The moment seemed to go on forever, all mixed up in her head: the ominous dark forms, the suffocating heat, Celia's sniffles, Cephas huddled on the wagon floor, Mother's colorless lips moving in prayer.

Then one of the men laughed. The sound seemed outlandish to Sarah, a bizarre contradiction to the danger. At first, she wondered if it could have been a cry of alarm instead, but then the others began to chuckle, too. She could hear them crawling out from under the wagons. Mother let out her breath in one long relieved sigh. Sarah widened the opening in the canvas with shaking fingers and peeked out.

The dark shapes were close, still moving low across the sand. They didn't look like horses and riders any longer, though. As Sarah watched, their large black forms lifted from the desert floor and flew up, higher and higher into the air, then wheeled around and flapped off into the blue sky.

"Just a flock of birds!" It was Mr. Smith. His voice held pure relief.

"Sure fooled us." The Major laughed. Sarah had never heard him laugh like that before, as if he couldn't stop. The men bunched together, slapping each other on the back and doubling over with laughter.

Sarah hugged Celia.

"Ceely, don't be scared anymore. It was just some big birds."

Cephas came out of his hiding place to look. Mother's lips still moved, but this time they curved upward, and a faint color came back to her face.

Now that her trembling had stopped, Sarah felt as

though she could walk across ten deserts, pulling the wagon herself and everything in it. The hot sand didn't seem so awful now that they were safe. It couldn't be too much farther. The men and Mother agreed that by evening they might reach the far side. She wished the Major would give the command so they could start up again and leave this place behind them.

What was Mother doing? She was lifting the lid of the trunk and rummaging around inside. Sarah thought of the silver teapot, hidden in the bottom.

"What are you looking for, Mother?" Sarah tried to make her voice sound unconcerned.

"My headache remedy," Mother answered. "I put it right here on top, but it must have slipped farther down."

Sarah waited, watching and holding her breath. Mother dug deeper and deeper, sliding her hands between layers of household goods and clothing, looking under each. Midway down, she stopped and pulled a small, wrinkled package from beneath some folds of muslin.

"Here it is," she said, smoothing things into place. "That scare has started my head aching."

Sarah began to breathe again. Her secret was safe for now. From outside, they heard the Major call, "Roll 'em out!" Mother hurriedly closed the trunk's heavy lid and slid onto the wagon seat.

Sarah made certain Ceely was safely on the bedding with her stick doll. She couldn't help noticing how skinny her little sister was now. Sarah knew it wasn't her place to fret about food, but she knew the flour supply was low again. The Major had a few days' worth, that was all. She wondered what Ceely would eat when it was gone. What would they all eat? There were no more beans and no more of the jerked meat Mr. Curry had given them when they parted.

Sarah jumped out of the wagon onto the hot sand, ready to finish the desert crossing. Mother said that after the desert came the Honey Lake Valley at the base of the mountains. Honey Lake. Was that something like the Sweetwater River, where the water wasn't sweet at all? She wasn't going to expect any honey or any lake either. She'd learned about places and names on this trip.

# CHAPTER 45

## MARY

Streaks of red shot upward from the setting sun while Mary cooked supper, but her eyes were on St. Lawrence as Americus led the big bay to the back of the wagon. The peculiar way the horse held his head made her pause.

"Is something the matter, Americus?"

"His throat is swollen hard as a brick, and he's not able to get his head down to the ground. I don't think he can swallow."

Mary's stomach clenched. St. Lawrence, the poor beast. Could he have labored this far only to meet his end just when reaching California's restful pastures seemed almost a possibility?

Americus tried over and over to dribble medicine down the bay's throat with a forbearance Mary hadn't seen since they left home. He spoke softly to the frightened animal and used his gentle hands to sooth the horse's throat. At last, with a stricken look in Mary's direction and a glance at the children, who were washing their feet in tonight's trickling stream, he led St. Lawrence off into the sagebrush.

"He's dying, Mary," Americus said when he returned alone. "We need to leave him in peace."

It was after dark when Mary heard St. Lawrence fall. By then supper was over, and the children were tucked in the wagon, even Sarah who had lain down for a moment to lull Celia to sleep and then fell into an exhausted slumber herself.

It was a terrible, heavy sound, as final as death itself. Mary realized she'd been listening for it as she banked the fire and put away the cups and plates. The Doctor heard it, too, from where he sat on the wagon tongue, and for a moment his haunted eyes met Mary's. Without a word, the two of them made their way to where the horse was lying on his side, thrashing his head against the ground. Mary knelt beside him, choking her good-bye. She laid her cheek on his neck and whispered into his ear, while Americus quietly stroked his flanks.

By morning St. Lawrence was dead. Mary's chest ached as she went about her chores. It didn't seem right simply to drive off as if nothing had happened and leave their old comrade lying on the hard-packed earth, alone and forlorn as a deserted friend. The children were crying hard; Sarah looked positively stricken. Mary took a few moments to hold them close and help them make a rough, fragrant cross from sage stalks to place at St. Lawrence's head.

The Major quietly hitched Blackey to the wagon and put a borrowed, dried-up milk cow in the traces where St. Lawrence should have been. Blackey's head drooped and his expression seemed to acknowledge his companion was gone, but at the Major's command he dutifully pulled the load onto the trail with the little cow doing her best to understand this new assignment.

With one last look and a silent prayer for St. Lawrence, Mary followed the wagons. Her throat ached from sadness, but she was determined to walk today. Blackey would have all he could manage without his old partner.

The heavy wheels turned slowly. Mary trudged ahead, firmly keeping her eyes on the horizon. When the Major noticed her dropping far behind, he halted and waited for her to catch up. Exhausted, she saw no alternative but to climb inside.

She lay on the bedding, grieving over the horse and fretting about her health. There seemed no end to this deadening fatigue. Even her desire to protect Blackey from her weight didn't change the fact that she couldn't walk more than the shortest distance. How would she cope if they reached California where she must set up housekeeping and till a garden and knead their bread and raise three children?

*Mother,*

> *Our good horse, St. Lawrence, died beside the trail like countless other pitiful animals out here. We grieve for him like one of the family. He was a fine, faithful horse who reached a terrible end. I feel great remorse at having put him through so much misery on this deplorable journey.*
>
> *At least we are through the fearsome desert! It is behind us now forever. I can see that I was indeed correct to assume that the fifteen-day jaunt I was promised from Rabbit Hole Springs to California will take much longer than expected. We are detained by all manner of things—bad road, failing animals, even a terrible, stinging dust storm that made us all run for our wagons. Mr. Barnard has taken sick and so has his lead ox, which has meant another delay. Despite it all, we press on in a westerly direction, racing (or at least crawling) for the mountains before the snow begins to fall. I am not sure of today's date, but believe it to be mid-September. The weather has given us signs of impending winter; however, in this arid country so different from Wisconsin, it is difficult to read the clues and know what to expect.*

*There is no recourse but to struggle on with just one horse. The road is worse here than I anticipated—a mere scraggly trail that seems as remote as anywhere we've been. Blackey pulls with all his might alongside whatever stray milk cow we can borrow. He is a phenomenal animal to stay alive under these conditions. I am doing much of the driving again since it tires me so profoundly to walk. (I am grateful to add that my sore ankle is healing nicely, however, and the pain is much diminished.) It spares Blackey the Major's much greater weight, but oh! such driving. It frightens me nearly to death, Mother, the sharp drop-offs and the terrible uphill stretches—those places my tired little Celia calls "heavy hills."*

*Mother, I am so afraid that the weakness of my body will govern my behavior for the remainder of the journey, and I am determined not to permit that to occur. I am trying so desperately to stay in charge of all that affects our progress, to watch over Americus and the children with love and compassion, and to continue my attempts to encourage the men in our party (for they are as worn out and disheartened as I). I can feel your hand on my shoulder, Mother, guiding me along with our Heavenly Father. Yet some days I fail entirely in my endeavors by snapping at Celia or tiredly ignoring someone who could use my helpful attention. I wonder if one's very character is shaped by this westward trek, this unforgiving landscape and the human frailties it exposes. In my thoughts, I rail against weakness and apathy, but try as I might, there are times when I am absolutely too weary to behave with courage and exemplary action.*

*I attempt to sooth myself with the peace and beauty of our surroundings. Sometimes even that is difficult when the land seems to be our adversary by blocking our progress and making our bodies miserable. I have asked the children to* search for the oft-hidden bright spots in this tempest of a journey, and have been proud at their cleverness in finding its few, small redeeming features. This will help, I am certain, to shape their characters and help them cope with life on the frontier.

Americus's behavior is much the same, although he sprang to life when St. Lawrence was dying, doctoring him with great gentleness and skill. It gave me hope that, when we reach California, he might occasionally be able to practice medicine. I have decided that if he is not able to support us, I will teach school. Certainly there will be a need for schoolteachers with so many newcomers flocking there. I've noticed that literacy is a rare skill in this rough country. The Doctor and Sarah and I, readers and writers that we are, are the exceptions.

I've rambled long enough, Mother, and must prepare for tomorrow. Please say a prayer for us as we approach the appalling chore of getting ourselves across the mountains ahead. It will surely be the challenge of our lives, and our very lives depend upon its success.

My love to everyone,

Mary

# CHAPTER 46

# MAJOR WHITESIDES

These men of his were like a batch of children, each clamoring for something different. A few were agitated about impending storms and were itching to start toward the mountains today. He had to admit he was edgy himself about delays when winter could blow in at any moment. On the other hand, this wide Honey Lake Valley grew tolerable grass that would build up the animals for the climb ahead. Some of the men wanted to lay over a few more days to rest the cattle. Maybe it was time to split the group in half. He couldn't forget, though, that there was strength in numbers, and if ever they would need their strength it was here where the mountains formed a great rugged barrier. Best to stick together and get over them now.

Trouble was, he was honor-bound to take the Powers family across, but they simply had to rest their horse, at least overnight. He regretted his agreement to see them as far as the Sacramento River, since it might compromise the safety of his own men. Too bad the doctor's big bay had died, along with most of the extra animals his men had brought along. Not to mention his own oxen.

His supply of flour was gone, too. Mrs. Powers was now baking biscuits for a few of the other men in exchange for a few to feed her children. It might be another week before they could reach the Sacramento. In the meantime, it seemed probable that Potts and Smith could snag a deer or two in the mountains, but food would be sparse.

The Major kicked a stone into his dying fire and pondered the situation until hoof beats interrupted his thoughts. A hatless rider approached carrying nothing but a canteen. The man was short and stocky with muscular limbs and a tan shirt that was frayed at the elbows. He and his horse seemed a matched pair, both sturdy and purposeful and covered with dust. He rode straight to the Major's wagon, as if he somehow knew the Major was in charge.

"Morning, sir. My name's Haverfield. I've settled here in this valley, and I make it my business to help folks cross the Sierras. Heading out soon, are you?"

"As soon as we can, at least some of us."

"I don't charge much for my services, just enough to get by. I know these mountains like the back of my hand. And I have a few provisions for sale. Flour and such."

The Major studied the man. He looked as though he'd been over the trail a time or two.

"Matter of fact, we have a problem. Most of us want to get moving today, but we have a family with us that needs a layover until morning to rest their horse. They're bound for the Sacramento. If we went on ahead, could you see them across?"

"Gladly."

"When could you go?"

"The sooner the better. Tomorrow morning sounds fine to me. They don't want to delay much longer than that."

"So we understand." The Major glanced at the sky.

"It takes awhile to cross with a wagon. I'd take them straight to the old ranch on the Sacramento. That route isn't used much any more, but it'll land them right on the river. I've been over it a couple of times."

"That's the road we're planning to take, too. We'd best buy provisions from you, since we're mighty low."

"This family I'd be seeing across—how are they situated for animals?"

"Their horses have died, all but one. You have extras?"

"Ready and waiting. Oxen."

"Good." The Major turned to scan the area for Mrs. Powers and saw her a little ways off braiding her daughter's hair. The Doctor sat nearby on the bare ground, his empty tin cup dangling from his fingers. Their wagon was behind him, dirty and slightly lopsided, as tired as the family that drove it. "Come with me. We'll ask them."

The rider dismounted and tied his horse to the Major's wagon. Together they approached the Powerses' campsite, where smoldering embers sent wisps of smoke into the afternoon air. The Doctor rose warily as they drew near, unfolding to his full height like a gangly puppet; the woman stopped braiding the girl's hair and came to greet them with a smile.

"Good morning, gentlemen."

"Morning, ma'am." The Major paused a moment, waiting for Americus to join them, but the man stood rooted to the dirt, his arms crossed over his chest, his sunken eyes watching them. The Major went on. "This is Mr. Haverfield. He's in the business of helping folks over the Sierras. Since my men want to start out now—but you folks need to rest your horse—he's offered to see you to the river, starting in the morning. He has extra animals and a good strong back, and he says he doesn't charge much for his services."

The woman's eyes opened wide, and she smiled. She glanced at her husband, whose gaze had shifted off across the camp.

"We truly need the help, and it would free everyone else to start out at once. What is the cost, Mr. Haverfield?"

Haverfield hesitated, confused by this woman talking business while her husband stayed in the background. He raised his voice slightly so the man could hear that they were negotiating.

"Actually, ma'am, I don't have a set price. I usually trade for whatever folks are willing to give, or I take coins if you have any left. Most folks don't by now." He fingered the rip in his sleeve. "It takes awhile to cross depending on the weather and the condition of the road."

Mrs. Powers glanced at her husband again and then pulled herself taller. She tilted her head just slightly.

"We'll be ever so happy to take you up on your kind offer, Mr. Haverfield. Our horse is in such sad condition that we do need to accept the use of your animals. All we could offer you is our extra cook pot, a water keg, a good length of muslin, and one wool blanket of fine quality, for now. Perhaps when we are settled . . . ."

"I'll be here in the morning, then. About sunrise?" He reached out his hand to shake on the agreement, but hesitated. Instead he nodded and strode over to her husband, hand out-stretched, and waited while the man slowly extended his own.

The Major looked down. "Our men will move out then, Mrs. Powers. The river we're speaking of is the Sacramento, so we'll consider this arrangement the fulfillment of our contract. We'll leave shortly, since you are well situated. I wish you the best."

"Thank you for all you have done for us, Major. Thank you with all my heart."

"Don't mention it."

The Major saw Haverfield back to his horse, feeling

lighter than he had in weeks. Then he gave the word to his men and watched their flurry of preparations. A few passed by the Powerses' wagon to say good-bye. As he watched, one of them— Charles Brookins, a slight, wiry fellow of about twenty-five who worked hard and spoke little—led his donkey to their campsite. Cephas was building a fort in the dirt near the front wagon wheel, arranging small stones into a stockade when Brookins brought the short, muscular animal near. Cephas looked up, squinting his eyes in the sun. As the Major watched, Brookins bent over and placed the donkey's frayed rope in Cephas's small hand. He spoke a few words. Immediately the boy's face lighted up; there was an answering grin on Brookins's face. The donkey stretched its neck toward Cephas as if looking for a handful of grass while Brookins strode away alone.

Back to work. It was time to hitch up. Another few days of this grueling travel and they'd all be in California, where gold nuggets waited for those with strong, willing backs and a few hundred hours to spare.

# CHAPTER 47

# MARY

Morning dawned blue skied and sunny, but Mary was hunched on the wagon tongue, a dirty slip of paper trembling in her hands. She read it again. Americus peered over her shoulder.

*Took sick. Can not take you accross mountians. so sorry.*

*Clive Haverfield*

When the boy galloped up on the horse Mary recognized as Mr. Haverfield's, her knees got weak, and she had to sit down to read the message the boy handed her. Now that he was gone, the full implications plowed into her mind.

The mountains lay in wait, the formidable barricade the guide book described as "perilous." The book didn't report on this exact route, but Mary had memorized its strict warnings about the other trails with their sheer cliffs, rocky overhangs, and tortuous ascents. She knew about the churning rivers and streams that must be crossed, the dense undergrowth with massive piles of deadfall, the violent mountain storms that blew up without warning, the Indians who inhabited the foothills.

The guide book saved its most dire warnings for the early winter blizzards that could swirl up from behind the peaks in no time at all, hurling icy flakes so thick that travelers were forced to stop in their tracks. A blizzard could clog the trail with deep drifts in a matter of hours while its howling winds froze livestock and emigrants to death. Building a fire or adequate shelter in such conditions was almost impossible. Mary had covered her mouth in horror when she read about one party of travelers who froze to death huddled in makeshift tents of sticks and cowhide on the wrong side of the Sierras.

By now, it was nearly hopeless to overtake the Major and his men. In despair, Mary took stock of the scene around her. The Honey Lake Valley stretched out empty to where the mountains waited. Every last wagon was gone, driven with urgency toward the far-off passes. To the east lay only the enormous, deserted landscape domed by cavernous sky. Mary strained her eyes, but she could see no moving specks that would indicate other late travelers. She glanced again at the western sky. Who knew what lurked on the far side of those terrible mountains? Chances of bad weather increased with every day, every moment, they delayed.

The fire smoldered. Beside it was the Powerses' lone wagon, sagging into the dirt as if it could never move again. Picketed nearby, Blackey and the little donkey Cephas called "Smoke" grazed peacefully, but Mary could see Blackey's ribs beneath his hide and the tired droop of his head. The Doctor had stretched out on the dirt now with his eyes closed, oblivious to the insects that crawled over his face. She wondered how he could relax at a time like this when her own body was taut as stretched canvas.

There was the added complication of low provisions. When was the last time the children had eaten a proper meal?

Haverfield's boy brought a sack of flour when he delivered the note, and Mary gave him her spare cook pot in return. The unopened sack still lay on the ground; Mary couldn't muster the strength to make biscuits. Besides, she'd better make the flour last. It was all they had, along with a little coffee and some mint leaves, until they reached the old ranch—if they reached the ranch at all.

Mary rubbed her face with one rough hand. Would it be best to stop here, build a cabin for the winter, and tough it out in this windswept valley? Watching her husband's chest rise and fall, she decided that constructing even a rude shelter would be more than Americus could manage now. Providing meat would be beyond his capability, even if he had a rifle. They would die here as surely as the blizzards would come. Should they turn back then? Mary dismissed the thought. California was far closer than any civilization to the east. Perhaps they could leave the wagon and cross the mountains on foot, but she knew she could never walk that far. Besides, it would mean abandoning their only shelter and most of their supplies.

They had to press on with the wagon; it was their only choice. She took a long breath and got to her feet.

The ground twirled beneath her as it often did when she stood up suddenly, but Mary ignored the momentary blackness and hurried over to the Doctor. She tapped the sole of his bare foot with her own toes, suddenly furious at his indifference. With effort, she controlled her voice.

"Americus, will you hitch up Blackey and the donkey? I see no choice but to attempt these mountains on our own. We'll have to try to overtake the Major."

Americus opened his eyes and squinted up at her. Wordlessly he sat up. Mary turned away and hurried over to the wagon.

"Cephas, help your father hitch Blackey and the donkey, won't you?"

"Smoke has never been harnessed before, Mother."

"We'll have to teach him then, Cephas. Blackey can't haul us over the mountains by himself. Sarah, be quick. Load the breakfast things into the wagon. We're starting out right away."

"Alone, Mother? Without that man to help us?"

"He's taken sick, Sarah. There's no other way." Mary tried to smile reassuringly, but for once her face refused to respond.

In a moment Cephas came up leading the donkey. Americus was still sitting in the dirt, so Mary helped Cephas harness the surprised animal. She knew she looked grim, but this disaster was too much to bear. The sky above her seemed empty, as if God had vanished. She felt like an inconsequential speck in His great scheme, abandoned and forgotten! Sternly she shook her head, but anger and fear pulsed in her veins. What else could possibly turn awry and heap more misery and trouble upon them? She closed her eyes for a moment.

"Mother?" Cephas was looking up at her, his forehead creased. "Are you sick?"

"No, Cephas." She forced herself to focus on her son. She could no longer fool Sarah with her false smiles and brave, cheerful words, but Cephas was younger and more easily comforted. She forced a light tone. "Do you think Smoke is ready to tackle the mountains? He surely is a strong little fellow, and he likes you best, Cephas. It must be all that grass you fed him along the way."

"I like him, too."

"I just hope he can learn to pull. Let's hitch Blackey beside him to show him what to do."

Americus slowly rose to his feet and pulled up Blackey's

picket stake. Mary let him hitch the horse while she went to help Sarah finish loading the wagon. It seemed roomy inside without the Major's pile of belongings.

In a few minutes they were ready to go. Mary climbed into the driver's seat. Her sunbonnet hung down her back, and she pulled it into place and tied it securely. Small good it did. Last time she'd been brave enough to peer into the looking glass, she'd recoiled at the sight of her windburned complexion. It seemed a lifetime ago when she had worried about keeping her skin white and smooth. Lovely skin was not essential to survival. She'd learned that much out here.

Clucking to Blackey, she watched the donkey. The stocky, short-legged animal looked around and balked for a moment, but then fell into step beside the much larger horse. The two made a comic pair, a mismatched team that Mary knew was utterly unequal to the task ahead. At a rock in the trail, the donkey stopped, and Blackey halted, too, surprised. Americus walked over and pulled on the harness, and the team started up again.

The sun was barely overhead, but Mary could tell by the color of Sarah's face that she was already getting tired piggy-backing Celia. In another few miles they would need to stop for a meal. Mary could hardly bear to take the time. She could imagine the Major gaining ground up ahead as Blackey and the donkey plodded along at their excruciating pace.

But she was forgetting. The sun was shining, the children were healthy, and Blackey (bless his soul!) was still pulling them closer to their destination. There was much to be thankful for, if only she could remember to see it.

# CHAPTER 48

# AMERICUS

Americus took a deep, slow breath. The air in these foothills was refreshing, scented as it was with the pitchy aroma of pine. All around him, towering trees thrust into the sky, as tall as any he'd ever seen. He almost liked these open stands of pine. Even the sky cooperated by staying a deep azure, regardless of the fact that September—or was it October?—was marching its way toward winter.

The Major was far up the trail by now, despite Mary's brisk pace, but he had made one parting comment.

"This route isn't as heavily used as some of the southern passes, Powers. Its heyday is about over. It's supposed to wind through some mighty nice country, though, heading due west just south of Mount Saint Joseph straight to the trading post on the old Lassen Ranch."

From the grim look on Mary's face, she was expecting the worst from this mountain crossing. Just ahead the road made a sharp turn to the south and he could see a bad spot coming up. The tracks jutted straight up a rocky hillside gouged with deep ruts and washouts and obvious signs of struggle.

They drew closer, and Americus sized up the incline again. Blackey and that ridiculous donkey couldn't begin to pull the wagon up this hellish spot, although Mary had set her chin and straightened her back and given them the command.

Americus stood back to watch. Blackey started up, straining to pull the weight behind him. Beside him, the donkey planted his sturdy feet and pulled surprisingly well for such a small animal. Together they hauled the wagon a short way up the hill before the front wheel hit a rut and the wagon jolted to an abrupt halt. Mary struggled to keep her balance on the seat, and Blackey stumbled backward a step or two, but then held on.

Americus knew they couldn't inch the wagon up with just a rope, their bare hands, and two inadequate animals, even if they unloaded. As he watched, Mary carefully backed the wagon down to level ground and tried again. Blackey's muscles quivered as he and the donkey strained upwards, but the wagon moved only a few feet before it faltered and stopped. Americus lugged a big rock to the wagon and dropped it behind the rear wheel.

A sudden strong breeze rustled the treetops, and the sun went out as quickly as a doused campfire. Americus saw Mary glance at the sky, and then look again. He studied the wind, which he hadn't noticed a few minutes ago. Here in the mountains, it sounded different than it did as it tore across the plains or picked up stinging sand in the desert or flattened the grasses along the Bear. Here it swished through these pines with a sound all its own, something like the rush of water or the sweep of a thousand brooms. He listened as it grew stronger. In the distance, the mountainsides began to roar with its power.

Above the swaying trees, dark gray clouds were scudding past, obliterating the blue sky.

"It's going to storm, Americus." Mary's face was pinched.

"It will just be rain, Mary. It's too warm for snow."

Still, a man didn't relish a lashing rainstorm in the midst of these giant trees. Given a strong enough wind, it seemed as if they could topple like sticks, crushing whatever lay in their paths.

"Let's get the wagon under some shelter." Mary's voice interrupted his thoughts. He shoved the rock away from the wheels. Mary backed down the short distance and then drove the wagon under a tree so huge that Americus thought it must have been rooted there since the Pilgrim colonies began. The canvas cover snapped in the wind and strained against the bows but it was somewhat sheltered by the thick clusters of needles above. Mary unhitched the team and tied the jittery animals to the wagon's back end.

Then, glancing up at the wildly swaying boughs, some as large as tree trunks themselves, she bundled the children into the quilt and hustled them under the wagon. She crawled under, too, her torn shawl scanty protection from the wind. Americus, seeing her wisdom, joined them. The temperature was dropping, and he wished he had grabbed a blanket.

The rain followed, falling lightly at first and then ferociously pelting the wet earth. The smell of damp wood and dead grass and sage arose, a fresh fragrance that was a sweet contrast to the storm's fury. Above the roar of the wind, there was a loud crack and a heavy thud nearby. Americus saw the branch that fell, large as a full-grown apple tree. It missed the wagon by 20 yards or so and landed just north of the trail.

This was a fine state of affairs, stuck here with a stalled wagon and no possible way to overtake those who could help. He shivered and wondered what his brother David would think of him now, stranded out here with one poor horse, huddled under the wagon like a cowering dog. According to their plan, Americus should be in California by now, building a tight lumber house for Mary on acres of burgeoning ground, his teams of fine horses grazing in the sunlight. How had things gone so dreadfully wrong?

Even the squirrels had disappeared when the storm hit. Americus wondered idly if they were edible, and the vision of bubbling squirrel stew made his mouth water so suddenly that he swallowed in surprise. He couldn't fathom eating a squirrel. He wasn't that far from losing his gentility.

He glanced at the children. Cephas crouched on his heels, digging roads or trails or some such nonsense in the dirt with a stick. Sarah sat quietly, almost too quietly, with her head leaning against Mary's shoulder. Celia was on Mary's lap, shivering and sucking her thumb, whispering something into her mother's ear. Americus caught the word "hungry" over the wind.

The gray afternoon light was fading when the storm ended. Mary crawled out, straightened her back, and began looking for dry firewood, clutching her old shawl around her with one hand. Occasionally she stopped to rub her temple. He, too, crawled from under the wagon. Raindrops fell from the wet needles in cold splats that trickled down his bald spot and soaked through the thin cloth covering his shoulders. If Mary could get a blaze started tonight, it would be a miracle.

# CHAPTER 49

# SARAH

S arah paused for a moment and turned to look back. It was a wonder they were up here. Yesterday she thought they would be stuck at the base of this ridge forever.

Cephas said they would have to leave the wagon behind and walk all the way to California. Sarah couldn't stand the thought. Imagine sleeping on the bare ground where all those ants could crawl right up your legs. Any passing cougar or bear would find you, too. And they'd have to leave everything behind they couldn't carry on their backs. Lucy. Mother's hidden teapot.

That was before Father wandered off. He was gone long enough for Mother to start furrowing her brow and watching for him to come back. When she finally saw him, she glanced at the sun and left the wagon to meet him.

"It will mean a long detour to get the wagon over there," Father was saying when they got close. "But it's a much gentler slope. Blackey can do it, I'm sure."

"Then let's try it. Anything is better than being stranded here."

Father sat down in his usual place on the wagon tongue as if settling in for the day, but after a while he rose with effort and grabbed the axe. While the morning sun moved high in the sky, he led the way off the trail, chopping off an occasional young tree in his path. Cephas and Sarah followed, helping him lug rocks and drag fallen logs out of the way. Sweat ran down Sarah's back, soaking through her dress, and she could tell her face was red by the color of Cephas's. Mother brought them a tepid drink at noon and a few biscuits. Bit by bit, they cleared a trail through the open timber and the dense, woody tangles of undergrowth, and diagonally up the gentler slope to the north.

By the time the sun was low, Blackey and the donkey were able to haul the load to the top with Mother and Father both pushing. Sarah hoped they would camp at the top, but Mother wiped her brow with her handkerchief and looked at the sky. "We've fallen terribly behind today," she said, studying Blackey's heaving sides. "We must try to make up a few miles if we're ever to overtake the Major." She handed everyone a dry biscuit. "We'll need to drive until dark."

Sarah wanted to curl up in the wagon and sleep forever. Her hands were raw, and she had a gash on her forearm that oozed blood. She sank down on a log.

Mother looked down at her from the wagon seat.

"Are you all right, Sarah?"

"I'm just tired, Mother."

"I know, dear."

Sarah marveled that Cephas wasn't as worn out as she was. He was standing in the trail, craning his neck to watch something in the treetops. She could tell her brother loved this place where the land lifted up from the plains as if reaching for the sky. The reddish ground was strewn with fallen pine needles that gave off a baked, pitchy smell. Huge cones, the biggest Sarah had ever seen, lay scattered. Between the trees, scrubby bushes with round, leathery leaves twisted up from the soil, but the land ahead looked open and inviting, as if a giant had cleared the way for the wagon.

"Sarah, come over here. Let's see if we can reach around this big tree trunk," Cephas called to her.

Sarah's legs felt limp, but she went. They stretched their arms as far around the trunk as they could, but they couldn't touch each other's fingers. Their noses pressed into the cracked bark. It smelled delicious, almost like fruit.

Mother called from the wagon seat. Then she straightened her back and clucked to Blackey. The wagon started up. Reluctantly, Sarah fell in step.

Was it three or four times they crossed that mountain stream before it got dark? Even then, Mother didn't stop. The last hill was another steep one, although, thank goodness, it was short. Blackey and Smoke had to rest twice on the way up, but they made it. The other side was a straight slant down to the stream. Father set the brakes.

Mother bit her lip and gave her full attention to driving while the wagon crept halfway down. Then, without warning, the brake gave way. Sarah screamed as the wagon roared down the rest of the awful slope. Blackey and Smoke plunged ahead so they wouldn't be run over and plowed into the water at the bottom. The wagon followed until the wheels hit the submerged rocks and slammed to a stop. Mother lurched on the wagon seat, but somehow kept her balance. The team, their sides heaving, dripped water from their flanks.

Sarah didn't see how Mother had avoided being dashed to pieces. Even in the darkness, Sarah could see the stark, pale oval that was Mother's face, and she could feel her own heart hammering. It seemed a long time before Mother spoke to the animals in a voice that trembled, urging them to the far bank.

There she stopped and climbed down.

There was no moon and not even any starlight. Mother started a tiny fire, just enough to heat coffee for Father, but it soon went out.

Sarah, Cephas, and Celia got into the wagon. For an instant Sarah was afraid. It was so dark it was as if she had suddenly gone blind. She wiggled her fingers in front of her eyes, but she couldn't see them at all. Then Mother's voice came out of the blackness, and Sarah could see again the blanched color of her face.

"Children, I have some tea for you before bed."

Obediently, she fumbled for the cup Mother held out to her in the darkness, but she didn't want tea. Tonight she knew what the saying "dead tired" meant. She made an impolite face that no one could see and took a halfhearted sip. To her surprise, this mountain stream water made the tea taste clean and delicious.

Even exhausted as she was, she couldn't sleep for the longest time. Something rustled in the bushes outside the wagon and a twig snapped. She squeezed her eyes shut.

# CHAPTER 50

## MAJOR WHITESIDES

When he saw the dilapidated wagon laboring up the trail behind his stalled crew, the Major felt dread settle into his stomach. Even in the pewter predawn light, he would recognize that dirty, ragged wagon cover and the poor black horse anywhere, but he saw no sign of Haverfield, the guide. Ignoring the heaviness in his gut, he wondered if perhaps the man had gone ahead hunting or scouting. It seemed unlikely, since the trail passed within a few feet of this unplanned camp. Maybe Haverfield was behind, skinning out a deer or some such thing—or more likely, keeping his distance from the surly doctor.

This mountain crossing wasn't turning out as he had planned. With the end nearly in sight, it was almost as if luck and stamina and even food were running out. Maybe it was the cold night air, but Potts and Barnard both were so sick they could barely crawl out of their wagons, and when they did they looked like walking ghosts. Worse than that, Smith had broken an axle two days ago crossing a rocky stream—a strange accident if ever he saw one, since they had traversed many places more treacherous. The Major suggested abandoning the wagon in the interest of time and safety, but Smith refused, so while the Major checked the skies a thousand times, the men cut and fashioned a new axle. The job was done now, finished by fire-light late last night. That pine axle was hardly adequate, though. This soft western wood was no match for the durable hardwoods back home. The new axle might last just long enough to reach the valleys ahead.

This morning the wagons were ready to move out again, provided Potts and Barnard could manage. The Major scanned the trail again in both directions. Irritation flared in his chest. The unexpected arrival of the Powers family seemed like one burden too many.

He couldn't help smiling, though, when little Cephas cut away from their wagon and ran toward him, a grin all over his face. He almost wished the boy were his own. He lifted his hand to wave, and the child shouted, "Mr. Major!" as he ran through the woods, leaping over logs and bushes, darting around trees. The boy's legs were bare to the knees and covered with scratches and bruises, and his light hair flopped across his forehead. His eyes were glued to the Major as if he were afraid the man might turn into a mirage and disappear. Panting, he ran up and stopped so near that the Major could feel the heat from his little body.

"We found you!"

"You sure did, Cephas boy." He patted the child's shoulder and let his eyes drift back to the Powerses' wagon, which was closer now. Mrs. Powers was driving, so it wasn't Haverfield at the reins. Her husband was walking near the team. The Major blinked and looked again. It was ludicrous, but the man actually had harnessed that little donkey with the black horse. What about Haverfield's fresh animals?

"Cephas boy, what happened to that fellow who was going to help you folks through the mountains?"

"He took sick."

"Sick? When did he take sick?"

"The day after you left. Mother has been trying to catch up to you."

"She's done that, all right." He kept the grimness out of his tone and tried not to think about his men's reaction to this new development. How such an unlikely team had managed to pull a loaded wagon all the way from Honey Lake Valley was incomprehensible. The up-and-down contours of these mountains were enough to stall anyone's progress.

Mrs. Powers drew up beside the camp and stopped the wagon. The doctor disappeared around the back. After a glad wave and greeting, she stepped down. The Major rearranged his frown. He'd best remember his manners and at least appear pleased to see her.

"Greetings, ma'am. Cephas here told me about your misfortune with Mr. Haverfield taking sick."

She tilted her head and smiled, relief at seeing him written on her face as clearly as if it had been labeled. He wondered that she had confidence in his ability to help them through. He no longer took much stock in himself.

"Yes. You can't imagine how glad I am to see you all. We've had some harrowing days by ourselves."

"We've had a few tough times ourselves. Delays, especially. But we're prepared to leave again this morning. Coffee? I was about to pour out the rest."

"Oh, yes, please. After the cold tea we had early this morning, that sounds heavenly."

She grasped the cup he handed her with eager, trembling hands and took a long drink. A few of the men gathered to greet her, and the Major watched as she smiled and spoke to each one by name. Some hung back around their animals, glancing warily in her direction. He knew what they were thinking, yet saw no alternative but to pack up and move out, Powers family and all.

And they had better do it now, before the clouds rolled in.

*Dear Mother,*

*This letter shall be short, as I am writing at our midday dinner stop. I simply must tell you that we have overtaken the Major and his men! Their ill luck became our good fortune; a wagon breakdown delayed them long enough for us to catch up. You can't imagine my relief when Cephas spotted their stalled wagons through the trees.*

*I coped with this most recent stretch of solitary travel to the best of my abilities, though. You would have been surprised to hear me handing out orders like the soft-spoken general I have become! Could you ever have imagined that I would turn into another George Washington out here, leading my troops into battle? That is how I felt as our little family faced these mountains alone. I am at the reins in more ways than one.*

*We have come across some very bad places that made my heart stop in fear, but none yet like the guide book describes along the more southern routes. We have not encountered the "treacherous cliffs" where one must hoist the wagons up over precipices with ropes, nor the "devastating early-winter* storms" *that could mean our demise. Although we still have miles of these mountains to traverse, it appears that I have fretted and worried much more than necessary.*

*It brings to mind, Mother, the words of an old French verse I've read quoted by that contemporary New England poet Ralph Waldo Emerson:*

> *"Some of your hurts you have cured*
>
> *and the sharpest you still have survived,*
>
> *but what torments of grief you've endured*
>
> *from evils that never arrived!"*

*I have certainly suffered enormous "torments of grief" over the evils of the Sierra Nevada, and so far, mostly for naught. Today our Heavenly Father has given us a bit of paradise through which to travel. It is a parklike, meadowy place that would make a beautiful setting for a Sunday picnic. The sun is shining from the deep blue sky as if this were a carefree spring day.*

*Now that I am not so intent on my single-minded goal of overtaking our comrades, I can see how beautiful these mountains are—and how lovely the weather. We've seen countless deer (I'm afraid I fail to notice their delicate beauty, but instead see visions of venison steak!) but fortunately no cougars. For this I am thankful, since a cougar will stalk and kill a child.*

*I must stop now, Mother, so we can resume our travels. Although the urgency within me has subsided a bit in today's cheerful sunlight, I don't delude myself. There will be plenty of challenges in the trail ahead.*

*I am finishing this letter to you later. Tonight, as I write by firelight, the black silhouettes of the trees stand out against a sky filled with glittering, diamondlike stars. The air is cold—we are using every last piece of our bedding in these mountains—but I am rejoicing, for the clear sky seems to indicate another sunny day tomorrow. I can't help but believe that God has heard my pleas for no blizzards and has shed His grace on us. I am humbled and ashamed by my fear a few days ago, for it is clear to me now that He held us safely in his hands, even then. Our little fire crackles cheerfully against the cold, and I shall try to keep it burning brightly all night.*

*I made some more biscuits, but our small supply of flour is dwindling quickly. It is a frightening thought. There must be some edible plants in these mountains; however, I do not know what they are and am afraid to try swallowing unfamiliar things for fear of poisoning ourselves. If we would ever stop long enough in the daylight, perhaps my smart little Cephas could catch a fish.*

*Americus is still regaining his strength, Mother, but I am tired every minute of every day. I am barely able to perform my chores adequately. I am hoping that the Doctor will be able to offer me some healing remedy once we are finally settled in California. For the first time, it almost seems possible that we might reach our destination.*

*Despite the fire and my shawl—which, by now, has holes and rents everywhere—I am shivering, Mother (can you tell from my shaky penmanship?) so I will go now and crawl in the wagon beside my warm, sleeping family. For once, perhaps I will be grateful for their very close proximity. The close quarters in the wagon might offer just the warmth I need to sleep tonight.*

*When we reach California where at last I can actually receive letters from you, remind me, Mother, of the lessons I have learned here in the mountains, and save me from the "torments of grief" over "evils that never arrived!"*

*Love from so, so far away,*

*Mary*

# CHAPTER 52

# CEPHAS

Cephas crouched under the wagon, listening. They were lost in these big mountain meadows! Mr. Major said they took the wrong road early this morning, and now it was suppertime. He pointed to something on the map and talked in a loud voice.

Mr. Smith said so, too. He said they had wandered around all day, making the teams tired but going nowhere. Mother stared at the map, rubbing her forehead. She kept looking over at Blackey.

Lost! Being lost was worse than seeing all the cougars and bears in these mountains. Worse than being sucked into a river's current! His heart thumped in his chest.

But Mother was here. And Mr. Major. They would know what to do.

"We've got to turn back. Go until we reach last night's camp and take the other fork. That has to lead us directly to the trading post on the river." Mr. Major jabbed at the map again. "And we'd better take time to cut and dry some grass. There's supposed to be a long dry stretch ahead."

Cephas crawled out from under the wagon. He didn't want them to see him listening. His toe hurt, and he stopped to look at yesterday's gash. It had broken open and was bleeding again.

If he weren't tired, he wouldn't mind going back. He liked traveling after dark. The trip seemed more like an adventure then. That was when the air was soft and quiet, and the stars seemed near enough to touch. Once he even tried jumping high to grab one, but of course it was too far away.

It was a lot easier traveling here, even though there were creeks and marshy places to cross. At least it was level. He was glad the steep places were gone for now. Little Celia was such a baby. She could hardly stand up on the downhill slopes. He and Sarah always had to help her. Sometimes Sarah told her to sit down on an old flour sack and slide down. Other times she just lugged Celia down herself.

He wished Father would make their new home here in these big meadows. He loved the open sky and the cool autumn breeze. He especially liked the view of that far-off snowy mountain. The leaves here were orange and tan and yellow. Along the streams there were nice muddy places that felt good under his bare feet. Under the clear water, bright green plants grew in the current. Birds gathered here, too, as if it were a meeting place.

He thought he would find gold here. People back home said gold chunks lay everywhere in western streams. He spent yesterday evening wading in a cold creek, digging with his toes, searching for the flash of a big nugget. Mother always said his sharp eyes could spot anything, but he couldn't find any gold. That's where he had hurt his toe.

"Ho, Cephas boy. You all right?'

"Yes, Mr. Major. My toe is hurt, that's all."

"Better keep up with the wagons. Plenty of Indians around here."

The sun was setting. Cephas ran after the wagons, trying to jump on his long shadow. It leaped away too quickly for him to catch. Chilly air blew down his shirt. He wondered when they could stop so Mother could make a fire and find some supper. Cephas couldn't wait. Last night he had dreamed about the johnnycakes Mother used to make back home. Now there was nothing to eat except venison.

The other men let Mother borrow their teams on the worst hills, but otherwise Blackey and Smoke were in the harness. When they stopped, Blackey's head drooped and his eyes closed. Sometimes he shook his head back and forth as if to say "enough." Cephas stroked his nose, but Blackey didn't seem to care. Smoke was dead tired, too. He didn't even notice Cephas anymore.

Cephas heard a noise behind him and glanced back. Father was striding up behind him. Cephas walked faster, but his father's gruff voice stopped him.

"Son, wait."

Reluctantly the boy obeyed. His father caught up and reached down for Cephas's hand. Startled, Cephas pulled back, but Father grabbed his fingers and slipped something small into his palm. Cephas looked down. It was a beautiful amber stone, so smooth it looked polished.

Cephas tried to say something, but no words came. He looked up at his father, who gave him a quick wink and strode off again after the wagons.

Cephas hurried to catch up and fell in step.

# CHAPTER 53

# MARY

The high mountain meadows were far behind them, and now this ridge lifted stubbornly in front of them, steep as any they'd encountered. It looked insurmountable to Mary, who knew she would have to tackle it on foot. She tried to put the ascent out of her mind: each aching lunge toward the crest, each labored breath, the constant backsliding on slippery gravel where it would take two steps to gain one. For a moment she wondered how Celia would ever manage here, but then she realized that Sarah was already over in the trees zigzagging the little girl to the top.

Mary knew it would take the entire day for the sweating teams to draw the wagons up. She needn't hurry her own ascent, but she wanted to put the climb behind her while it was still morning. Later in the day her strength would fade entirely.

She took a few steps. The slope was vertical enough that she could claw her way up with her hands. She dug her fingers into the loose dirt and stones and pulled herself a few feet, grasping the tangled dead branches of manzanita for support.

"Hello, down there, Mother!" It was Cephas, already at the summit, holding one of Celia's hands while Sarah held the other. Mary lifted her hand for a quick wave. The children's hair ruffled in the breeze, but here on the hot gravel slope the air was still and the heat oppressive. She wished for a bit of shade where she could sit and catch her breath.

"Mother!" It was Cephas again. "Sarah's coming back down to help you."

Sarah was, indeed, angling her way back down. Mary rubbed her forehead and tried to breathe more slowly as she watched Sarah navigate the slope. Tenderness and pride for her daughter tightened her chest. Sometimes she had to remind herself that Sarah was only twelve, especially at moments like this when the girl took on the responsibilities and cares of a woman.

"Do you need help, Mother? Here, loop your arm over my shoulders, and we can climb together."

"Thank you, dear."

Sarah was strong as a young doe. Hundreds of miles of walking and toting Celia had made her lean and muscular. Mary leaned on the girl's shoulders and concentrated on climbing. They stopped to rest and then resumed their struggle. Sarah's neck was damp under Mary's forearm, and her dress showed a dark stain down the middle of her back. Mary stopped again, panting. It seemed a long time before they finally reached the crest.

Mary dropped to the ground in the shade of a gigantic pine, heedless of the stones and powdery dust under her. A light breeze blew across her forehead as she looked down at the wagons still to come. The men were swarming around the teams, hitching six pairs to Americus's wagon. Her husband was lugging the grub box from the back. Gradually, the pounding of her heartbeat subsided and her breath came more easily.

It was then that she turned and looked west.

The land dropped off in an incredible slide to the western

horizon, perhaps miles or more in the blue distance. Below her, the heavily forested foothills stretched out in the morning sunlight, which smoothed out the sharpest contours and lent the scene a gentleness she hadn't expected. The vast sky was a deep, dazzling blue. Up close, the few massive pines loomed over the slope, their shiny long needles swishing slightly in the soft wind, and their warm, brown bark giving off its sweet smell.

What caught Mary's eye, though, and caused her to draw a sharp breath, was a clear, unobstructed view of the astounding peak that had shown glimpses of itself for the past few days. Mount Saint Joseph, the Major called it. They had caught occasional hazy views of its far-off, massive slopes, but nothing had prepared her for this breathtaking vista. They were much nearer now. Her awed eyes took in its stunning height and beauty. Immense, snowy flanks rose from the blue-green foothills to a towering dome that dominated the landscape to the northwest. The stark white peak rose like a huge monument that dwarfed its surroundings.

She took another deep breath as she admired its spellbinding slopes. Then her eyes slid back to the foothills. With a sudden shocked realization that made the blood rush to her head, she knew that she was overlooking California's long-awaited valleys—what the guide book called "the land of milk and honey." The valleys! Somewhere out there—perhaps even within view! —lay the end of the trail, a place where she could finally stop and make a home.

A small shiver went up her back. She warned herself not to anticipate too much, but she couldn't stop the images that flashed across her mind. A safe cabin. Fresh vegetables to eat. A rocking chair. Soon she would never again have to sleep in the crowded wagon, or eat old beans, or depend upon anyone's charity. Never again have to perch on the driver's seat and pray the brake would hold, or shiver through another lightning storm, or carry boulders—or watch her children go hungry. It wasn't so much farther.

# CHAPTER 54

## AMERICUS

Americus felt the splintery boards press into his raw, angular shoulder. He braced his feet in the gravel and pushed. Beside him, Smith and the Major leaned into the wagon as well. With all of them holding it, the wheels stayed where they were, halfway up this blasted slope, giving the animals time to rest for a moment. How many more of these miserable obstacles would they have to navigate before they were through?

"Good thing you were able to catch up with us, Powers," Smith commented, panting. "Or you'd have been on foot a long ways back."

Americus didn't answer. It was indisputable he couldn't have made it up these bad spots without the Major and his men and animals. He didn't need to discuss the fact with anyone.

The wooden boards were bruising his shoulder, and he was glad when Barnard cracked the whip again. The wagon's weight lifted as the oxen strained upward. Americus pushed with both hands, his body rigid and every muscle at work. The wagon ground its way up the hill.

Already he was tired, and there were still the other wagons to come. Potts's was a small, light affair, but Americus dreaded Smith's—a heavy lumbering farm wagon modified for the trip west. It was always the most difficult one on these un-relenting hills, whether going up or down.

The children had reached the crest long ago, and even Mary, with Sarah's help, had already labored her way to the top. Americus had watched their long ascent. His daughter was nearly as tall as Mary now—when had that happened?—and from this distance the two of them might have been sisters, one flushed from heat and exertion beneath her tanned skin and the other with a pallor and dark circles under her eyes.

Finally with a last mighty shove from the men, the wagon crested the hill and stopped. Americus climbed inside for a moment to catch his breath. The trapped air was hot, but he needed to rest. Outside, the men were exclaiming over the view to the west, and Smith hollered out, "Ho, Barnard, come over here. You have to see this mountain!"

"Mount Saint Joseph. Just look at the size of it." The Major's voice held a hint of awe.

It wasn't often that these trail-worn travelers got so ex-cited. The last time was when that quiet young fellow Brookins found a chest full of brown leather-bound books discarded be-side the trail. Americus hadn't known the man was literate until he let out an uncharacteristic, delighted whoop and began reading off the gilt titles one by one. The men gathered around, interested at first but then unimpressed, until Brookins packed the chest away in his wagon. The Major was disgusted about the added weight, but Americus could understand a little of the younger man's enthusiasm. In the past, he had felt that way about books himself.

Smith was still hollering for Barnard to see the moun-tain. It must be quite a sight. Curious, Americus stepped out of the wagon and walked to the edge of the ridge.

Smith was right: It was worth exclaiming about.

The astounding peak had to be thousands of feet high. Compared to the restful, rolling land back home, its impressive slopes and radiant summit made Americus rub his hand over his eyes and look again. No wonder they called it Mount Saint Joseph. It was saintly enough, rising as it did above all the others like a protective fatherly presence.

There were no clouds in the afternoon sky. Below and beyond the mountain, the landscape became foothills that leveled out into a vast, broad valley. Looking out over the panorama, Americus knew one thing with startling certainty: This downhill sweep was the beginning of the journey's end.

Suddenly it seemed as if a heavy, sodden coat were slipping from his shoulders, relieving some terrible dead weight upon him. Despite the altitude, his breath came more easily. He knew now that they could finish this monumental undertaking. They could make it through to the Sacramento River in one piece, without starving to death or being stalled in some lonesome spot with only vultures for company. He was alive. His family was alive.

And this, he told himself in disbelief, was the place he'd awaited all these long months. The place where he could finally rest his gaze upon the California valleys.

Mary put the tip of her pen to her lips. How could she ever describe the complexities of yesterday's emotions? The feelings that flowed through her while she gazed down upon California were only a part of them. Earlier in the day she'd despaired over her physical weakness, and blinked away tears at Sarah's kindness when her daughter helped her climb that last endless hill. Her cheeks had flushed with gratitude when Mr. Smith handed her a raw, bloody venison steak. She recoiled from touching the wet, shiny mass, but once it was hung over last night's fire, the delicious smell nearly made her mad with hunger.

What stood out in her mind, though, was her absolute shock when Americus approached her as she crouched at ridge's summit at sunset examining a sliver in Celia's finger. He awkwardly took her hand in his. Stunned, she had been unable to speak, so she looked up at him, and he had said quietly, "Come with me, Mary."

The children's mouths gaped as he led her away from the others and helped her to the best overlook. Once there he released her hand and pointed to the vivid pink and gold light of sunset reflecting from the magnificent mountain to the northwest. He sat quietly next to her as she rested and absorbed its splendor. Later he took her elbow and helped her down the hill again. Mary was still in a state of confused wonder about the incident. She shook her head and laid her pen aside.

The wagon was loaded and ready to begin another long day. She looked around for the children, and noticed Celia crouched beside the wagon crying quietly. Sarah and Cephas knelt beside her.

"What is it, Celia?" Mary went over to her children.

Celia lifted her wet cheeks and tried to answer, but her breath came in gasps and her thumb was wedged in her mouth.

"She's lost her stick doll, Mother." Sarah brushed the tears from Celia's face.

"Oh, Celia! Did you look for him?"

"We've looked everywhere," Sarah said. "In the wagon, under the trees. I even shook out the quilts." She turned to her little sister. "Ceely, we'll find him. And if we don't, I'll make you a new one. And a stick pony to go with him, like your old one that you left behind to keep St. Lawrence company. Would you like that?"

"No," the little girl wailed. "I need that same stick man."

At that instant, the Major gave the signal for the wagons to pull out. Mary gave Cephas and Sarah permission to stay behind for a few minutes to search, but when they came running to catch up, they were empty handed. Mary cuddled Celia with her in the driver's seat until the little girl nodded off into an exhausted nap, her breath still quivering.

It was noon when the Major halted again. For once he seemed relaxed and in no particular hurry to get back on the trail. Mary again took her pen and paper from her apron pocket.

*Dear Mother,*

*You won't be able to believe what I am writing, for I can scarcely believe it myself. We are in sight of California's promising valleys! I am filled with the joyful prospect of finally finishing this fearsome journey. Can you imagine it, Mother, after what seems like eons of travel?*

*After encountering some rocky downhill grades, we have stopped for dinner in a sunny clearing. This place is as close to heaven as I have ever been! Everything is golden: the bright autumn leaves, the amber sunlight, the beautiful dried grass. The men are relaxing under the giant pines, tossing cones at each other. Americus is napping in the sun. This morning he strode out, looking at the scenery instead of just trudging along with his eyes on the ground.*

*All around are the tallest pine trees; if the children and I stand beneath them, we must severely crane our necks to see their tops. Their needles, fallen in a layer upon the ground, give the fresh mountain air a delightful pungent aroma. These are wilderness trees, not the lovely hardwoods we have back home, but they are beautiful nonetheless.*

*We are winding along beside a pretty mountain stream with delicate, bright green plants growing along its banks. Sarah actually drew water in the bucket for the team instead of leading them to water's edge, for she didn't want their clumsy hooves to crush the fragile leaves. There is a spectacular vista to the north, dominated by a gigantic mountain called Mount Saint Joseph, or occasionally, Mount Lassen. I have never witnessed such a thing. It rises regally above the others, a splendid snowy dome that almost seems to float above the lower mountains around it. I wonder if the trail will take us closer, for it would be a wondrous thing to stand at its imposing base and look up, up, up to its lofty heights.*

*Cephas is fishing. Thankfully, he and the Major have caught a whole string of small troutlike fish, which we shall have tonight for supper. Earlier today, he was busy filling up the wagon with "treasures," hiding them so Americus won't find them. I've found little stashes of golden leaves, glittery stones, even the small fragile skull of a mouse. Recently it has been gigantic pinecones, which don't hide well, but don't add any weight to the wagon. Americus tolerates them somewhat.*

*Mother, I crave the company of other women so badly. The men in our party are all very kind, but oh! how I wish for some privacy and an escape from the dull things that they discuss! The conversation around their evening fire might include the ailments of ox hooves, and the relative strength of chains versus ropes, and the uses for axle grease. Whenever I yearn for a good heart-to-heart talk with another woman, I fetch my pen and paper. I do hope you won't be overwhelmed by the volumes of pages I've written to you.*

*Love, Mary*

# CHAPTER 56

## SARAH

This had been the worst day yet. Sarah dried her eyes again on her apron corner. Poor Blackey was gone, left behind on the trail. Today he had reached the end of his endurance at last. She could hardly bear to think of it. Every time she did, she could still see her good old friend watching them leave, unable even to follow.

They had been traveling for what seemed like days along a high, dry ridge where there was no water. The men called it a "mountain desert." To reach the creek, they had to scramble down big drop-offs and fight their way through undergrowth for a long distance. Coming back up with buckets of water was nearly impossible, so there hadn't been much for the animals to drink. Smoke held out, but poor Blackey. He finally could not go another step. Mother unhitched him and gave him precious water from the keg. Father tried everything he knew, but nothing helped.

The Major said there was no choice but to leave him. It was almost like deserting Ceely or Cephas! Sarah felt worse than when St. Lawrence died, because Blackey knew they were abandoning him. He watched them go with the saddest eyes she had ever seen. Mother and Cephas had tears streaming down their faces. Once Sarah thought she even saw Father's eyes glisten.

She wiped her cheeks again. Blackey's dusty hide with bones poking out was all that was left of his body, but his spirit was still strong inside, she could tell. If only he could have made it just a little farther to the valley, he could have rested forever. Mr. Potts let them borrow his old, lame red ox to help pull the wagon. Every time Sarah saw the clumsy animal limping along in Blackey's place, her tears started all over again.

As if that weren't enough, this afternoon they had passed an awful place on the trail. It looked as if a whole wagon party died there, even though they were on the safe side of the mountains. Mother did her best to distract them, and Ceely did pass by without noticing. But Cephas and Sarah couldn't help staring. It was the remains of a camp, but not just a dead campfire and some trampled ground. There were shredded tents with the poles falling down, and old pieces of wagons and coffee mills, and someone's precious trunk with the lid torn off. Sarah saw clothing scattered about that looked as if it had been out in the rain for a hundred years. There were dented tin dishes and old rusted gun parts, too. Worse than that, there were animal skulls lying on the ground. High above them, their ropes and harnesses were still tied to the tree trunks. She puzzled about why the ropes were up so high, but then she overheard Mr. Smith say that there must have been deep snow here when the party died. It was enough to send shivers down anyone's back! She ran ahead so she didn't have to look anymore.

At least one good thing had happened today. This afternoon, they had come upon an unexpected little outpost beside the trail. Sarah thought the man who lived there was a real mountain man. He had long gray hair and a scraggly beard that was stained yellow by the corners of his mouth. His eyes appeared black, but he squinted so much she could hardly tell. His ragged clothes looked as though they had never been washed. She didn't care, though, because he had a little flour and side pork for trade. Mother had to give him four of her spoons, but they received 20 pounds of flour—enough to see them to the Sacramento. The side pork was like a miracle. She could hardly wait for supper.

Something was poking Sarah's leg through her apron pocket. She pulled out Ceely's new stick man. Sarah had made it the day her little sister lost the old one. Cephas helped her search the undergrowth until they found the perfect twig. Then Ceely watched, her thumb in her mouth, as Sarah tied on the arms and the lichen hair and sewed its clothes. Despite her efforts, though, Sarah kept finding the new toy deserted on the ground or lost in the bed quilts. Last night Cephas almost accidentally kicked it into the fire. Ceely was filling her pockets with pretty stones now instead. Sarah had seen Father showing her where to look.

It was time to put her little sister to bed. She went to sleep so sweetly if Sarah crawled under the quilts beside her and told her a story as they snuggled down. Ceely always thought Sarah was going to bed, too. Wouldn't you think she might notice Sarah still had her dress on? After Ceely fell asleep, Sarah explored the camp with Cephas. Other times she helped Mother wash the dishes or make campfire biscuits.

She was in the wagon when she heard Father's low voice outside, speaking to Mother.

"Potts says I can borrow his last horse and go back after Blackey if I'm of a mind to," he said. "I think I will, first thing in the morning. He's a valuable animal, and we'll need him in California. After today's rest, he should be able to follow along if he's still alive."

Sarah clapped her hand over her mouth and jumped to her feet. It wouldn't do to utter the unladylike glad squeal she felt rising in her throat, but she couldn't contain the wild rush of hope that filled her to the brim.

# CHAPTER 57

# AMERICUS

Steep Hollow. The name didn't begin to tell the story of this long, nearly vertical drop-off. It made a man dizzy to stand at the top and look straight down to the bottom. Getting up the other side would be just as bad.

Americus's muscles tensed as he stared at the wreckage below buried in scrub oak and dense, brittle thickets of manzanita. Bashed wagons and wheel parts, a broken trunk, and snapped-off wagon bows were jumbled together like piles of castoffs. The Major was hunched on a boulder looking over the mess below; Potts and Barnard, both pale and skinny but recovered from their fever, were discussing the best way to get the wagons down.

"If I didn't need mine for farming, I'd be tempted to leave it here," Potts commented.

"Yep," Barnard replied. "Looks like we could lose 'em anyhow."

Americus settled onto the wheel hub. Up on the ridge a few miles back, scattered vantage points showed him how close the valley was. There were worse things than losing a wagon here, although Mary would disagree. He wished that blasted left brake were in better shape. After it gave way that evening with Mary at the reins, he hadn't trusted it much.

He watched as the Major stood up and began giving orders. They'd take Potts's wagon down first—his was the lightest—by setting the brakes, looping the heaviest chains around the axle, and then attaching ropes to the chains. It would take every bit of manpower on the ropes to hold the load back and slide it slowly down. If there was a disaster with Potts's wagon, they'd learn a thing or two about this Steep Hollow.

"Keep the children away from the bottom, ma'am," he told Mary. "No telling what could happen."

Nothing did happen except for the slow inching of Potts's wagon to the bottom. By then Americus was sweating with the rest of them. Dirt stained his rope-burned hands and his muscles quivered from exertion, but Potts's wagon was still upright and intact.

There were six more wagons to go, including his own. Just the thought made him weary. He glanced over at Mary, who had started a small blaze on a rock outcrop and was using the time to bake biscuits. He wondered how she would ever be able to make her way to the bottom, even with help. Her face was peaked, but she worked steadily, mixing the dough with her hands and poking the fire now and then.

He hadn't made note of much on this trip, but one thing had penetrated his thoughts: Mary rarely complained, even when she was most miserable. He remembered that back in Wisconsin she had considered complaining the height of self-pity, and he guessed she felt the same out here. Once in a while, she disappeared from camp and returned with her eyes suspiciously bright, but her lips were pressed silently together. Her pockets bulged with those everlasting letters she was writing to her mother. She insisted on carrying them with her, even though he no longer minded their tiny extra weight in the wagon. It was beyond him why she wrote them, since there had been no place to post them for the past thousand miles or so. But then she would square her shoulders and go on.

As he watched, she gathered a handful of dead grass and took it to where Blackey was picketed. He couldn't forget the look on his older daughter's face when he rode up yesterday leading the horse back to the family. Sarah flew out of the wagon and nearly spooked the poor animal by throwing her arms around his neck and crying out his name. When Americus dismounted from Potts's horse, she gave him a shy, whispered, "Thank you, Father." She spent the evening currying Blackey until the worst of the dust was gone. Then she braided his mane and put liniment on his scratches. When she thought Americus wasn't looking, she gave him the rest of the day's water from the bucket, all the while talking aloud to him as though he were a person. But the horse looked like a skeleton. Americus wondered if the animal could actually finish the journey, even free of the wagon's load. If it were simply downhill all the way, Blackey could probably stumble his way to the valley. These unexpected, devilish up-and-down spots were quite another matter.

Americus wished Mary's biscuits were done; he was famished. He needed a good long drink, too, but the seasonal rivulet down in Steep Hollow was dried up. Mary still had a little water in the kegs. They'd better make it last.

The Major was giving orders again. Americus watched as Smith jockeyed his wagon into place for the descent and unhitched. The Major crawled underneath to wrap the chain around the axle.

"Powers, yours is next after Smith's. Better get that trunk out of there to lighten your load."

The Major barked his instructions as though Americus

were a child. Americus bit his tongue. He could finally admit that he needed these good men, irritating as they could be. It was a few more long, hard days to the valley.

He rose heavily and went to wrestle the trunk from the wagon—no easy chore, buried as it was. He gave a quick look around, wondering what else he should salvage in case the wagon met its demise here. Nothing. There was nothing at all from this disheartening trip that he wanted to save, and nothing much of value with which to start a new life in California. Then his eyes fell on his medical kit, dusty and forgotten where it had slipped unnoticed behind the trunk. He startled at the sight of it, as if it were an artifact of an earlier life he had forgotten. He grabbed it and stuffed it into the top of the trunk.

Once the trunk was safely on the ground, Americus hurried to his place at the rope. When the Major gave the signal, Smith's wagon tilted over the brink and began the long slide to the bottom.

# CHAPTER 58

## MARY

She could see the distant Sacramento River from the wagon seat, silvery blue in the afternoon light. There was a scattering of far-off cabins, too, beckoning like an outstretched hand. Beyond them, the land unfolded to the far horizon, but Mary's eyes were drawn to the smoke from their chimneys and the dark specks that must be livestock grazing the verdant river grass. She smiled. They had actually made it to this place alive. The mountains she had dreaded from the outset were behind them now. She turned to look at them. They seemed low and benign today, an artist's painting against the sky, their rocky gullies and arduous trail hidden beneath peaceful summits. From here the trip would be easy, for they would simply follow the river downstream. Along its curving banks would be trading posts and settlers glad to welcome newcomers.

Mary stretched her arms over her head. A light breeze fluttered through her fingers, and the sun was warm. She watched the children run ahead, eager to reach the long awaited valley. They were thin and malnourished but otherwise healthy despite it all.

The road had been rough today as the wagon descended

the last stretch of this high ridge between Deer and Mill creeks. Mary had endured the wagon's constant jolting and crashing over rocks as long as she could. She felt as though she'd been tossed around like cream in a butter churn. Lifting her thick knot of hair, she let the sun shine on her aching neck as she looked ahead at the narrow, steep track. There was one last hill before the road reached the valley floor and meandered toward the river. Sitting on the wagon seat, she suddenly knew she had to walk down this final slope into the Sacramento Valley. She needed to finish these foothills on her own two feet, conquer this one remaining downhill stretch herself.

She slid to the ground, leaving Americus to drive. As the wagons pulled away, she wondered if she could manage, for her legs trembled after only a few steps. Taking a breath, she concentrated on placing one foot ahead of the other. The wagons were creeping downhill, but still they were leaving her behind. She sank to the ground for a moment and then struggled to her feet again.

When the wagons reached the bottom, they stopped to wait for her. Mary leaned heavily on her walking stick. The rest of the distance looked intimidating.

"Mary, hurry up, can't you? You're keeping the entire train waiting," Americus hollered up to her.

"I'm coming," she called back with effort. For once the men would have to wait. She took one step, then another, forcing herself on. With each step, she left the Sierras farther behind and dragged herself to the valley floor with slow triumph. The men's attention had been diverted to one of the oxen and its sore hoof, so she came up to them unnoticed until Mr. Smith turned to look at her.

"Mrs. Powers, are you all right?" He jumped to her side and put his hand under her elbow. Americus turned then, and after a quick look at her stark white face, grabbed her other arm.

"Mary!" There was alarm in the Doctor's voice. "What's wrong?"

"Only tired," she managed to say. "Very tired."

The two men lifted her into the wagon, and Americus helped her lie down. The wagon cover was spinning, so she closed her eyes. The Doctor covered her clumsily.

"Can you tell me what's wrong, Mary? Do you need water? Are you hurting?"

She was too weary to answer and was asleep again when the wagons started up. Here in the valley, the road was smoother, so she didn't awaken until nearly dark when the motion stopped and the smell of wet earth filled the evening air. She felt better, much better, and could hear water flowing by— not a trickle or small gurgling but a river. The sound was so welcome that tears formed in her eyes. The Sacramento. She needed to touch it, feel its presence. Could it be true that they were, indeed, stopped on its banks?

*Dear Mother,*

*I must keep my letter short tonight. Today I very nearly collapsed after simply walking down a long hill, so I must not try to do more than the sheer necessities for now. But although my body is tired (oh, so tired!) my heart is singing, Mother!*

*We have outlasted the trail! The continent is behind us, and we are camped in the broad valley of the Sacramento River at long last. Tomorrow we will reach the settlers' cabins. I am looking forward to visiting those little homes, crude though they may be. Perhaps I will encounter another woman.*

*Despite my eagerness, I shrink from calling upon anyone*

*in my present state. Perhaps, since they have made this terrible journey themselves, they will understand our ragged appearance, but I am ashamed of my tattered dress, my hair, which is once again snarled and dusty, and my shamefully rough and windburned face. You should see my hands, Mother. They have soot and dirt so embedded that it no longer washes away. My fingers are red, scarred, and chapped with broken, dirty nails. I look, I am sure, like a perfect scullery maid. The children are no better, and you would hardly recognize Americus.*

*The men believe there may be a boat that travels this river that could take our little family to Sacramento and beyond. Wouldn't I be glad to trade our dusty, lurching wagon for a gently gliding boat and a swift end of our journey?*

*Love from the valleys of California!*

*Mary*

The guide book was right about one thing. This was awe-inspiring country, as rich and lovely as a slice of heaven. Americus sat on the nearest wheel hub and bit into a cool, sweet slice of watermelon while his eyes wandered over the life-giving river and the fertile land beyond. Any place that could grow something this succulent had to be extraordinary. Sugary juice ran down his throat, and he closed his eyes for a moment, savoring the thirst-quenching liquid, sweet as candy. If this was a taste of California, perhaps it was worth that desperate trip.

The evening air was balmy in the last pale light. Idly, he looked at the children sitting in the grass gobbling up the rare treat. Watermelon juice dripped off Celia's elbows and chin, soaking the front of her dress, and both of Cephas's cheeks were stained where the curving slices wrapped around his face. For once his little brown torso bulged.

Americus was grateful for this reassuring day. Earlier, three men from the sparse settlement had eagerly approached the wagons to welcome the newcomers. When they saw the children, skinny and trail worn, they sent them scampering to their nearby cabins for thick slices of cake and warm bread with butter. The good women in the shanties sent them back laden with onions, cabbages, tomatoes, and a watermelon, plenty to feed them for days to come.

Blackey and the donkey had grazed all day, chewing up the long-stemmed grass as if it might disappear at any moment. Americus was glad he had summoned the strength to go back and fetch the horse. On the practical side, Blackey—once he recuperated—would be needed for working the fields when they got settled. More to the point, Americus had become attached to the creature again. The horse was a perfect picture of devotedness. If not for that one lone animal, he and Mary and the children would be nothing but a few sets of dry bones scattered across a parched desert or strewn in some godforsaken mountain gully.

Tomorrow they would move upstream to Tehama to catch the boat to Sacramento and San Leandro. Americus pondered what to do with the horse and wagon. Surely one of the settlers would keep them for the winter. He could return for them in the spring—or perhaps immediately, weather allowing. The seasons in this warm country where grass grew as tall as a man's shoulder weren't like Wisconsin, that was certain. Back home, cold winds had already brought the long days of summer to an early end.

Mary approached him, and by some earlier habit that surfaced like a long-lost child, he got up from the wagon hub to allow her to sit.

"Thank you, Americus." A surprised look crossed her face, but she went on briskly. "I came to say that we must get an early start in the morning so we'll have time to make arrangements with the boat captain for our passage. Mr. Potts says he'll winter in Tehama, so he has offered to keep Blackey and the wagon for us. I imagine you'll want to return for them at some point."

He nodded. When in the world had Mary taken charge of all the arrangements this trip demanded? No matter how fatigued she was, she was always in full command now—not in a domineering, demanding way, but with a reluctant determination. Back home, she had been content to leave the planning and decisions to him, but somewhere along the route that had changed. He ran his hands over his face and tried to remember.

"I hope that suits you, Americus. We'll be in Sacramento before we know it, and we can rest before deciding if we want to continue downstream to San Leandro, as you mentioned."

That was Mary, ever considerate of his feelings. But he could see now that beneath her refined and gentle surface ran a new strength so powerful she could alter her very personality to take charge of a trip like this. He reached out and took her hand. For an instant, he thought she was going to snatch it away, but she let it linger.

"We'll leave before dawn, so we'd best bid the Major good-bye tonight." She rose. "I'll get the supper dishes packed."

The Major. Americus wondered what the man and his companions thought of him. They had kept a wary distance from him for the most part. Fatigue seeped into his bones when he thought about approaching the noisy bunch and thanking them for their help. Maybe he could just leave that duty to Mary.

He climbed into the wagon and lay on the quilt. Sometimes it seemed as if his old self—the Doctor, the father and husband, the hardworking man who had disappeared back there on the trail—was reappearing to him now, ducking in and out of his grasp like an elusive ghost that he yearned to touch but could never quite seize. Other times the dreaded fatigue and dullness gripped him again. It puzzled a man. He felt as if he were clawing his way out of some strange darkness, but there were glimpses of light ahead.

Outside the wagon he could hear the river swishing by and the children playing in the dusky light. Farther off, there was an occasional guffaw from one of the Major's men as they sprawled around their fire. He relaxed, his stomach pleasantly full.

He lay there for a moment, but only a moment. Then he stepped down from the wagon and walked swiftly to the men's fire. Ignoring their shocked looks and the abrupt end to their jocular conversation, he stood among them and looked around the circle at each man's face. Before the silence stretched on too long he spoke.

"Thank you all. We couldn't have made it without your help."

He moved then, straight to the Major, and held out his hand.

# CHAPTER 60

## SARAH

Sarah lifted her face to the wind and breathed in the damp smell of river water and mud. Mist blew across her skin: She could feel the tiny cold droplets on her closed eyelids. The breeze tugged her braids, and her ragged gray shawl tried to flutter into the river. She pulled it closer, shivering.

Even as cold as she was, she couldn't bear to leave the windy bow of this big boat and join Mother and Father and Ceely in the sheltered spot behind its cabin. Sarah loved the way the boat rocked on the green water and made a great splashing riffle that roiled up behind its stern. Between stops, it glided down the swift current as smoothly as a dandelion seed on a soft breeze. It was high and strong and safe, not tippy like the covered wagon had been as it sloshed its way through too many rivers to count. She watched Cephas sitting on the back deck, dangling his brown bare feet over the edge and trying to dip his toes into the frothing water. His legs weren't long enough to reach, so he kicked at the flying droplets instead.

Sarah could see scattered cabins on both sides of the river. They settled lopsidedly into the soft ground near the river bank. Most were crude and small, without windows or even doors, and Sarah tried to imagine what it would be like to live in them. There were swarms of children playing outside the doorways. She wondered how their big families all crowded into such tiny shacks. Until today, she had thought it never rained here in California, so settlers could practically live outdoors. Today's chilly dampness said otherwise.

After yearning for months to be finished with this journey, Sarah now wished it could go on forever. Already her family had traveled effortlessly down the river more than 100 miles, past Sacramento's dirty smokestacks and the stale, fishy odor of its docks. Today they were pressing on to San Leandro, where Father said they would settle. She thought she would never tire of the changing sights and the luxury of riding like a duchess instead of trudging beside the wagon. She lifted her face again to the mist.

"Sarah," Mother called softly. "Come have your dinner, please."

Sarah concentrated on walking in a straight line toward Mother, but the deck rocked beneath her feet and made her veer to the railing. She grabbed it and followed it to the bench where Mother had prepared sliced tomatoes and halved biscuits. Mother's face was greenish gray from seasickness, and Sarah noticed she didn't take any of the food for herself. Her forehead had lost its furrows, though, and the set of her mouth was relaxed. Somehow she had mustered the strength to prepare dinner for the rest of them. Sarah thought Mother lived up to her name: Mary Rockwood Powers. She was solid as a rock with a power all her own.

The only trouble with the boat ride was that they were indebted for the price of their passage. Mother had neither coins nor goods left to trade for this last part of the journey, so they were even more in debt to Mr. Potts than before. Mother was fretting about it.

Sarah pulled up her shawl to hide the back of her head. The young men who made up the boat crew were not shy about speaking to her boldly and lifting their caps, even though she had never met them before. She lowered her eyes and ducked her head when they came near, and once she heard Father speak sharply to one of them.

The wind was becoming much stronger, riling the river until the boat began to buck and shudder. She wished the waves would subside again for Mother's sake, but Father said it wasn't likely so near to the ocean bay. She watched Ceely and Cephas making a game of trying to walk across the rolling deck without falling. Every time Ceely went sprawling, she laughed. It was a sound Sarah hadn't heard for a long time.

Up ahead, the river widened, and Sarah could see the open water that was San Francisco Bay. She had never seen so much water in one place. As the boat churned closer, whitecaps crashed against its sides and made the vessel roll and toss. Sarah looked for the muddy bottom, but she couldn't see it at all. She wondered how long it would take to reach San Leandro.

Once they reached the bay and turned south, the shoreline crept past as the boat struggled against the wind and waves. Sarah could see mile upon mile of reedy marshland, and above it, hundreds of geese and ducks flying against the low, dark clouds. Father said this was a place where the tides ebbed and flowed and made a good home for waterfowl. The children would have plenty to eat, he told them, even before his crops were ready, for the flats were full of shellfish, too.

Off the other side of the boat the bay was so wide and deep that Sarah didn't like to look. Cephas, though, stood in the wet wind, his hair whipping back, and tried to catch the flying water drops on his tongue.

"Try this, Sarah!" he called to her. "The water tastes like someone put salt in it!"

It was many long hours before they drew close to their destination. A light rain fell. By then, Sarah was chilled enough to retreat to the lee of the boat's cabin. When the boat turned slightly toward the shore, Mother stood up and put on her sunbonnet despite the drizzle. Sarah saw her take several deep breaths and straighten her skirts.

"We're nearly to San Leandro, children," she said, with a doubtful look at the wet, gray shoreline. Buildings, both new and weathered, showed amidst the vegetation. "We must thank our Heavenly Father for bringing us safely to this place."

It felt strange to Sarah that their journey should end here. It seemed as though they had reached their destination when they drove the overland trail's final mile and halted the old wagon on the banks of the Sacramento. This boat ride felt too easy to be a part of the same toilsome trip across the continent.

But they were here at last. This was the place they would call home, this leaden-skied land. Sarah tried not to be disappointed, yet where were the golden fields of rich harvests and the year-round sun she had heard about for so long?

"Sarah, you children stay here while Father and I go ashore and inquire about a place to live. No one will disturb you. The crew will take its leave, and you'll have the boat to yourselves. We'll return for you later today after we find a suitable place."

The afternoon light was fading when Sarah finally saw them picking their way back through the mud. Mother's face was drawn, and she held Father's arm as they walked, stopping now and then to rest. As they got close, Sarah saw Mother put a smile on her face—the same smile she used to encourage Cephas and Ceely when things were bad on the trail.

"Come, children! We've found a little shanty where we can settle for now. It's small and empty-looking, but we'll make it into a livable home." The false cheer in her voice didn't deceive Sarah. She wondered why Mother used the word "shanty" instead of "house" or "cottage" or even "cabin."

The shanty wasn't even a shack. When Sarah saw it, she felt as dull as the weather, for it was no bigger than a pantry or the smallest lean-to. It stood in the middle of a sodden field, dwarfed by the muddy acres around it. Its weathered walls were dark with rain, and Sarah could see wide spaces between the cracks in the old boards. A crooked door hung open on leather hinges. Inside, the floor was dirt, hard packed and lumpy, and the air felt cold and damp.

The five of them would hardly be able to crowd inside to sleep. There was no chimney—nowhere, in fact, to build even the smallest fire to ward off the chill. Mother kept the brave smile on her face, but Sarah noticed that she kept glancing at the littered dirt under her feet and pulling her shawl closer.

"Americus, do you think if we had the wagon here, we could use it for sleeping?" Mother asked, eying the heavy spider webs draped in the corners.

Father hesitated with his shoulders slumped, but then he straightened up.

"We're going to need it. If you and the children can make do here for a few days, I'll go back after it."

"Well, we've food and quilts, and the roof is quite sound." Mother looked up. It was true that not a drop of rain filtered through the overlapping boards overhead. "We'll sweep this awful floor, be rid of the cobwebs, build a fire just outside the door, and then we'll be warm and comfortable, won't we, children?"

Sarah didn't answer. Cepahs looked unconvinced, too,

and Ceely clung to Mother's hand watching a big unfamiliar insect make its way up Father's pant leg.

"When the sun comes out again, we'll look for the school and a dry goods store," Mother went on, looking at the three of them. "We have a new home to explore." The firm tone in her voice told Sarah it was of no use to complain.

———

It took Father nearly two weeks to return with Blackey and Smoke and the wagon. By then, the rain had stopped and the sun dried up the mud. Mother had swept the shanty's floor so many times that the powdery dirt was smooth and clean, and she had constructed a rude table of old boards. The spider webs were gone. Sarah and Cephas kept a fire going in the stone circle they made outside the doorway.

When Father returned, Mother immediately washed the quilts, which were gray from lying on the earthen floor in the shanty, and made the bed in the wagon.

"I believe the first thing we must do after planting is add a room to the shanty, Americus," Sarah heard her say. "With the dampness and dirt, Celia is beginning to cough. I've considered how we could build a new section with a floor and perhaps even windows."

Sarah's spirits lifted. Maybe they would have a nice cottage after all.

Now that the first hard days were over, she was beginning to like California a little better. When the sun came out, this new place was more like the warm paradise people back home described. The air smelled good, like the sea and the teeming marshes, and there were a few comforts, just like Wisconsin. Down the winding, rutted track that ran past the shanty was a dry goods store. And of course Mother had found the school, about 2 miles away. She promised Sarah and Cephas that they could start soon. For now, though, Father needed Cephas to help prepare the fields for planting.

They had been in San Leandro just over a fortnight, but the overland journey seemed a long time ago. Already, Sarah couldn't completely remember what it had felt like to be desperately hungry or thirsty or bone tired. When memories crossed her mind that made her sad—St. Lawrence sprawled dead in the sagebrush, Mother's purple swollen ankle, Ceely's crying face, her father's vacant stares—she simply forced herself to stop thinking about them.

When she put the remaining pictures together in her mind, they resulted in something like artwork, she discovered. She arranged them in a vivid mental collection like a series of daguerreotypes, but in color. She could still see the snowy slopes of Mount Saint Joseph jutting into the royal-blue sky. Bright glowing sparks from a campfire flying off into the dark night. An Indian mother and baby with shiny black hair that fluttered in a creek's breeze. Ceely's little stick doll wearing its red gingham clothes, and icy summer snowballs, and Cephas proudly holding the dripping water keg that saved their lives. Brilliant green water plants beside a sparkling mountain stream, and golden wildflowers blowing with the feathery silver grass. Blackey's big trusting eyes, Mother's gracious smile, and Father's hand reaching out in thanks to the Major.

Someday she would try to put them into a painting.

*September 1, 1857*

*Dear Mother,*

*I am sitting in my rocking chair for a few moments before I begin making a cherry pie for supper. The sun is pouring in the window, and the door is open to the breeze. I can see Americus and Cephas in the fields working the crops, their caps pulled low over their eyes to shade them from the San Leandro sun. To the east are the lovely hills we look upon each day, and to the west, a bright glimmer of the saltwater bay. The rumors about settlers finding gold in every stream here in California were false, of course, but there is a sort of gold here that defies the imagination: The air itself has a lovely golden tinge that is beautiful beyond all comprehension. Each day when the mist rolls in from the bay, it glows with an almost heavenly light.*

*The twins are asleep in their cradles, and Sarah and Celia have walked over to visit our neighbors, so I have a rare moment alone. In the year we have been here, such a quiet hour has come to me only once or twice. I expect the babies, one or both, to awaken soon, and then I will have to put this aside.*

*I have your most recent letter in my apron pocket. Like the others, I have read it a hundred times until the ink is fairly worn from the pages with my frequent folding and unfolding. Although your news is old by the time I receive it, I am eternally grateful to hear about my sisters and friends, and most of all to find out that you are well. Thank you for writing so faithfully to your wandering daughter, Mother.*

*I do wish I had a daguerreotype of the children to send you. Sarah is a beautiful young woman now, with rosy complexion and slender, feminine build. Her hair is exactly the color of mine and her face has taken on her delicate adult features. She is sewing much of our clothing, and recently did the finish work on a new dress for herself. It is patterned after one of mine, and she looks so comely in it that I am certain we shall soon have suitors knocking at our door!*

*Cephas, at eight, is tall and brown from the sun. He still loves to explore the creeks and marshes nearby, but for the most part he uncomplainingly helps the Doctor with the many chores necessary on a farm. I can almost see him growing day by day, and am happy to have an abundance of good food now to feed him. My little vegetable garden is doing well in this balmy climate.*

*You would hardly recognize Celia, Mother. She is no longer the toddler you knew, but instead is a sturdy child who is learning to read! I have been teaching her myself until she is old enough to start school. This little girl, who was my "baby" for so long, has fully recovered from the traumas of the journey west. With a sparkle in her eye, she is into every mischief until I am ready to tear my hair! I keep her busy with small chores to prevent her from dreaming up her own schemes.*

*And my sweet babies, Mother! How I wish you could see them. Little Mary Catherine is delicate as a wild rose, with blue eyes that remind me of Father's. She rarely fusses unless she is hungry, and who can blame her for that? She has the most perfect, regular features and plenty of shiny dark hair, and she smiles readily at us all. How I love her!*

*Little William Henry, too, is a fine looking baby who entertains us with his cleverness and guile. He is especially fond of his brother, who plays with him on the floor (did I mention that our cabin now has a good, clean wood floor with my rag rugs scattered over it?). Cephas never tires of rocking little William's borrowed cradle, too, when my own foot gives out.*

*The good Doctor works hard to support us all, and I join as his partner in our endeavors. He treats me with great affection, and there is not another man in the world who cares so much for his family. His odd and distressing behaviors from our trail journey—the gruff irritation, the poor decision-making, the stony silence, and the constant sleeping—have vanished. I simply do not comprehend the changes and have stopped attempting to understand what happened. Instead, I try to enjoy and appreciate his attentions and return his affections. Once again he is the devoted, fastidious, and patient man I married, and I thank the Heavenly Father every day for that. He no longer seems intent on practicing medicine, although he takes good care of me and my lingering ailments, but is content with his farming. His first crop of potatoes paid most of our trail debts and helped build this fine new room on our home.*

Mary paused as William Henry began to stir in his cradle. A hummingbird explored the rose cuttings planted just outside the door. The low buzzing of its wings made her look up. In another year or two there would be rose blossoms, just as there had been back home. She knew she would never see Wisconsin again, but the grim knowledge didn't hurt as deeply as it had at first. This foreign land with its strange saltwater smells and unfamiliar fog was at last beginning to seem like home. The cabin, too, finally seemed like her own, not merely a stopping place. She already had friends, plenty of them, and was learning to decipher the quirks of climate, unusual plants, and multitudes of unknown birds and animals that at first had made her feel like a stranger. She thought her health was improving, too, although the twins' birth had set her back.

She had worked hard to make this small new room homey. One night she sat up late sewing curtains for its two square windows from her old blue trail dress. The calico was thin and faded, but after she starched and ironed the new curtains and tied them back with a bit of her mother's lace from the trunk, they looked crisp and pretty. The light inside the cabin reflected its honey-colored walls, and the black stove filled one corner. On its surface, a pot of the thick tomato soup she had learned to make filled the cabin with its aroma. A bright yellow cloth covered a makeshift table in one corner. The old trunk was pulled beside it to provide the children with a place to sit, and for now a board across two heavy stumps created a bench for Mary and Americus. Behind a curtain in the cramped original section of the house was the bed.

Americus had taken time one rainy afternoon to build a shelf over the table for her grandmother's silver teapot, an act of apology that Mary appreciated. She gazed at it now, remembering that it was only months ago her husband angrily demanded she abandon it near the sodden banks of the Sweetwater. She had gasped in surprise the day Sarah pulled it from the trunk and set it in her lap and told her the story of its rescue.

Today it was filled with the wildflowers Cephas brought her from the fields. Glimmering in the corner of her eye as she went about her work, it made her think about the way silver linings slipped unnoticed into life unless one learned to be watchful for their small joys.

Mr. Curry was one such joy, although he certainly hadn't slipped into her life unnoticed. She thought of him every day, but without the sadness that had first assaulted her when she was forced to go on without him. Now she felt simply a warm gratitude. He had saved her life in more ways than one, and she intended to pray silently for his well-being each morning for as long as she lived.

She looked out the window and saw Sarah and Celia returning from their walk. They came back by way of the fields instead of the road and stopped to talk to Americus and Cephas. Sarah plucked something from the ground and walked over to where Blackey and Hudson were hitched to the wagon—the potato wagon, they called it now that the canvas and bows were removed. Mary had used the canvas to make a cover for the woodpile until Americus had time to build a woodshed.

Blackey stood patiently as ever, twitching his glossy flank now and then to discourage insects, and accepted Sarah's offering. The new horse, Hudson, was younger and stronger, but Mary loved Blackey with a warmth she'd never felt for any animal. She sent Celia out with tidbits for him almost daily—a half an apple, a raw carrot, a handful of wheat—and Sarah curried him without being asked. Pulling the potato wagon was his only responsibility now except for occasional trips to the dry goods store. In between, Blackey grazed and napped for hours in the sunshine or the protection of the trees, depending upon the day. At night, Americus led him to a deserted shed at the edge of the fields and covered him with a horse blanket to keep him from the damp fog that drifted in from the bay.

*Mother, I had best finish this epistle to you so I can post it tomorrow. Little William Henry will awaken soon, and my girls are returning from their afternoon visit with the Hart girls. Their mother, Lucinda, is our nearest neighbor and my best friend here. Sarah spends many happy afternoons sewing and whispering with Lucinda's eldest daughter, Susan.*

*I am still tired every day and have given up the hope of recovering from whatever it is that ails me, although I believe I shall feel stronger when the children are older and do not require my constant attention day and night. I have learned to keep working no matter how fatigued I am, for there is no other choice!*

*I am a different woman than I was when we left home, Mother. Although I seem the same outwardly, the qualities I earned on the trail have not faded away simply because Americus has recovered his mental state. I like the new person I have become, and here in the West it is not uncommon for a woman to be strong and confident and to have a definite say in all matters. No longer can I simply acquiesce to Americus's wishes without question, and I am often the one to make decisions. The Doctor is willing to accept that, and only once or twice have we experienced minor discord about it. For harmony's sake, I try not to contradict him in a confrontational way, but simply make decisions and go about our business the way I see fit. He has few objections.*

*It is satisfying to be a part of this great movement to start a new civilization. I am pleased to be among the women clamoring for new schools and churches, libraries and civic refinements. We mothers have great power to shape our children's destinies here. Just yesterday, for example, I located a woman who has a piano in her home and who is offering music lessons for a small fee. I am hoping that when our new potato crop is sold, I might be able to send Sarah to her for music training.*

*My girls are home, and the cherries are calling me. I would like the Doctor to have a pie for his supper after such a long, hot day in the fields. Let me close this letter by saying that I love you all, Mother, and I will never let you stray far from my mind. Our lives are like a symphony, with crescendos and decrescendos, soaring high notes and mournful low tones, but the music itself flows on and on. My life is at its crescendo, and you may rest at ease knowing I am safe and warm, and above all, at home with myself.*

*Love, Mary*

# EPILOGUE

Historical accounts indicate that Mary Rockwood Powers was able to enjoy being "at home with herself" for only a short time before she did, indeed, make the ultimate sacrifice from seeing her family safely across the continent.

In a letter to her mother dated January 5, 1858, she wrote that her new baby daughter, Mary Catherine, died in infancy, and shortly afterward little William Henry also succumbed. Less than a year later, Mary herself died after a short illness that her physician husband described as "a severe congestive chill." Writing to break the sad news to Mary's mother back home, Americus Powers told of the large procession of friends and neighbors that turned out to honor her, and noted that, despite the short duration of their life in San Leandro, Mary had "gained the universal love and esteem of all who knew her."

Without Mary by his side, Americus Powers struggled to raise his remaining children. Sketchy historical records indicate that Cephas and Celia may have died later in childhood, but Sarah reportedly lived with her father through what was possibly another episode of mental instability. It is said that she grew to adulthood near Hollister, California, with Dr. Powers, who was by then a recluse, and that she married in 1867 and eventually became the mother of thirteen children. Late in her life, she visited the old family home in Wisconsin, where she was finally able to see again the places of her early childhood that had claimed her mother's heart.

# ACKNOWLEDGMENTS

If there is one truth about the process of writing fiction, it is that it takes a village to create a novel. To the many "villagers" who helped with this project, I am very grateful.

First and foremost, I am indebted to Mary Rockwood Powers, who, despite terrible obstacles, wrote down her powerful saga so long ago. Without her account, the story of her journey West would have been lost—and this novel could never have been written.

I am also thankful to the many other pioneer women who left behind diaries, letters, and other records of their westward treks. I have studied—and then borrowed—their voices, their experiences, and their knowledge to ensure authenticity in this story.

In my own village, there were many who offered support for my endeavors, but none so faithful as friend and fellow writer Maggie Plummer, who suggested this book and encouraged me to pursue it. I am grateful for her creative suggestions, her patient and expert critiques, and her unfailing presence.

To Melissa Guyles, who drove through hundreds of miles of sagebrush, thunderstorms, and mountain canyons with me researching the overland trails, I offer my heartfelt thanks. Not only did she contribute her interest and enthusiasm to this project, she gladly put all those dusty miles on her car.

Many thanks are due, also, to Erin Turner, my editor at

The Globe Pequot Press. I have appreciated her clear vision for this story and the steady guidance she offered throughout the writing/editing process. Her fine suggestions, as well as her knowledge and expertise, have helped in countless ways.

I am grateful, as well, to the many other publishing professionals, including copy editor Megan Hiller, who saw this project through the complicated process of turning a manuscript into a finished book.

I would also like to thank my late father, Dr. George H. Barmeyer, as well as Dr. Steve Irwin, for their medical expertise in helping me decipher and understand the various illnesses, medical conditions, and nutritional problems that possibly affected the Powers family as they made their way along the overland trails.

Further, I thank my family and friends for their support and encouragement:

—my husband, Dan, for helping me create the time to take on a project of this scope and for keeping my computer up to the task.

—our daughter, Jennifer, for reading the manuscript with her careful eye for detail and for offering her accurate and helpful suggestions.

—our son, Kevin, for his clear ideas about structure, characterization, and style.

—our younger daughter, Katie, for her thoughts about how twelve-year-old Sarah Powers would act and react on a cross-continental journey.

—the "Sibs Club," of course, for their love and for being faithful "fans."

—Debbie Ofstad, for her genuine interest and continual support.

—Mac Swan, Milana Marsenich, and Liz Grant, for reading early chapters and offering suggestions and encouragement.

—Barb Claude, for firsthand information about Wisconsin's flora and fauna.

—Woodeene Koenig-Bricker, for sharing the Emerson quotation with me.

—Cynthie Preston and Paula Lowder, for helping with the details of horse behavior.

—Cathy Plummer, for offering facts about the climate and topography of San Leandro, California.

To the many interpretive rangers, webmasters, history writers, mapmakers, librarians, and curators who have enriched my understanding of the 1850s and conditions on the overland trails, my sincere thanks, especially to:

—Eileen Spencer of the Eagle Lake (California) Ranger District, for information about the Nobles Trail and the Lassen Trail, and what early travelers there would have seen and experienced.

—Kimberly Missman of the Chester, California, library for facts about the area's climate and vegetation.

—Steve Zachary, Education Specialist at Lassen Volcanic National Park, for details about what covered wagon travelers in the area might have encountered.

—Douglas S. Prather, for the descriptions and information contained in his Masters thesis "The History and Archaeology of the Lassen Emigrant Trail," (California State University,

Chico, Fall, 1996). His section on Steep Hollow was especially helpful.

As always, I am indebted to my co-workers at Polson City Library, especially:

—Library Director Marilyn Trosper, for her expert research assistance as well as the ongoing support she offers in so many ways.

—Assistant Librarian Allison Reed, for her prompt help in locating materials through interlibrary loan as often as they were needed.

—former Youth Librarian LouAnne Krantz, for locating the original source and date of the Emerson quotation, and for finding the voices of pioneer children for me.

I also acknowledge and thank the many other novelists, especially Montana writers, whose works I have read and studied for years in preparation for writing this work of fiction.

# ABOUT THE AUTHOR

Mary Barmeyer O'Brien was born and raised in Missoula, Montana, and received her B.A. from Linfield College in McMinnville, Oregon. She is the author of three previous books about pioneers on the overland trails: *Toward the Setting Sun: Pioneer Girls Traveling the Overland Trails*, *Heart of the Trail: The Stories of Eight Wagon Train Women*, and *Into the Western Winds: Pioneer Boys Traveling the Overland Trails*. She has also written a biography for young readers called *Jeannette Rankin: Bright Star in the Big Sky*, and her magazine articles for both children and adults have appeared in many national magazines. Mary works from her home in Polson, Montana. She and her husband, Dan, a high school science teacher, have two daughters and a son.

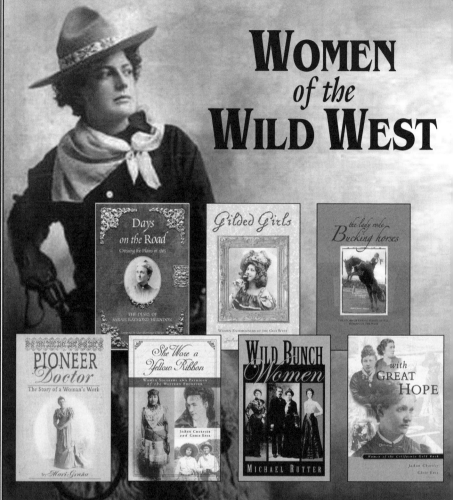